MW01113864

The Stolen Crown

C. A. Moltzau

Edited by Dr. Jay Moltzau

The Stolen Crown is a work of historical fiction. Beyond the well-known people, events, and location in the narrative, all characters, events, and locations in this book are fictitious. Any similarity to real persons, dead or alive, is coincidental and not intended by the author of this novel.

Copyright © 2020 by C.A. Moltzau, pseud of Christopher Moltzau Anderson

All rights reserved. No part of this publication may be reproduced or transmitted in any form or by any means, without permission in writing.

Published in the United States by C. A. Moltzau

First edition 2020

ISBN Paperback 978-1-7346879-1-0
ISBN Ebook - EPUB 978-1-7346879-0-3
ISBN Hardcover 978-1-7346879-2-7

Library of Congress Control Number: 2020906376

Printed in the United States of America
Washington Crossing, PA

www.camoltzau.com

Book design by 100 Covers

10 9 8 7 6 5 4 3 2 1

To my Mother who is my inspiration; I love you

Acknowledgement

I would like to acknowledge the people that throughout the years have helped me to become the writer I am today. I am very grateful to them. To Mark DiGiacomo, my high school history teacher from Pennington, and Professor Paul Milliman from the Department of History at University of Arizona. Both have shaped the foundation of my writing through history. To Paulus Wildeboer who was my role model for his guidance, support, and encouragement. To Mario Kreft who is like the father I never had. To all my friends. To my wonderful mother and sister for everything and anything they do for me.

Thank you

HUNGARY, 1439

Chapter 1
Search

Blood was coughed forth, warm and scarlet red, while the cold winds of the night howled against the shrouded world and all in its path. Trees shivered and swayed, as they whined at the cold that burrowed into their bark. Faint flakes of snow and ice accentuated the cold and fell on slated roofs and those that guarded them. Though, for what strength and defense a holy structure could bear, it was defenseless against the blight that had already burrowed within.

Incomprehensible mumbles filled the halls, and shadows danced on the walls. From those of humble origins who simply served, to those born into silver and gold, conjecture and doubt reigned. Yet, for the congregation that gathered, there was one group among them that seemed different, both for where they stood and the role they played; the physicians.

"Where is Janos?" Tomas asked, throwing his dark eyes and messy hair on the figures he could see with cautious glances. His arms hung from his sides like ropes, tired muscles struggling at the thought of so much as a wave.

"That's not important," Peter, his fellow physician replied, scratching his fair hair and trying to wipe off the grease and sweat that was endlessly proliferating his face. "We need a plan, before our heads are on pikes."

"We need Janos, where is he?" Tomas asked again.

"He is with the Queen, again…" Peter replied with a nervous demeanor; once more wiping his nose and rubbing off the filth on his sleeve. "Keep your voice down, before you get us killed. And help me think. We need a plan."

"He is with the Queen at a time like this, even though the King is—?" Tomas began to ask, though before he could, he was interrupted by the presence of another who forced a shiver up his spine.

"The King is what?" A man by the name of Istvan demanded to know, marching towards the door they loitered before and throwing off the flakes of ice and snow that clung to him. He stood taller than both men, his thick neck stretching from the large, but richly ordained body below. Fine fabrics of rich colors called any eyes that wandered, though it was the opulence that came in the form of gold and silver that kept it. Yet, for all the gold and silver, it could only do so much to keep eyes off his thin mustache and combed over dark hair. "Go on, speak, I haven't got all night!"

"My lord!" The two physicians said, in a panicked unison as they bowed.

"Did I ask you to lick my boots?" Istvan asked with a tumultuous tone. "Answer my question, now. Or so help me, you very well will know what I stepped in when you lick them."

The two physicians stole a glance to one another, silently holding a conversation with their wrinkles and eyes. "My lord—" Tomas began, though quickly trailed off and bit the inside of his own cheek.

"The King... The King—" Peter added with nervous uncertainty, though he could not finish other than with a faint weak mumble. "The King..."

"I suppose I should go and see for myself!" Istvan proclaimed. "You two going to wait out here while the man you're here to see goes unchecked?" He demanded to know, pressing past them. "Get out of my way and get back to work!"

"Right..." both mumbled.

With a hard push that threw open the door, Istvan strode into the room. It was a crowded space, the furniture and decorations lost to the mob of nobles that occupied it. Whispers filled the scene, seeming to advance and retreat, much like the waves of the tide. With nods and glares, and a half dozen daggers behind every smile, Istvan was quick to distinguish friends from foes. Though it was the King that called his attention, as it did everyone.

On a bed alone, lay the man they had all been summoned to see, the man whose blood and authority held the Kingdom in place. Yet, at that moment he was all but drained. His skin was pale, drenched by sweat, the hairs from his head clinging to his skin and doing little to hide his sickliness. Drool hugged the pillows, and the indignities of his own body lay apparent by smell alone. His eyes, when opened, held a look of pain that glazed over all sight in his view, while the panted breaths of his lungs raised his chest in a manner that screamed of what was to come.

In the company of the whispers, Istvan took a knee besides the bed, though quickly shuffled over when a wetness pressed against him.

"Sorry," Peter said softly, as he returned to his post and glanced at a piss bucket. "I spilled some... Something there earlier."

Istvan scowled ignoring the comment and smell as best as he could, while turning his attention to the task that lay just out of hand. With a reach, he extended his arm and opened his hand to clasp the limb of the King he served.

"My King?" he asked softly, though to no audible reply, as the mumbles of a groan were all that left the royal lips. "My King?" Istvan asked again much to the same result. With a sigh, he rose and turned to his fellow nobles, though not before ordering the physicians in a manner to gain praise. "The two of you, get back to work."

With quick movements, Tomas and Peter hurried to either side of the bed and began their tasks once again. They brought forth a multitude of objects and dried plants, waving to one another with discreet orders. Though, time and time again they turned their eyes to their books for guidance, each page revealing the harsh reality of a situation they already knew.

"This could not have come at a worse time," Istvan said in anger, as he took his place beside the other nobles. "The Ottomans are on our borders waiting for the moment to push into our territory. If there is no figure of authority to rule, they will take advantage of the weakness. We need a plan, if this gets any worse… When this gets worse."

The room roused itself with the harsh words of what the future could bring, noble men already cutting the kingdom apart with their desires and preparations. All the while, the truth of the scene lay apparent to only the two physicians.

Tomas and Peter watched with wide eyes, as they stared at the King, who had finally fallen still. His gaze was endless, staring out at something none of the living could see. His breaths were still, and the drops of blood that had pooled, were left to run dry. With a glance to one another, they pressed their ears to his chest. There the two of them lingered for a moment, before they silently shared a look of fear, while the mumbles and greed of those in the room were oblivious to the still heart before them all. With a nod to one another, the physicians slowly shuffled their way to the door. Step after step, they moved in silence. Yet, before they could reach the door, a voice held them in place.

"Where the hell do you two think you are going?" Istvan demanded to know, his voice loud enough to quell all others in the room. "Get back to the King and help him!"

Tomas and Peter held their place, beads of sweat pouring down their faces. They took turns opening their mouths, yet were both unable to say anything.

"We can't…" Tomas finally croaked.

"Maybe a priest…" Peter followed.

"What?" Istvan demanded, as his eyes leaped from his patron to the two physicians and back again.

"He's gone…" Tomas whispered softly. "The King is… Dead…"

All eyes fell to the tranquil King, a somber silence befalling the room. Like the still surface of a body of water, a calm lay on each guest's face, though below the veiled mask each wore, a turbulence quickly drew to the surface.

"Where is she?" Istvan demanded to know, his voice finally asking what all those besides him thought. "Where is the Queen?"

Chapter 2
The Beginning

A still tranquility enveloped the room, as the faint crackle of the fire whispered to the smoke. The warmth it exuded soaked into the rich wood furniture, ornate tapestries, and the two living souls occupying the room.

They stood in the embrace of each other's beating heart, listening and feeling each rise and fall of pressure. Their warm breath tickled against each other's soft skin, the clothes between them doing little to stop what act they were committing.

With each moment that passed, the man held his place, his eyes closed, as if waiting for something. The soft red ordained gown that belonged to his companion, was all that kept the sharp features of his face and long loose hair from touching her skin. Though, before he could discern what he was waiting for, the sound of heavy feet rapidly approached.

With a hard 'thwack' the door swung open with a fury.

"You can't go in there!" A voice that would have otherwise been heavenly said, as she tried to stop the unexpected and uninvited guest.

"Move!" Istvan ordered with a bark, his heavy feet carrying him through the threshold.

"I am sorry your Grace," a woman by the name of Helene Kottanner said, hurrying to stop him. The simple yellow gown she wore hugged her thin, yet tall body, while the faint hint of her golden hair fell from her braided locks, obstructing a few of the scattered freckles that kissed her skin and climbed down her thin neck. Her eyes held a gentle color of a calm body of water, as the soft pink of her lips invited a second glance, though not at that moment.

"What the hell is going on?" Istvan asked with wide eyes and anger, catching the two in the act they had been entwined in while the King had passed away.

"You should knock," Queen Elizabeth said softly with a tilt of her head. Her unbound red and golden hair fell to her shoulders, as the exposed skin that flowed down her neck to the cusp of her shoulder held a tantalizing purity devoid of a blemish or mark of labor. Her eyes peered at her guest with a calm expression that was made evermore soft by the hazel color they held. Yet, while her soft red lips seemed as delicate as her voice, they held an authority that forced all to attention, if for only a moment.

"And you!" Istvan shouted, as he pulled his eyes from his lingering stare of the Queen and threw them onto the physician, Janos. "What the hell do you think you're doing with your head on her chest? And while he, your King, is still warm no less! I should have you in chains for the mere thought of such a thing!"

The fingers of both Queen Elizabeth and Janos were quick to reply, as both held their index fingers extended demanding silence; the first on her soft lips, the second suspended in the air. For the embrace that was shared was no lay in the biblical sense, or any such connection that bound two and made them one. Rather, one sat in the chair, while the other pressed closely against her, listening for the secrets that were within her.

"Why, you--!" Istvan began to protest, though before he could, he was rendered silent by a third finger, that of Helene who moved to stand in his path.

Silence held the air for a moment, as Janos continued his labor. He wiggled his ear, searching for a beat hidden within a beat, until suddenly with a nod and his eyes thrown wide open, he pulled his ear off of the Queen and turned his attention to those in his company.

"It will be a boy." He explained with a calm, yet confident tone. "I am sure of it. The King and you, my Queen, will have a son."

"What the hell were you doing?" Istvan demanded to know, storming over to him and swallowing him in his shadow.

"I was checking her heart, as well as that of the King's unborn son," Janos calmly replied.

"Son…?" Istvan asked taken aback.

"Yes," Elizabeth answered. "As I have long suspected. I will give birth to a son."

A loud scoff and a roll of his eyes was all that Istvan did, as he collected the right words on his tongue. "The King is dead."

All eyes fell to the Queen for a moment, as words from her company fell precariously close from being spilled from each of their still lips.

"A shame he has passed without knowing that he will have a son," Elizabeth finally said, as she lowered her head and offered a payer. "I can only pray now that God will tell him."

With a loud grunt, Istvan bit his tongue in frustration and held the words that wished to wiggle forth from escape. Though, he did not hold it at bay for long, as he turned his eyes to the physician whom he held authority over. "Where the hell were you? Where were you when the King, our King, was coughing up blood?"

"There was nothing more that could have been done when he was alive," Janos replied. "He was doomed. The forces that were saw it so. Nothing more I could have done than hold his hand. Therefore, I saw to tend to his memory and tend to his wife and unborn son, as was requested of me."

"Other men would call abandoning him traitorous," Istvan said softly, staring the man down so closely that the smell of his last meal filled the air between them.

Janos held his gaze for a moment, before fanning the smell and warm breath out of his face. "Onions?"

Like a beast, Istvan's nostrils flared wide and a low snarl formed in the back of his throat. His knuckles cracked as he fisted them into balls and the muscles on his thick neck tightened. Yet, before he could do anything, he was interrupted, and his bravado sapped.

"If there is nothing else, I would like a moment to collect myself before I see to my husband," Elizabeth said, standing from her chair. The gown she wore shifted with her weight, the soft cloth hugging her body and its curves, though the bump that was her pregnancy drew each person's eyes, further accentuated by the cupped embrace.

"This way," Helene said with a gesture towards the door, waving the men out. "Right this way please."

"My Queen," Janos said with a bow, taking his leave.

Istvan however, was far from cordial, as he lingered and watched the other man go.

"My lord," Helene ordered, pulling his attention and making her point with a raised eyebrow and a nod of her head.

With another grumble, Istvan turned to leave, mumbling a faint measure of respect. "Queen."

As the two left and made their way down the hall, there was still one who remained with the Queen.

"Is there anything else that you need?" Helene asked.

Elizabeth, was silent, merely staring out beyond the light of her room and into the hallway where the whispers of footsteps were all but gone.

"My Queen?" Helene asked softly as she stepped closer, placing her hand on her arm.

"What?" Elizabeth asked back.

"Is there anything you need?" Helene asked again with a look of concern.

"No, no," Elizabeth replied softly, lingering between her thoughts and the question at hand.

"Then I will leave you for now," Helene said as she pulled away and made her way to the door. Her fingers touched the smooth surface, though before the hinges could begin to whine, they were made still at the request of authority.

"Helene," Elizabeth said.

"Yes, what can I do for you?" Helene asked back from the doorway.

Elisabeth opened her mouth, though no words escaped her lips. With swift movements, she moved to the door and forced it closed. "Since I was born and given my name, I have known this life for twenty-nine years. I know what is coming."

"My Queen?" Helene asked. "Is something wrong?"

"Helene," Elizabeth said with a soft voice. "I have a favor I must ask. I don't need an answer now, but I must ask it."

"Anything," Helene replied with a smile, oblivious to what words would come.

Elizabeth stroked her belly as if she touched her unborn child, though when she turned to Helene, a fire burned in her eyes. "Would you really do anything? Would you risk your life?"

Helene was silent, unable to reply.

"Would you do anything?" Elizabeth continued, as she stepped closer to her friend. "Even at the risk of your children's lives?"

Chapter 3

For an Answer

The cold winds blew against the loose folds of a cloak, as the figure that wore it moved with heavy feet around the structures of the village. His pace was a quick one, only ever made slow when the winds tried to rob him of his balance and sap him of his strength. Though for each gust and the howl that accompanied it, he marched on, past the structures and the warmth that slowly left the corpse of the King.

"Damned physician," Istvan grumbled to himself, kicking the small pile of snow he came across. Heavy breaths forced the air from his lungs and into the night with a grumble. He bit his nail, standing just beyond the rays of light from one of the structures, before quickly throwing his hand through the air in frustration. "This is a disaster. A God damned disaster. Stuck in this one-horse village with nothing to do other than wait. This is—"

Before another word could be uttered, a voice interrupted him, reaching out beyond the light. "What seems to be the problem, Istvan? Can't think of a good plan?" The figure said from the shadows with the whisper of a snake.

Istvan's eyes narrowed, trying to make shape of the source of the voice within the shadow. "Who's there?"

Approaching like the winter's cold, a figure slowly emerged into the light. The silver hilt of a sheathed dagger was the first thing to reveal itself, as the shimmer and gleam of the finely crafted instrument demanded attention. It held the eye, but as the wielder stepped forward and took shape, it lay second to him, though only by nail. His hair was curly, his posture lousy and the slight inclination of crossed eyes seemed to mark his vision. What features he had were far from pleasant, whether superficial or deep, though they were productive.

"Fodor Gorgein," Istvan said with a hiss. "What the hell is your ugly self doing here?"

"What has you so flustered?" His revealed company asked with a laugh that ignored the words just spoken. "You look like you just stepped into something."

"The King is dead," Istvan replied in anger, protruding his jaw and grinding his teeth.

"So?" Fodor asked indifferently. "People die all the time. You never get worked up about it. Well, generally speaking."

"This is different," Istvan replied. "This is a King... This is the King."

"We have had Kings before him," Fodor said. "Will have many more after."

"He was a good King," Istvan explained. "He was a man that knew the threat of the Ottomans. He was a man that knew that strength was needed. And he knew to support us."

"We still have a Queen," Fodor replied, though by design striking a nerve. "She already has a daughter. Besides, good might be a stretch."

A roll of Istvan's eyes began his reply, as a scoff of frustration left his lips. "Don't give me that. You know why that will not work. No, that will not work. Not at all."

"You're really going to make me ask?" Fodor inquired with a slight laugh. "Come now, we all know what it is you do. You always have a plan. You always have some scheme up your sleeves. So, what is it? You're among a friend, my friend."

Istvan held a long stare at the self-proclaimed comrade before he finally revealed his teeth with a scowl. "Weren't you the one that saw some of my wealth taken away a few years back, my friend? With Sigismund."

"You sure it was me, it could have been anyone," Fodor said, as he turned his eyes up to the sky.

"It was you, I am sure of it," Istvan replied.

"Indeed, I was," Fodor calmly admitted with an indifferent roll of his shoulders and a smile. "Indeed, I was. Though, I should remind you that you were just one among many."

"A means to an end then?" Istvan asked.

"A means to an end," Fodor replied with a nod. "Took out the wealth and authority of many lesser men who were in the way. You, along with a few others simply got pulled along."

"And gained support of the last King…" Istvan added. "Well, now it would be the second to last King. Must be difficult for you falling so far out of favor now. Especially with the Queen, who never much liked you."

"Well, the wealth that was taken was used in part to secure the power to fight the Ottomans," Fodor said, as he leaned against the closest wall and crossed his arms. "That should make you happy, but I think you already knew that. But, as you say, yes, I have some concerns on my mind, especially with the succession. She never did like me, don't know why."

"Probably because you're as ugly as a shit covered shovel," Istvan replied, as he moved to turn his back to his company and stare down the darkened path he had come. "I know you're there. Come out!" He ordered, as he watched and listened, waiting for a flutter of any shadows within the dark.

"Thought you were being watched?" Fodor asked with a grin.

Istvan slowly turned his attention back to his company with a narrow gaze. "I may be blunt, but I am not stupid. I gave you the chance to put that dagger in my back and reveal what might have been hidden. As well as scare anyone who might have been listening."

"So, then you are satisfied?" Fodor asked. "Able finally to speak your plan?"

"No," Istvan answered, a sinister smile stretching his lips. "I will not tell you the details of it now. But I will say that we must gather power and work to steer the Kingdom down the right path. A path that sees our interests secured."

With those words cast, Istvan began to walk away, though like before, Fodor's voice reached out to him from the shadows. "So, you do have a plan. Good to know. Let me know when you want to tell me."

Chapter 4
Awakened from Sleep

The morning light shone through the gaps in the wall as if it was an open window. With a soft glisten, the reflected light of the snow and ice shimmered with its soft fall, though its embrace was far from wanted on the skin of a man.

With a grunt and a whine, he rolled out of the ever-reaching dawn's light, trying to stay away from its warmth and its simultaneous awakening.

With heavy feet through the hard dirt and melting snow, a stout, tall figure marched his way from beyond the shelter of his home and company, towards the slumbering man's bed. "Hey, Paulus," he said, as he entered the barn hunched over to fit through the door. His brown hair lay combed carefully to the side, as not a speck of dust or dirt made its home on any part of him. "I need you to get up. I got work that needs doing and not enough time to do it all. You better not still be drunk."

"Just another hourglass, Mathias," Paulus mumbled, pulling the cloak that was his blanket over his brown hair and soft features, with his heavily scarred and branded hand. "Just another few hours…"

"Don't make me get the water, not again," Mathias warned, waving his finger in a stern warning. "You know I will. I've done it before. I'm not going to feel sorry for you, you know. I will get the bucket. You know I will. And you know what will happen in this cold."

A grunt and a whine filled the air for a moment, followed by a plume of warm air leaving Paulus's mouth like a chimney. "At least close the door. It is freezing. I might lose something important. Something the women of this world can't live without."

"It was opened when I got here," Mathias replied with a sigh. "You're lucky none of the animals suffered."

"I could have caught my death," Paulus said, as he shuffled back and forth and looked for comfort. "Maybe I should just lie down for a little longer. Make sure I'm well enough to go and work."

With another sigh, Mathias ran his hand through his hair struggling to find the right words. "You're still drunk. I'm going to get the bucket. Yeah, I'm going to go and get it."

"You don't have to do that," Paulus replied with an annoyed sigh of his own. "Why do you want to do that? Do more work and for what? So, you can feel good about yourself? So, you can tell your wife that you came and bothered me? Big man."

"You stink," Mathias quickly stated, as he turned and made his way back the way he had come. "You have been laying in the same spot for who knows how long. And don't talk about my wife." His pace was quick, though not quick enough to escape the words that followed and burrowed into him.

"You really are under that woman's thumb," Paulus said bluntly. "Always knew you were weak, but to choose her over me, shows what a man you are. A short one. And I'm not talking about your height."

"You leave my wife out of this," Mathias replied in saturated anger.

"I'm just saying, you could at least be honest," Paulus said, as he closed his eyes and remained in the trapped heat of his makeshift bed. "Instead of that passive thing that you and every other woman does."

"You really want honesty?" Mathias asked, growing louder with each word. "You want honesty, fine. What type of a man are you who had it all and lost it because of stupidity and greed, and then does nothing but moan and drink, when he's not begging for a handout? What kind of man brags to people about the brand he got on his hand, when those very same people not only put it there, but laugh behind his back? And what kind of man walks to the capital to beg, when he has good limbs to work with? You still drunk now, or just hungover?"

"That's not fair," Paulus replied with a stoic tone. "I also eat. And what about you? We used to do good work together. Made enough for you to live here, didn't I? Or did you forget that?"

A twitch pulled on Mathias's eye as wrinkles gripped him. "Yeah, you helped me! But I helped you too! I remember—" he grew silent for a moment as he shook his head and waved his hand before his face. "You know, I have had it with you. Not even related to you and I'm treating you better than I do my own son. My own son!"

"Well, I would feel bad for your boy, but you're not bothering him right now, are you?" Paulus asked back. "He just has to worry about getting your looks, or hers…"

"What was that?" Mathias demanded to know.

"What was what?" Paulus asked back, with an act of ignorance, as he turned his eyes to him. "Did you say something?"

A stillness held the air for a moment as the two men stared each other down, the only sound permeating between, the subtle drip of the fading snow.

"So, are you going to go?" Paulus finally asked, as he pulled his cover over his head. "Like I said, come back in an hour. I need the sleep."

"You know, I have seen lepers work harder than you," Mathias replied as he waved his finger. "And that's not even a joke. That's a truth. Even with their faces falling off and dealing with all that shit people give them. Seen them at least get out of bed."

Paulus peeked his head out of his cover with a long silent stare, as if debating to release the words on the tip of his tongue. "That's no way to talk about your wife."

Mathias grew still and silent, holding the stare with eyes that grew wider with each beat of his heart. "To hell with the bucket, I'm getting my shovel," he finally warned with a hiss, as he turned around and stormed out of his barn.

A grumble and a reassuring sigh left Paulus's lips, as he pulled the makeshift blanket over his face once again. "He's not coming back," he said with a sigh and a faint laugh, as he turned onto his side and closed his eyes. There he remained, his breaths steadily rising and falling. Though, before he could find comfort and peace, one again the sound of footsteps drew near, and his vision was drawn.

With a shovel in his hand, its spade still covered in mud, Mathias returned with a look of rage across his face. He stood a few steps shy of his friend, his fingers coiling tightly while he readied himself.

"You're not going to use—" Paulus began to say with a laugh, though could not finish.

"GET OUT!" Mathias shouted, as he raised the shovel high and rapidly advanced towards him.

The sound of confrontation and turbulence filled the early dawn, as only one phrase by Paulus could be heard through it all. "Not the face!"

Chapter 5

Her Decision

Rains battered the window with a tumultuous sting, while as if frightened by it, a lit candle fluttered on its sheltered side. Stone floors echoed softly in the candle's company, as drops of rain found their way onto them through the carried embrace of a cloak. The one who brought them in was slow to advance, while a slight trail of mud and water followed her.

Through the short and narrow hallway she went, her pace gripped by too much labor and too little rest. Step after step followed one another, until there before a dark door, she fell still. With a slow whine, the door that kept the sheltered flame at bay opened, as she stopped at its threshold.

Like a treasure, the room held something that called her gaze and forced her to linger despite the dark bags that pulled on her tired eyes. There they lay, what she had traveled to see, the very same thing she had traveled to provide for; her children.

With a soft gaze she watched as her two children slept peacefully in the company of each other. They each lay wrapped by love and the warmth of their blankets, as the cold of the night seemed to be a distant dream.

Though, her presence in the structure did not go unnoticed and from the depths of its shelter there came another. With a shadow cast far and wide, a figure that was familiar to the woman in the doorway approached. A trimmed beard and mature hair graced him, as the bushy brows between them lay scattered and disorderly.

"You're back," he said with a soft whisper, wrapping his arms around her and pressing himself close to her. "I heard what happened, Helene. Terrible."

"Yeah," she replied softly, persisting in the embrace. "Back for a little, Johann. Only a little. I think the Queen will want to have me running off somewhere else soon. I think I will have to."

"Is it true?" Johann asked.

"I would think all the world knows," Helene replied with a sigh.

"But is it true?" Johann pressed.

"Not now," Helene replied, as she continued to watch her children. "I'm tired. I just want a moment."

"Sorry," Johann said pulling away. "I will wait for you in the other room. I got some food there. It's cold. Thought you would have been back earlier, but it's good."

"I will be there in a little," Helene replied. "I will tell you what happened."

With receding steps, Johann left Helene to the slumbering company of her children. She stood there with her eyes on them, as their gentle breaths raised and dropped the blankets that gave them warmth.

"I can't," Helene finally said to herself with a whisper, as she slowly and quietly closed the door. "I am sorry my Queen, but I can't. I cannot risk them."

With slow steps, Helene made her way through her home and eventually reached the sanctuary that lay laden with food, drink, a place to sit and some company. The room was simple containing a table lacking splinters with a few cups and bowls and a pair of benches on either side of it. With a sigh she took a seat and rested there with her eyes closed for a moment.

"Tired?" Johann asked.

"How were the children?" Helene asked, ignoring the question.

"Fine, they missed you though," Johann replied, moving his limbs and bringing forth some wine and bread for his wife. "You know you made a mess when you came in. Dragged in a bit of mud with you."

"What about the Queen's daughters, Anne and little Elizabeth?" Helene asked, ignoring the stray in topic.

"They are fine," Johann stated. "Do you know what will happen to them? There is already talk. Quite a bit of it."

Helene was silent as she stared out towards a sight that no one other than herself could see. "Talk?" she finally asked with a whisper.

"I overheard some nobles say that they would push for the Queen's children to be married to secure the border and gain better claim on the other kingdoms," Johann explained, seemingly to himself. "They don't think the Queen will be able to maintain her authority without her husband. Would not be so bad if it were not for the Ottomans. They are talking about having her marry someone else. And don't even get me started on the unborn child. Some say if it is a girl, they will see her sent to the Ottomans as some form of tribute. And if it's a boy, well you don't even want to know. But, I don't know, I just don't know. I can't help but think, what are we going to do? I mean, will we have work for much longer? Should we be looking to the nobles? Maybe we can take care of some of their children instead? We have a few pieces of silver saved, but that won't last us long if we have to leave."

"The Queen will look after us," Helene replied, finally turning her gaze on him.

"Yeah, but how do you know?" Johann asked, as he tore a piece of bread and put it between his teeth. "She doesn't even have a husband, how is she going to take care of herself? Right now, the nobles are working to tie a leash around her or worse a noose."

"She will look after us," Helene echoed, her tone a note higher.

"You say that, but how do you know?" Johann pressed, searching for some measure of comfort. "I mean, she is in no position to—"

"I know what I have to do," Helene suddenly interrupted as she spoke to herself with a tone that silenced her husband. "I know what I have to do."

"What?" Johann asked. "What do you mean?"

"Nothing," Helene replied. "We will be fine, and the Queen will be fine. And before you ask, I know because I will look after her and she will look after me."

A momentary hiatus settled, as the conversation was left in a lull, only the faint sounds of his chewing filled the air. Finally, with a sigh, Helene pressed against the table and rose back onto her tired feet.

"Where are you going?" Johann asked, mouth half full. "Shouldn't we talk? At least about the funeral? At least about what we're going to do?"

"Bed," Helene stated more than replied. "I am tired."

"But you haven't eaten," Johann said, as she turned away. "And we haven't—"

"Just clean up when you're done," Helene whispered as she vanished.

Chapter 6
Leads to the Capital

Under the high sun, an engulfing wall of water, dark stone, and brick reached into the sky, as the faint winds carried the scattered clouds and their shadows over the barriers of men with ease. The towers and the archers that manned them could do naught against the tide that brought them forth. Though their eyes were not turned to the vast space above, but rather to the mob that snaked their way through the city, all for the chance of a view of a motionless body that held royal blood.

In Székesfehérvár they gathered, their bodies pressed against each other, from the rich to the laziest of beggars, as they crossed below the gatehouse and into the shadow of great cathedral.

Its tall two towers tried to scratch the sky, as their ornate design left the jaws of those to see them fall to the ground. Though, while most gazed up at it with the wonder of a child, those of wisdom and invitation kept their eyes focused on the closed doors as they waited.

With a sudden sound that shook the sky and forced the birds that clung to the city to take flight, the bells rang loudly. Their rings echoed one after another, summoning all to heed the event and forcing the mob to grow vibrant and restless.

"LOOK!" a soul in the mob shouted.

A procession of substance and wealth, those of nobility, affluence, and connections rode their way through the city streets, past the eyes of the world beside them and into the cathedral. There they embraced the scene of some who mourned in its sheltered embrace, while for the majority, they cast aside such commotion and settled into the politics that dominated even a widow.

Queen Elizabeth stood draped in black, her position fixed and her eyes on the altar and those who contended with the ceremony. She watched, as those who had been granted entry made their way to her late husband and offered the illusion of respect, before they quickly vanished to their task of securing their purses and coffers under the rhetoric of a once again great Kingdom. They gathered in their groups, buzzing to one another like busy bees. Though, while they caught the Queen's eyes, her gaze was suddenly pulled as her own daughters made an appearance at the altar.

They stood side by side, under the watchful eyes of the world, one with fair hair falling to her shoulders, the other with dark hair nestled tightly beneath a hairpiece and accompanied by Helene's husband Johann. Though, even such things as being left to mourn could not go undisturbed.

"How are you my queen?" Count Ulrich Cillei said with a bow. Silver trimmed his hair, as the otherwise brown head and dark eyes gave him an air of elegance and grace. Only the stubble of a beard permeated on his face, though a large gut pressed out his belly.

A weary smile formed on Elizabeth's lips as she reached for his hand and took it in hers and ushered him to rise. "I am well, all things considered. Tired, but I seem to have my health."

"And your daughters?" Ulrich asked, gesturing to them. "They seem to be taking it well. It seems they have inherited your resolve."

"I fear it is because they did not know their father that well," Elizabeth confessed. "All day with the nanny or tutors.

Interactions with their father were limited to a simple passing embrace, where masks and customs must be worn and enforced. It is a hard thing to feel sorrow for a stranger and they are too young to know any better. I think they will one day understand. I know I eventually did."

"The cost of power some would say," Ulrich said with nod. "I'm sure they will one day understand. As we will as well."

A faint smile grew over Elizabeth as she gave the man a subtle nod. "Even though my husband, the King, still lays above the ground, there seems to be no shortage of men who wish to fill the void left by him."

"If there is anything you need, you simply need to say the word," Ulrich quickly stated. "Anything. As you are the Queen and may shape the world to your liking. I would be happy to lend you my support."

"There was something," Elizabeth mentioned. "More of a question than a favor."

"One often comes before the other," Ulrich replied with a smile. "I will try to complete both if able."

"Well it is something I noticed," Elizabeth said softly as the ceremony progressed. "Where are the Crown Jewels?"

For the briefest of moments, Ulrich was taken aback, as the weight of the words seemed too heavy for his shoulders to bear. Yet, while he seemed trapped by the Queen's words, he stroked his beard, washing away the shocked expression and replacing it with a deep look. "They were moved. They were moved to Plintenburg Castle for safety."

"Why were they moved there?" Elizabeth asked.

"Customary," Ulrich replied suddenly and seemingly calmly, as if contended to the path he had chosen. "Unfortunately. The Bishop of Gran died and now with the succession it must be held carefully to avoid a disaster. That is what the new keeper of the Crown, Count Gorge, along with all the others are thinking. Can't have any fool that wants to simply put on the Crown and claim the throne. Too dangerous, even for an unjust successor. Could you imagine, anyone you wanted could be made King."

"I can only hope then that it will be kept safe," Elizabeth said giving a few nods to those who passed before her. "I would not want anyone getting their hands on it. Not until they are needed for a rightful heir."

"That would be very hard," Ulrich said as he too gave a few nods to those that passed before them. "It is under Count Gorge's watch. The man is not good at much, but at defense and keeping a tight grip, he is second to none."

"And with women," Elizabeth added. "Spends a lot of time chasing women. Married women, noble women, women who do not want his attention or advancement. All manner of women."

"And with women," Ulrich agreed with a nod. "That he does too. That he does."

"One might think that it would create a hole in the Crown's protection," Elizabeth said, pondering out loud. "But I'm sure that there are other means besides one man to cause the Crown to be taken."

"Indeed, there are," Ulrich replied with the faint hint of a smile, though quickly brought his hand to hide it. "But the structure that it is kept in makes up for certain shortcomings, or as you said, holes. Many call it a castle, but it is much more than that. It is one of the greatest structures in the Kingdom, in terms of defense and security. Anyway, the structure it is in now, is one of the great ones. It could hold out for months in a bad situation. And in a good one, possibly years. Its walls are thick and high…" Before he could finish, he drifted off for a moment, as the stifled hint of a smile grew once again.

"Thinking about something thick and high, perhaps?" Elizabeth asked, as she forced a faint and nearly indistinguishable blush on her company's cheeks. "Your wife?"

A faint cough left Ulrich's lips, as he shifted his weight back and forth from one leg to the other. "Right then. Where was I?"

"High and thick," Elizabeth replied, much to the amusement of Helene who giggled and smiled under her veiled hand before moving to tend to the next task required of her.

"Well, there are many guards," Ulrich continued with a nod. "Many within on watch. Many on the wall on watch. Many on the towers on watch. Even many on horseback to depart and peruse on watch. We can thank the Ottomans for the need of so many."

"And I suppose that the stone and men are not the only obstacle?" Elizabeth asked.

"Quite right, then there is the door," Ulrich confirmed with a nod. "I don't mean to say the door to the castle, which in itself I would call impenetrable without the right numbers. No, not the gate. I mean to say, the door the Crown is kept behind. That is as thick as the royal vault and with locks that would take ages to break. But, that is just my observation. One observation I have made in person a few times, but one none the less I have made."

Elizabeth was silent for a moment, as she mirrored the nods of those that continued to pass by; playing her part as widow.

"By the sound of what you have told me, it would seem that an army would be needed to get the Crown from where it has been placed," she finally said. "Either that, or another way in."

"I pray you don't take this the wrong way," Ulrich began to say, as he searched for the right words. "But, you seem to have an interest in this."

"That is why I ask," Elizabeth replied. "Is that not why we have interests, if not to inquire on them?"

"No, no," Ulrich explained. "I mean to say, if someone like me were to hear what it is you were saying, they would get ideas."

"I merely wish to see what options lay before me," Elizabeth replied. "The world may gather what ideas they wish. All that matters are actions in the end. Anything else and, I think it would be safe to call it gossip, or speculation. And there is no need to fear that, is there, my ally Count Ulrich?"

Ulrich nodded slowly turning his eyes to the scene before him. He nodded to those that passed, throwing a few fellow mourners looks of condolence, accentuated by a certain shimmer in his eyes. "My Queen, I do not know what the future of the Kingdom may hold, but I am sure that it has ideas with you. Whatever they may be, I hope you know that I will gladly aide in whatever way I can. Whether it be from my informants, my wealth, or my allies. I only pray that if that day should come, you do not forget who was happily by your side."

"Thank you, Ulrich, I will not soon forget it," Elizabeth replied pulling the faintest hint of a smile from her hiding. Though, before it could blossom and grow, before it could spread, it was stunted like a flower that tried to touch the sun in a late winter storm.

"What are you two whispering about?" Istvan asked approaching with rolling shoulders.

"Probably the same thing you have been talking about over there," Elizabeth replied with a point of her noise and a calm face, to the nobles he had departed from.

"A fitting ceremony," Istvan said, as he shifted his eyes across the room in an attempt to disguise those whom he had been with. From one to the next he watched with a long stare, deciding who would be his next company before he returned his attention to those before him. "You have done well to arrange it so quickly. I think the King would be pleased. If there is anything that you wish to discuss, anything that you want me to convey to the other nobles, don't be afraid to ask. I am someone they will listen to." With a subtle bow bound by convention and the eyes of the Kingdom upon him, he readied to take his leave, but was stopped in his tracks before he could.

"I do have a question for you," Elizabeth said. "Have you seen Helene, my governess?"

"That woman," Istvan replied with a grunt. "Why would I have seen her? You're the one who sends her out on errand after errand. Have her running all over the Kingdom. Travels more than a merchant who peddles foul goods."

"It sounds like you care," Elizabeth stated. "You do know she is married."

A scoff a tad bit too loud echoed in the holy place, as eyes searched for the source that was Istvan. "The placement of one servant is hardly worth an eye."

"Are you trying to say she has your eye?" Elizabeth asked as she subtlety taunted him.

Istvan opened his mouth to protest, though before a word could emerge from it, he pulled it closed and held his silence, if for only a moment. "I will take my leave, Queen Elizabeth. I have a great deal of other nobles I must meet with."

"I'm sure you do," Elizabeth replied. "As do I."

"Oh, just one last thing, my Queen," Istvan said with a grin. "You can cry if you want. It would be expected of you."

A smile that was nothing but forced grew over Elizabeth's lips, as she held the man before her gaze. "I thank you for your concern. As well as what is expected of me. But, I should only say, that if you want to see some tears, you can let them fall. It wouldn't be the first time, would it? It is the chatter amongst many of the nobles, as well as the commoners. But, I'm sure you already know that, right? It was what you have been talking about with the others?"

Istvan was silent, as the drum of his heart rose and rang in his ears. With a jerked nod that was an offering not of conviction, but of custom and necessity, he turned his back and quickly stormed off into the crowd, his face red out of rage and embarrassment.

"Well, let's get this ceremony started," Elizabeth said to herself, a faint smile growing over her lips as she savored the temporary victory.

Chapter 7

The Beggars

With feet that stumbled over every stone in the road, a familiar man made his way through the winding streets. The scene of the world lay just at the periphery of his view; all the while, the excitement of the sun played through the city rousing the spirits of those who lived for the day. Shops tended to the task of pushing the last of their goods, as they raced to clear their stands before the encroach of the inevitable event that would swallow them whole. Though, it seemed to do little to the one whose face was covered black and blue.

With a stumble, Paulus fell to the ground, just on the cusp of the busy street, staying in the company of only himself and the shadows cast by the people who walked by.

The fresh bruises on his face, marked his skin, as the faint outline of a shovel left only the questions of who and why. From the folds of his clothes, he pulled forth a small purse, no larger than a pouch and gave the tanned item a shake. Not even the faint hint of a jingle permeated from within it, as the sobering silence brought about an unwanted reality. For a short while, he sat there, his eyes closed, the cold touching him and his extended unbranded hand, as he silently begged for a few coins.

Time and time again, stray figures that crossed through the otherwise narrow space gave Paulus little more than a glance, as they worked to avert their eyes and hide their wealth. Though, compassion was soon to arise, as one who rushed past, threw two green copper coins at his feet.

With a sigh, Paulus slowly began to move, reaching for the coins and quickly putting it into his previously empty purse. "I guess I will be able to get a drink... Don't really care to see what's going on. I just wonder if the inns will be open now?" Yet, before he could rise, a figure at the far end of the alley caught sight him.

"Hey you!" A loud and commanding voice suddenly bellowed, matching down through the alley. His armor chimed, as the metal that made it struck his long spear and accentuated his rough features. "No beggars allowed in the city, especially not today! Get over here!"

"Well, I guess I should see what is happening..." Paulus quickly said to himself, rapidly leaping up with the grace of a squirrel, rushing out the alley and vanishing into the crowd that grew larger with each passing moment.

The crowd pushed and buckled, as the weight of each of them pressed against one another, like the waves that met a cliff.

"What's all the commotion about?" Paulus asked, pressing against the crowd and struggling to find space. "Something I should know about?"

"The King is dead," an old man alongside him replied, keeping his eyes forward on the scene.

Paulus was silent for a moment, reflecting on the words with a blank stare. "I should have been clearer. I should have said, is it something I should care about?"

"Without a King the Ottomans will invade," the man replied with an angry tone.

Paulus was quiet for another moment, turning his eyes in the direction of the others. "So, is something supposed to happen here?"

"They brought the King's body already," the man replied with anger. "Now shut your mouth, I can't hear!"

Taken aback, Paulus stood there with the others, like a sheep in the herd, unbeknownst to him that a pair of quick hands made even faster work of his newly acquired wealth and the purse it lay within.

With fingers that knew where and how to climb, a hooded figure plucked from its place, Paulus's purse and added it to his own. Though, like an awakened dragon, he was voracious and searched for his next prey. Moving a few souls over, he eyed his next easy task, blind to what was about to occur.

"I'm going to get that drink," Paulus mumbled to himself with a faint smile finally satisfied. Yet, before he could depart, his eyes grew wide, as his hand reached for his lost purse. Throwing his eyes about, he searched for where it had gone, finding nothing. His eyes combed the ground to no avail and before his heart could flutter, he looked to those besides him. With a hurried set of steps, he rushed to catch that which caught his eyes. "Hey. Hey! The hell you think you're doing? The hell you think you were going with my purse?"

The pickpocket was silent, his brown eyes staring back in shock. Barely a stubble grew on his chin, though the wrinkles that were his shock forced a temporary jump in his age that was otherwise half of that of his unexpected and unwanted company.

"What! What do you think you're doing?" he demanded.

"Caching a pickpocket," Paulus replied with a tighter grip.

"What makes you think—?"

"Don't bother," Paulus warned, as he interrupted. "Just give it here and we won't have any problem. Everyone gets one. And I need to get my drink before my hangover catches me. So, give it here and I won't point you out to the watch."

A silence held the scene between the two men, the turbulence of the procession pressing just beyond them. The rumble of the steps, and the cries and mourns that forced the birds to take flight, seemed like an island in the middle, somehow untouched by the drama of the world beyond.

"Just leave it!" The pickpocket ordered, suddenly pulling his arm back, giving Paulus a shove and rushing off. Pressing through the crowd, he fought against the seemingly endless wall that lay before him.

"Don't say I didn't warn you," Paulus grumbled, with his eyes fixated upon him like a beast on the hunt. "Get back here! Don't make me run!"

With a glance, the pickpocket looked over his shoulder and saw the man that was his shadow quickly approach. He tried to break through the mob, a jingle to his step, as the purses he held in his embrace were dropped one after another. With stumbling steps, he broke through the wall that was the mob and began his unobstructed run through the city. Lefts followed rights, as panted breaths flowed from his lungs. Beads of sweat fell down his skin, his face growing red. Though, at every turn, at every step that he hoped was an opportunity to grasp at the victory of an escape, there behind him continued his pursuer.

Paulus's breaths were heavy, his limbs growing weak and his pace seemed to slow. Though, before he could succumb to his own limitations, with all his force, he threw himself forward with a lunge.

"I got you!" He shouted with a mix of pride and anger, as he grasped him and held him to the ground.

"Just leave it fatty," the pickpocket replied, pulling and pushing to free himself. "Just leave it..."

"Fatty?" Paulus asked through panting breaths. "I might not have worked in a while, but I am no rich man and I am no fatty."

"It was a compliment, just take it," the pickpocket ordered, grinning through his heavy breaths. "Next time I will call you old man if you're that offended."

"It was not a compliment," Paulus grumbled, raising himself and lunging once again after the man. "And I'm not old."

"Older than me," the pickpocket replied with a faint laugh and smile, as he once more began to run, though was quickly stripped of his smile. From his periphery he caught sight of his pursuer but a finger's reach away. His pace hurried, trying to force the gap between himself and his victim to grow, though his efforts were too little too late. For just as he reached the edge of the alley, and back into the embrace of the busy crowd and all it brought, a hard tackle sent him forward and to the ground.

Both men fell gasping for air, though there was no relief as they lay on the ground. Flailing their arms at one another, both tried to subdue the other, though to little avail. Their strikes were weak, and their placement wrong, as they struggled to hold onto their dignity.

"HEY!" A voice called from nearby.

Both men paused their struggle, looking to the source.

A captain of the guard by the name of Andreas filled their sights, storming towards them, his weapon drawn and ready. A pink scar ran from his chin to his cheek, as his head lay devoid of hair, with merely the stubble of what had once been. Moving as fast as his limp would allow, he approached with a retinue of half a dozen men along with him.

"The hell is going on here? What are you two doing? Who attacked who? I want an answer! NOW!"

"He didn't attack me," Paulus quickly explained, raising his hands and gently pushing the point of the spear out of his face and towards the pickpocket. "Was a... it was a bee."

"A bee?" Andreas demanded. "There are no bees this time of the year! What do you take me for?"

"Yeah, a bee..." The pickpocket echoed, slowly pushing the spear point back towards Paulus. "A big bee. It looked fat and old. Ran right into me, caused all this trouble, sir. But, I don't think it will be any problem now."

"Bee ran into me first and stung me, had to deal with it with a little bit of force," Paulus added. "I can say we are sorry. And if you leave us, we will be out of your hair... I mean—"

"Clear the road, before I have you both in the pillory, or worse," Andreas warned with a rage on the tip of his tongue, running his fingers over his barren head.

"Right," Paulus agreed, standing up and taking his purse out of the pickpocket's possession. "That's mine," he whispered, yet before he could take it and vanish, he was suddenly stopped in his tracks by a tight grip that burrowed into his shoulder.

"I didn't realize it before," Andreas said, showing his teeth to the sun. "You were begging earlier, weren't you? You were the one who ran away from me, weren't you?"

"Who me?" Paulus asked back, quickly shaking his head. "No, that wasn't me. I wasn't in any alley."

"I never said anything about an alley," Andreas replied, the smile growing even larger across his face. "I remember, you were in the alley over there earlier. Isn't that right? The one who didn't listen. The one who tried to get away. Isn't that right, beggar?"

"Looks like you are in trouble," the pickpocket said under his breath with a slight laugh, as he raised himself off of the ground and began to make his departure. "Have fun with your friend. I have places to be."

"Where do you think you're going?" Andreas demanded to know, quickly moving his free hand to Lucas, and holding him tightly in his grip. "You really think I'm going to let the second beggar go while I deal with the first? Do you think this is my first day on the job? I know your kind always go in groups."

"I was, ugh, I was just going to clear the road," the pickpocket replied, his voice soft and his composure pulled back. "And I'm not a beggar..."

"Oh, no, no," Andreas said, wrapping his thick arms around the two and beginning to lead them forward. "Only a beggar would wear such patchy clothes. And as to the road, I have a better plan. You see, I have a place where I like to put people. A place that is currently empty. A place I think both of you will enjoy spending a little time."

"It's not a dungeon is it?" Paulus asked.

"You think you belong in a dungeon?" Andreas asked back, his smile growing unsettlingly large. "You want to go in one?"

"No, not what I said," Paulus whispered.

"I do have family I need to get back to," the pickpocket stated, trying to wiggle free of the grip, but finding heavy fingers burrowing deeper into him instead.

"You don't have to worry about that," Andreas replied with a sinister smile. "You see, all you and your friend here did was a bit of begging and a bit of a brawl. Right?"

"He's not my friend…" Paulus mumbled so far under his breath, that not a soul heard.

"And we have a fitting punishment for people who see my time wasted," Andreas continued. "You see, I could have you flogged, but I think a little time in the pillory will suffice. What do you think about that?"

"Are those the only options?" the pickpocket asked. "Maybe a warning instead? A firm warning always worked with my old man."

"There is always the dungeon," Andreas replied smiling. "We like to brand those that make their way to them. So, what's it going to be beggars?"

Chapter 8
A History and Legend

A black pot grew hot, the water within beginning to bubble, as it lay suspended over an open flame. The timber beneath crackled and slowly gave way to ash, steam rising from within. Though, no soup or stew boiled within its darkened black curves, but rather a plain body of warm water; one that would soon become larger, as a hand came upon its handle.

With a great deal of strength that pulled against her whole body, Helene carried it to the center of the room and poured it out into a nearly filled bath.

"It's ready," she said, wiping her brow from the labor. "Sorry it took so long."

"You have nothing to apologize for," Elizabeth replied, putting to rest the page of parchment she read. "Water takes the time it needs to get warm. Besides, it has been an eventful day…" for a moment she drifted off into her mind, staring blankly at what she had been reading.

"While you get ready, I should tell you," Helene explained, contending with the many tasks that demanded attention. "Your children have been taken care of and are already asleep."

"That's good to hear," Elizabeth replied. "I hope they can sleep. It will be busy in the coming days. It will be busy. It always is…"

Helene was silent, gazing out blankly against the wall in patience and deep thought.

"I forgot to thank you, Helene," Elizabeth said, as the soft cloth that draped her skin fell to the floor and she was left with only her undergarments. The lump of her belly called the eye, and had any been there to peak, they would have stared. "I know you would have liked to stay for the funeral, but I needed you to do those tasks. So, thank you, Helene."

"No need to thank me," Helene quickly replied, turning further to avert her eyes. "I was just doing what was needed of me. That's all."

"You were doing much more," Elizabeth said, stripping the last of her vestment and letting the mix of warmth and cold touch her skin. She pressed against the sensation of the air and dipped into the warm bath, letting out a sigh of relief. "Ahh, that is what I needed… My bones were aching… I think I could sit here all day, or until the water gets cold. Almost makes you wish you could do this every day."

Helene grew the faintest of smiles, turning back to the Queen, though as she stood there, it was relatively quick to vanish. "My Queen," she finally said as she lowered her head. "My Queen I—"

"My Queen?" Elizabeth interrupted with her eyebrows raised. "Helene we are not in anyone's company. There is no need for such things. I told you this when we became friends, you don't have to act that way." She fell silent as she stared at her, "what's wrong, Helene? You can tell me anything."

"I am sorry," Helene began. "I am sorry for your loss. I am sorry I have not been more involved with your grief. I am sorry I was not there to take better care of you when you needed it. And I am sorry for not saying it sooner… but… but… I will do what you need of me. I will do anything you ask, my Queen. I will gladly serve you for your future."

Elizabeth was silent for a moment, before pulling her arm out of the warmth of the water. With a wave and a reach, she called to her friend and quickly held her hand in her own.

"Helene, my friend. You have nothing to apologize for. If anything, I should say that I am sorry. I did not mean to put so much weight on your shoulders. And I should not have asked, I should have—"

"No," Helene interrupted. "I'm sorry, but no. You do not have to apologize. I have to apologize. I should be the one who—"

With a laugh and a warm smile, Elizabeth broke the tension that gripped the room and brought about a levity that calmed the very soul.

"Is this going to be like that time we first met? When we went back and forth apologizing until we became friends? Do you remember that? Seems like just yesterday, but..."

"So long ago..." Helene added with a laugh of her own.

A silence held the air between them, as the warmth of the bath slowly faded away. Though, the warmth of the two hands and the pulse of the two beating hearts that flowed through them, held its constancy.

"I have a plan," Elizabeth said, lowering herself deeper into the bath and relishing the warmth.

"A plan?" Helene asked with a hint of surprise.

"Why are you surprised at that?" Elizabeth asked back.

"No, no," Helene replied with a slight wave of self-defense. "I didn't mean it in that form."

"I know," Elizabeth said with a coy smile, soaking in the last bit of warmth. "I'm just toying with you. But, I do have a plan. Want to know what it is?"

"I—" Helene began to reply, though was swiftly interrupted before she could.

"I know you said you would gladly serve, but…" Elizabeth explained with a somber tone. "I just want you to know that I won't think less of you if you don't. Nor would it jeopardize your position with me, or that of your husband. You have my word on that. We are friends, nothing will change that, Helene. And if my plan should fail, you would be spared of the direct consequences of my actions. So, before you answer please think one last time, because after I tell you, there will be no way to undo your choice. So, are you ready? And are you sure?"

"At first I was not sure," Helene confessed. "I grew afraid, not just for myself, but for my children. But, I know… I know that it is not something I can decide not to do. This is something I must do. This is something I must do for my children and their future, as well as for you, for your children, and if not for them, then for the Kingdom. So, now I can say, yes. I am sure. I am ready."

"Thank you, Helene," Elizabeth said. "And please believe me when I say thank you. I mean that… Let me ask you this, do you know the history of the Crown, Helene?"

"Well," Helene replied, shifting her head back and forth. "If we are talking about the Crown that belongs to the Kingdom, I know what they told me when I was a child. I tell those stories as well as I can remember to my own. But, I wouldn't call that history, more of a simple conversation to distract the little ones with."

"What of the legend?" Elizabeth asked.

"I know of that," Helene replied with a smile, as she moved to tend to her labor. "I doubt there is not a farmer worth their salt who does not know it."

"Would you tell me what you know?" Elizabeth asked.

"I think I actually told my little one this story just a little while ago." Helene confessed, throwing her a look mixed with joy and suspicion. "She was in the bath too."

A light chuckle left the Queen's lips as she tilted her head back and closed her eyes. "Then I will imagine I am a child again."

"Alright now bear with me," Helene said, clearing her throat with a cough. "I will tell you the shortened version… Long ago, back when the Kingdom was a child, just like you, a saint was given a crown by the pope after he had been blessed by a vivid dream of angels. Though, before the crown could be placed on the royal head, your great, great, great, great, great grandfather, Saint Stephen, offered the crown to the Virgin Mary. She accepted it and by doing so, a contract, divine in nature was made. That is how the Crown became holy, a halo for all those who wear it."

"Did she really come down for the Crown?" Elizabeth asked, playing her role. "Did she really touch it?"

"That is what the legend says," Helene replied. "You see, the Virgin Mary accepted the saint's divine contract and made the Crown divine, so that only those chosen by God may have the right to rule. And by doing so, the Virgin Mary became the patron saint of all the Kingdom. And with it, a purity, divine in nature governs the Kingdom."

"It is a good legend and you gave it justice," Elizabeth said. "Thank you."

"If only my children were so kind after I told them a story," Helene said while laughing, as she turned her attention back to her labor. "Half the time they demand another. The other half, they fall asleep mid-story."

"Isn't the point to make them fall asleep?" Elizabeth asked with a light laugh.

"Well I mean it is, but no one wants to think they are that bad at telling a tale," Helene replied with coy smile and a bit of a laugh. "It's like my mother told me, a blessing in one situation is a curse in another."

A lull filled the air between the two women, as they drifted off to the labyrinth's of their minds.

"Do you want to know about the history?" Elizabeth suddenly asked with a somber tone.

"Sure," Helene replied with a laugh. "I could use it in the next story I tell my young ones."

"The Crown has been used since the origins of the Kingdom," Elizabeth began with a calm demeanor, raising herself and stepping out of the body of water. Drops fell to the floor and the carpet, as she quickly found herself wrapped in soft clothes that grew wet as she dried. "It dates back to the first King. Made of gold and covered with enamels that were made in Constantinople, it was beyond valuable at the time it was made. And now, it is priceless. Though, that is not why it is so guarded. No, it is guarded beyond the reach of even armies for the symbolism it holds. It is so important, that no King can be recognized without it. So much so, that they say that the Crown is not for the King, but the King is for the Crown."

Helene fell silent and still, as she listened to the words and passed clean articles of clothing for her to put on. She opened her mouth to speak, though no sound emerged, as the words of the Queen lingered in her mind and kept her there.

"I think I stayed too long in here," Elizabeth suddenly explained, holding her hand out and showing the wrinkles that were on her skin from her bath. "Then again, at the same time I wish I could have stayed in longer." She added, finishing her process of covering her skin and emerging with a simple, yet unapologetically elegant green gown.

"Do you mean to say...?" Helene finally asked, though before she could add her thoughts and make them form deeper reason, she drew silent again.

"Come on," Elizabeth said, forcing the wrinkles out of her dress. "We are going to need help."

"Help?" Helene asked. "From whom? And for what?"

"Someone who can get into a castle," Elizabeth replied.

"I think your words could do that," Helene said bluntly. "You are the Queen, there is no one who can, or would for that matter, barricade their door to you."

"Without me being there," Elizabeth replied. "As I will be busy contending with the nobles."

"Many women in waiting could do that too," Helene replied, the hint of uncertainty and suspicion in her voice. "In fact, I could go and do that for you. You would just have to tell me what it is you would like to get and from which castle."

Elizabeth turned her gaze to her for a moment with a smile. "And into a vault."

"A vault!" Helene said with disbelief. "You don't mean to say, that you... That is your plan? The Crown?"

Elizabeth stared at her reflection, as the words spoken to her quickly vanished, though like the echo that whispered a truth back, she finally replied. "The one that is history and a legend."

Chapter 9

Count Gorge

With slow steps that echoed over stones and made their way down a lavishly decorated hallway, one figure followed another, a chime of nine to them. Past the ornate tapestries that hung on plastered and painted walls, past the fine furniture that only those of noble birth were welcomed to, and past the dark timber of a dozen ornate doors, climbing upwards.

Their shadows pressed along the walls and all the wealth, as the light of a flame they each carried fluttered against the flow of air. The rays of the high sun fell further and further away, as the windows lay cast aside by thick unending stones. Further into darkness and isolation they went, until they both fell still.

They stood before something that was more of a wall than a door, as timber and metal lay bent and bound against one another in a conformity that shouted, 'none can pass.' Its ten locks stood imposing, its weakness unapparent. It was a vault, an intimidating one and as impenetrable as the word would suggest.

Silently Gorge pulled from his place around his neck, a large black key and the fine silver chain that bound it in its place, holding it before him.

"Unlock it," he ordered.

"Right away, my lord," the armed man by the name of Demeter said, as he quickly hurried to the task. Black hair as dark as the night lay hewed short and lent the man the hint of age. Though, his hazel eyes and strong jaw saved him of any disparity and left him a desire to many. Clothes that were neither of nobility or of the common folk clung to him, yet the sheathed sword and its ornate handle spoke of his responsibility and authority. With all the force that he could muster from his wide shoulders he turned the imbedded metal of the key, until finally, with a click, the first lock released its teeth.

"Where is the Castilian?" Gorge asked, turning his eyes down the hall towards a small closed door. "Is he not supposed to be keeping an eye on the vault?"

"I think he was tending to something in the lower castle, my lord," Demeter replied, turning key after key, until the last one found its place.

"Open it," Gorge ordered, a slight nod to his head.

With a whine of timber and metal, the vault door was pulled open by Demeter with a great deal of strength and effort. A faint grunt left his lips, as the veins in his hands and neck grew exposed and red consumed his skin.

Light flooded into the vault, as it drove away in an instant the darkness that had been left to swallow what lay inside. With each whine the hinges made, it forced what had been hidden to the world, to reveal itself with an opulent splendor of shimmering and precious metals and the jewels that lay imbedded in it. The treasures and wealth of the Kingdom stared back at those who looked upon it, as a tempting call summoned them to do more than look. Yet what truly caught attention was directly in the middle.

On a solitary podium nestled atop a soft red pillow sat the royal Crown. Gold shimmered in the light, as the precious stones sparkled. Two rings of pearls around the base glistened, as the enamels that were an assortment of colors and shapes, each told a tale that called to be watched. Nine gold chains with pendants at each end reached across the pillow, as they waited for the Crown to be lifted and them along with it. While atop of all the ornate intricacies, there sat a golden cross, perfectly erected and ostentatiously displayed, that shouted to the world, 'gaze here, gaze at the Crown and King.'

"You know, I liked to check it every day when the King, my friend, was alive," Gorge explained with a raspy voice, stepping into the vault and moving his fingers closer and closer to the royal artifacts. "Seemed to be a necessary thing. Don't know if it was out of fear of disappointing him, or if it was a sense of pride to be honest, but that is what it was. Do you know then why I do it now?"

"I do not, my lord," Demeter replied with a calm and still expression.

"Neither do I," Gorge stated, lingering in the royal possession's embrace. "I don't seem to want to check it much lately. There are times when I find it such a chore. And then there are times when the act just seems to bring to mind the memory of the King. You know I couldn't even go to the funeral because his death was so sudden. I would have been at the center of it, had I gone to his funeral. I know what his favorite flowers were... Don't think even that wife of his did." His fingers moved closer to the Crown, yet again ready to touch it, though just before he could, his hand was halted.

"Everything seems in place, my lord," Demeter said from beyond the threshold of the vault.

"So, it seems," Gorge replied with a nod, his fingers pulling away. "So, it seems... Want to know something funny? The Crown is actually bigger than any man's head."

Demeter held his expression unchanged, staring at his patron. "Quite funny, my lord."

"Just so you know, I didn't try it on to know that," Gorge explained, leaving the side of the precious item and making his way back toward the vault's door. "As I told you before, I know the King... well, I knew the King. He's the one who told me about it before he put it on," he crossed the threshold and watched as the door was closed once again. "He said he had to wear a leather cap to make it fit and even then, it did not sit properly. That brings back memories. I do wonder one thing though, who is going to come and claim it? Would think the Queen would, but she would need a husband in line to take it. Can't give it to her without one. Or better yet, I won't give it to her. Suppose we shall keep a watchful eye and see what the future brings. I think I will check on it one more time before then. Maybe two. Don't really see much reason to check it much more. Takes too much time. And time is something I believe you can never have enough of. Just like gold, wine, and women. Not always in that order, depends on the wine."

"Is there anything else you need of me?" Demeter asked, as he checked the handle on the vault with a strong pull. "The vault is secured."

"There is one thing," Gorge replied, a grin growing over his lips. "Do you remember that young thing that was with me earlier? The fair haired one that you had your eye on."

"I do, my lord," Demeter replied with the hint of a nervous blossom.

"Where did that woman go?" Gorge asked with a slight laugh, as he looked up and down the hall like a dog in heat. "I think I must keep her busy with my company for a bit longer. Just a little bit longer. Woke up with my head full of vigor."

"I will go and look for you," Demeter replied, trying to compose himself.

"You go and do that," Gorge ordered with a laugh, placing the chain along with the vault's key back around his neck. "Just don't try anything with her. I know how you get around fair haired women. You're always so serious, that is, until you get around them." His laugh drifted off, as he began his march back the way he had come. "Problem is you like to stare at them. You need to be more confident around them…"

Chapter 10
The Pillory

The cold breeze of dusk descended further upon the world, as the city fell quiet, stripped away in the presence of the encroaching stars. Though, like any, there were exceptions to the norm. Like a ship tied to a dock, timber whined as each subtle movement fought against the tension of the knot, which in reality was a lock. It whined and rattled, as time and time again, like the consistency of the waves, it exuded a force that drove the nearest soul into a rage.

"Stop fighting," Paulus ordered with a flustered grunt, as his voice vanished into the night. He stood on two legs, though not upright, as his head and wrists lay bound by splintered timber. "That lock is locked. All your shaking isn't going to do anything more than put a thorn in my neck and split my head. You are just going to have to wait. You are just going to have to wait."

"Don't tell me what to do," the pickpocket ordered back, as he continued to wiggle. "Wouldn't be in this mess if it wasn't for you. So, now I'm going to get out of this on my own. I got places to be. And who gets put in the pillory for such a long time? And how hard is it to get free? I am a master at my work, don't you know? Everyone knows who the great Lucas is."

"Who's Lucas?" Paulus asked.

"I am," he replied. "I am Lucas. And this is all your fault…"

Paulus turned as far as his head could, before the splinters that were by his neck burrowed deeper. "Want to explain to me how this is my fault?"

"You couldn't just have let me get away?" Lucas asked back. "Couldn't just have turned the other cheek and just let me do what I needed to do?"

"You couldn't have just not pickpocketed me?" Paulus asked with a loud scoff.

"Not so loud," Lucas quickly hissed. "Want me to get branded? That guard could be anywhere."

"Couldn't have just given me my purse back after I caught you?" Paulus continued, as he ignored his company. "Couldn't have just returned it like a normal person? You had to keep your hands on my coins. You had to get in the way of a man and his drink. And that says a lot about a man, just so you know."

Lucas was still for a moment, waiting within his own mind and thoughts to pull together some words of a rebuttal, though only the opposite fell from his tongue. "Sorry, didn't know it was for a drink."

A faint sigh left Paulus again, as he rolled his eyes and ever so slightly shook his head. "So, do you have any friends of yours that are going to come back and save you from here?"

"I might…" Lucas replied under his breath. "Might not…"

"Yeah, I got one too," Paulus said. "If he hears about it, he might just come to hit me with a shovel."

"Shovel?" Lucas asked, a smile slowly dawning over his face. "Wait, is that what happened to your face—?"

Before he could finish, a spatter of filth spewed forth and struck both men on opposite sides of their faces. Chunks of vile rotten food from a long-spoiled vegetable clung to them, as what remained of the thing fell to the ground with the sound of a plop that mimicked a wet mop.

"HEY!" Lucas shouted, spotting some mischievous kids running off. "When I get out of here, you are both going to beg I hadn't! Don't you know who I am? That's right you better run! Run home!"

With a spit that cleared the edge of his lip of the green and brown filth, Paulus grumbled under his breath. "Just leave it. You're only going to make it worse. Those brats don't have anything better to do. If it wasn't this, they would be scratching some mark into the walls."

"Leave it?" Lucas asked back. "They need to know who I am."

"That doesn't make any sense," Paulus replied. "You're a pickpocket, you don't want people to notice you."

"Not so loud about that," Lucas ordered with a loud whisper. "You have to stop saying that, before I get into a lot of trouble. They only think I'm a beggar. They don't know the great thief that I am."

"You would deserve it," Paulus explained, turning his eyes towards the lock that bound him and growing a faint smile. "Me on the other hand…"

"How much longer do we have?" Lucas asked with a groan. "I have places to be. I have things I need to do. You know the night is a very important time for someone in my line of work. Especially today, with all the drinking and moaning people will be doing. It's very important."

"At least it's not snowing," Paulus replied with a sigh, as his eyes lingering on the lock and his fingers beginning to wiggle. "And on behalf of all those you would have robbed, at least you're not able to and are being held accountable."

"I can agree with you on the snow…" Lucas said, lulling with only the faintest of noises that whispered of fiddling. "And no one can see us anymore," he added with a faint smile, as he stared out into the darkness. "You want me to sing a song?"

"Look," Paulus replied with a sigh. "We just have to deal with each other for a few more hours, then we can go on our own way and never have to deal with each other again. What do you say?"

A still silence held the night for a moment, as not even the distant sounds of stray animals, or the turbulence of the drunks permeated, or even the trivial whispers of fingers at work.

"Sounds too good to be true," Lucas finally said with a faint laugh, returning to his task of attempting to wiggle free.

"It almost does, doesn't it?" Paulus said with a dwindling chuckle. "Now, stop that shaking or you're going to get it when I get out of here."

"Oh, yeah, and what are you going—?" Lucas began to ask, though was silenced by a sight that suddenly caught his eye. "My God!"

"What?" Paulus asked, taking notice of his company's composure and quickly catching sight of what lay before them.

Through the darkness eyes peered at them and seemed to burrow into their souls. It was not those of a human, but of an animal that lay just above the ground.

"It's a cat," Paulus said annoyed.

The two men and the cat looked at one another with suspicion and curiosity. Though, with a slow soft laugh that broke into the air, Lucas seemed to enjoy the company, as well as that of his own thoughts.

"What?" Paulus asked, as the cat rushed away. "What's so funny? It was just a cat."

"Hope this night does not end in a catastrophe," Lucas finally said, laughing loudly at his own joke. "Get it? Catastrophe. Cat."

"Cat?" Paulus asked, turning his head as far as he could, before looking at what he could see of his company. "I don't get it."

"What?" Lucas asked baffled. "What do you mean you don't get it?"

"It's not important, so be quiet," Paulus ordered, as his fingers continued to fidget until suddenly, the very lock and timber that bound him in place released its grip. "There we go."

"HEY!" Lucas shouted with wide eyes, watching him in disbelief stretching his legs. "How the—How the hell did you do that? Get me out, quick!"

"Not that hard," Paulus replied, rubbing his wrists and continuing to stretch his limbs. With a slow sigh, he lowered himself to the ground resting against the very timber that had held him. "And keep your voice down before you get me in trouble."

"Wait, what are you doing?" Lucas asked. "You going to get me out? Hurry. Let's make our break for it."

"No," Paulus stated. "No, I'm not."

"Wait, what?" Lucas asked in disbelief, trying to no avail to catch a sight of him.

"Not so loud," Paulus warned again, shifting where he sat and trying to find comfort.

"You're not going to run away?" Lucas demanded.

"No, that would just cause me more trouble," Paulus explained. "I want to come back into the city. If I'm not here when the guards get back, I will be in a lot of trouble. Don't want that."

"That doesn't make sense," Lucas replied.

"Well, then it means it's none of your concern," Paulus said. "So, what do you do? And I don't mean as a pickpocket."

Lucas turned his head as far as he was able with a sense of disbelief. "You being serious right now? Did you seriously ask me that?"

"You have something better to do?" Paulus asked back. "I suppose I could always close my eyes and get a little sleep before the sun comes up again."

"Wait, wait, wait," Lucas pleaded. "Fine, we can talk. What do you want to know?"

"What do you do when you're not robbing good people?" Paulus asked.

"I don't rob good people," Lucas replied. "Just fools."

Paulus was silent for a moment, staring out into the dark. With a faint scoff, he shook his head, closed his eyes, and began to snore.

"Fine, fine, fine," Lucas said. "I travel. I go where I need to go."

"You mean, you leave a place after you have taken what you need from it, but not before you are caught, is that it?" Paulus asked.

"You going to let me out, anytime soon?" Lucas requested.

"Sure, before the guards come back, but after the sun comes up," Paulus replied. "After that, you can call us even for stealing from me."

"Wait, really?" Lucas asked. "You're being serious?"

"No," Paulus replied, as he closed his eyes. "Just make sure you wake me up before the sun comes up and the guards with them. If you don't, then we will get in real trouble."

Time drifted away as the night gave way to the endless repetition of the heavens, yet there was one figure who advanced through the city streets ahead of the rising sun. His pace was slow, as his limp tried to drag him back. His armor chimed in his ears, while his spear tip pointed to the sky and its base thumped on the ground.

"I guess I was a little rough with those beggars," Andreas said to himself, as the faint and earliest rays of light began. "Wife always makes me soft… Except in one way."

He laughed to himself, approaching the slumbering fools oblivious to the consequences of his company. As when he would descend upon them, a fury filled with punishment would be theirs, all within the confines of a place far worse than the pillory.

Chapter 11
The Obstacles

In the company of darkness and shadows, a lone figure made his way over the stones with no direction other than that of pacing back and forth. With feet that would have shaken the stones below him had the mortar not held them in place, Istvan marched with anger. His tongue lay trapped between his teeth, with a force that lay just shy of drawing blood, as an ever-growing frustration blossomed with it.

"About time," Istvan said as the door finally swung open. "Do you know how long I have been waiting? Making me look like a common fool."

"I was busy and there were many eyes," Fodor replied with a taunting smile, as he entered with a lit candle in his grip and quickly closed the door. "I did not think it would have been smart to simply depart and bring them here with me. And being seen leaving at the same time is a good way to get rumors started. We are not yet ready to be seen as allies. Though I am sure I can go back and get some others if you would like."

"Enough," Istvan ordered with a growl, taking his place at the table with a hard fall on the empty stool. "Let's try to make this quick. You said enough about watchful eyes already. What do you have?"

"Always so eager to be done with things, where is your sense of politics?" Fodor asked with a light laugh. "That is half the thrill of life."

"I don't want that thrill," Istvan replied with a dismissive wave. "The only thrill that I want, is victory. Nothing else matters until a victory is had."

"All for a means to an end, is that it?" Fodor asked with a laugh. "There has to be more than that."

"There isn't," Istvan replied. "Not until there are no other obstacles. Then, and only then, can you indulge in the prospects of having no enemies left. And if we act quickly, we can see that it does happen soon. So soon, it could happen by the time we gather with the council. So, I say again, what do you have?"

With a smile made ever wider and his stained teeth exposed to the light of the flame, Fodor moved to grab a drink and quench his mouth. "I have missed the wine you collect. Even though I spend a fortune on the stuff myself, I can never seem to get anything as good as yours."

"Tell me," Istvan ordered. "What news have you uncovered?"

"From the Queen you mean?" Fodor asked back, filling his mouth with another gulp.

A silent nod was all that was replied.

"Well, that's the funny thing," Fodor commented, scratching his chin. "I have seen her talking—"

"As have I," Istvan interrupted. "Always chatting away."

"Playing politics perhaps?" Fodor asked.

"Perhaps, you don't know?" Istvan asked with a mixed hint of skepticism and shock.

"I know enough about her, that I know that she is playing at something, but nothing to be concerned with," Fodor explained. "She has—"

"From what has been going on, do you not find that suspicious?" Istvan interrupted, raising his voice above the other.

"As I was about to say..." Fodor continued. "That is her nature. A nature that has been suppressed after her marriage. A nature that I am sure will be suppressed once again. I care little that she has met with a few people. I care little that she—"

A knock at the door, pulled both men's eyes along with their breaths, as a silence swallowed them whole for a moment.

"Did you invite someone?" Istvan asked.

"Depends who's at the door," Fodor replied. "Shall we see who it is?"

A nod was all that Istvan ordered for him to go and check.

"Her claim is a weak one," Fodor said, as a sinister smile grew over his lips and he advanced towards the door.

"A weak one?" Istvan asked with suspicion.

"Yes, a weak one," Fodor explained. "I have a man that can explain it better than me. Come in, Father."

With a slow whine that did little other than add tension to impatient blood, the door swung open. There draped in a vestment that was not one of war or crime, but of a shepherd to those that were kept in a flock, stood a holy man. What hair he had lay hidden under a plain cap that hugged his scalp and kept it warm. Though while his appearance held the illusion of modesty, it was the cross that dangled from his neck that caught the eye with its glitter.

"Why have you—?" Istvan began to ask, but stopped as he caught sight of the books under his arm. "Is that what I think it is?"

Silently the holy man moved his way across the room and took his place in comfort between light and dark, pulling forth the books and placing them before him. "My lords, may God guard you and keep you and your estates safe."

"Thank you," Fodor said with a smile, turning to his guest and giving him a nod. "You may begin."

"I was indeed my lord," the holy man replied. "In these pieces of work behind me I have found the truth of legacy. And that truth is a simple one. The Queen of Hungary, Elizabeth, whose husband has just passed is the rightful Queen to the throne."

"What?" Istvan asked, a look of rage creeping its way across face. "What! That was not what I asked for! That is not what I need to hear! I need you to—"

"That was not the extent of what I found, my lord," the holy man interrupted. "No, what I found is while she is the rightful heir to the throne, she has no male heir to claim it. If she were to have had a child, one that was a male, she might have had the right to claim regency until he is of appropriate age. But, alas she does not."

"Not yet..." Istvan mumbled to himself, as the anger that gripped him slowly dwindled.

"Furthermore, there is the political situation at hand," the holy man continued to explain. "Given the current situation on the southern and eastern border, the need for a King would be argued to be precedent. And given that the council has been gathered, therein lies the opportunity to decide if the Queen has the merit to rule as she sees fit. Or, if she does not. The records I have found are her lineage, which protects her from being stripped of her position. But it does show that the council, by majority, can decide the next King, and arrange a marriage that the Queen will be forced to accept."

"And if she does not accept it?" Istvan asked, leaning forward. "What if she refuses to accept the will of the council?"

A silence remained between the three, while the echo of his question vanished.

"If she does not accept the will of the council, then she will be held in—"

Istvan interrupted the holy man, with a bellowing laugh that filled the air. "Thank you, Father. You have given me the information I needed. Thank you. Now then, if you would see yourself out."

"You will be paid as we agreed," Fodor added. "You don't need to worry."

With a glance to Fodor, the holy man did as he was told and took his leave, vanishing the way he had come without uttering another word. The only signs of his prior presence, the books he had brought with him.

"So then," Fodor said as he scratched his chin and studied the books. "What is your plan?"

A wide smile grew over Istvan's face, as he turned his attention back to his sole companion. "It is a simple thing really. We are going to pick the next King."

A loud laugh left Fodor's lips. "And you think the Queen will just agree with who we pick? She will never agree to that."

"If it was simply us two, then I would agree," Istvan explained, his smile growing wider with each word that flowed through it. "But what makes you think it is only us two? Did you not hear what that man said?"

"You don't mean—?" Fodor began to ask, before he was interrupted.

"But I do," Istvan continued. "Like the birds of spring I have begun to sing. And I have found that many sing the same tune. But, you already know this, don't you?"

"Who, me?" Fodor asked back with a hint of a coy tone. "After listening to what you asked of the holy man there? How would I?"

"We will have to move fast," Istvan said. "We will have to pick a man we can agree on. And one who will agree with us."

"And one that will benefit us," Fodor added. "Can't let the opportunity of deciding the next King be left to the Queen alone. She is after all only a woman, Queen or not. Let me ask you something, do you think I should pay that holy man?"

"I wouldn't," Istvan replied without so much as a second thought. "Always get payed before you do the work."

"Sound advice," Fodor said with a grin. "So, what do you want to do with the Queen?"

"This is an opportunity," Istvan explained. "We have been given a great opportunity by God to secure our future. A future built around us. We should do well to pick a man who will be grateful for our loyalty and in turn, will reward us for it. We have a few days before the council is to meet. That gives us until then to set things in motion in the way we wish. A few days to lay the obstacles we desire. And if you are going to add anything about the child, then I say wait. The odds that the child is born still, or of no consequence, are good."

Chapter 12

The Dungeon

Drops echoed, finding its way into the confines of chains and punishment. An unsettling cold held the stone, as their mere touch forced a shiver up every spine. A foul smell permeated the air, and any deep breath would force a gag upon the one who took it. Critters rushed over the ground in darkness, their limbs stuck to the dirt in search of some nourishment that did not seem to exist.

"Did you hear it?" Lucas asked, throwing his eyes to every corner of the cell, a beam of the sun's light the only source of illumination. "I know you must have heard it. I just know it."

"No," Paulus replied. "And stop asking me if I did."

"Can't believe that guard," Lucas said, stretching his neck back and forth and bringing about a multitude of loud cracks. "Don't know why I got into trouble too. I wasn't the one he caught out of the pillory. Why am I the one here that has to suffer? At least I can move my neck again... But, you should have said something!"

"All you had to do was wake me up," Paulus replied with a sigh. "Don't know how you couldn't manage that. And he wouldn't have listened to me."

"All you had to do was leave," Lucas said in frustration. "But, no… You wanted to stay. I don't even know why."

"Doesn't matter," Paulus replied, staring at the barren wall.

"Still not going to tell me?" Lucas pressed, seeming to grow frustrated by the thought. "Even now?"

Paulus was indifferent to the words, as he rose off of the ground and made his way to the door that kept him with his company locked up.

"You're not going to try to escape from here now?" Lucas asked with a hushed voice. "If this is what you get for trying to escape from the pillory—"

"Wasn't trying to escape," Paulus interrupted, yet his words seemed to have no bearing on his company.

"Think about it. What could be worse than sitting in a dark hole all alone—?"

"First, I'm not alone," Paulus explained. "I have your company."

"Ah, that's nice of you to say," Lucas replied, smiling happily.

"Not what I was saying," Paulus continued. "I'm saying, they are already doing the worst thing they can do to me right now. They have me trapped here with you. There is honestly not much more that can be done to make me suffer. Secondly, I'm not sitting, I'm standing. Because I don't want to sit anymore."

"I'm going to say, that's just the hunger talking," Lucas added. "I think they will bring us some food soon."

"No," Paulus continued. "That is the roaches and rats and anything else that is on the ground that is trying to grab me."

A lull filled the foul air, as Lucas cast his eyes all around him in search. "I don't see anything."

"Then stay down there," Paulus ordered, as he stood by the door.

"You know how much longer they are going to keep us down here?" Lucas asked, turning his attention to the critters that rushed by. "It won't be that much longer will it? It's already been a while... I think..."

"It will take what it takes," Paulus replied.

"That's not much of an answer," Lucas mumbled under his breath.

"I should remind you that we are in this situation because of your actions," Paulus explained pressing his back against the wall and finding some comfort against it. "If you hadn't been—"

"That was a long time ago," Lucas interrupted. "We should move on old man. Take each thing that happened and just forgive each other. That would be the best thing. Definitely."

"Did you just call me old man again?" Paulus asked.

"Yeah," Lucas replied with a laugh. "Just like the day we met. All things considered it was a pretty good day. I mean, not for the King, it was his funeral, but for everyone else it was pretty good. Don't you think?"

Paulus stared at him in silence, the only expression, an eyebrow raised. "I think you should just go to sleep."

"It's funny, but I'm not actually tired," Lucas replied with a laugh. "Funny right?"

"No," Paulus stated, the scowl on his face growing in the shadows and dark.

"You know, I heard that most people that find their way here have problems owing money," Lucas commented, once again trying to ignite a conversation with the spark of his thoughts. "Yeah, they apparently have not payed people back. I'm never like that. I always pay back what I owe. That's one of my rules. You got any rules?"

"No," Paulus replied, as yet again a silence consumed them.

"So, come on," Lucas said, continuing to press. "Tell me why you really didn't run away. You must have had a good reason. Right?"

Paulus turned and silently stared at him.

"Right?" Lucas asked.

"If I tell you, will you be quiet?" Paulus grumbled. "And before you answer, I mean, will you be quiet and not say another word to me until we are free from this place? Do you understand?"

A light laugh left Lucas' lips, as he grew a wide smile. "I knew it! Sure, I will be quiet. Not a word. Just silent and still."

"Fine, if you really want to know, I will tell you," Paulus said with a laugh. "When the guards caught us and were going to put us in the pillory, they took our stuff. I want what was mine back. Happy? Now be quiet, like you agreed."

"Wait!" Lucas shouted in disbelief. "Wait, wait, wait! They only took one thing from you! You wanted to get that back! You wanted to get back your purse! Wait, is that really it? I don't even know why? It was practically empty. Why would you wait for that?"

Paulus was silent, turning his eyes to the darkness and remaining in its still embrace.

"Oh, come on," Lucas pleaded.

"All your screaming and shouting is going to get us into real trouble," Paulus warned. "If I were you, I would be quiet. Before the punishment we get becomes more severe."

"What do you think they are going to do to us?" Lucas asked.

"If we're quiet, they will be better with us," Paulus explained, the words echoing in his ears. "They might listen to our plea. Then we will probably only get a few lashes before they kick us out."

"And if they don't?" Lucas asked back. "What if they don't?"

"Probably keep us here for a while longer before branding us, then give us a few lashes before kicking us out of the city," Paulus explained. "Just as long as they give me my purse back, I don't really care…"

Chapter 13
The Seal and the Letter

The light of a flame danced in the setting sun, as the one who worked within its embrace etched the last of her ink onto the piece of parchment, along with her thoughts and a part of her soul. She labored away, her hand made to curve, spin and stab, though while she did, her gown, exquisite in green, gold and design befitting of her royalty, was made slightly inept by the faint smudges that clung to it. With a final mark, she admired her work and basked in the labor of her own doing. She puckered her lips and blew a warm breath of air over the scratched grooves as she dried the ink.

"It's ready," Elizabeth said, holding the unsealed letter out to her company.

Helene, who had waited by her side was quick to take it in her hands.

"What do you think?" Elizabeth questioned.

"I think you made a mistake here," Helene commented, her eyes glancing over the piece of work and the seemingly innocent words that lay within. "Did you misspell this word?"

"Let me see," Elizabeth said. "I don't see anything."

"I think you made a mistake with the way you spelled her name," Helene explained.

"That's not a mistake," Elizabeth replied with a smile, as she passed it back. "That's a smudge."

"Want me to write it again?" Helene asked.

"No need," Elizabeth said, leaving her seat to ordain herself with pieces of gold and silver jewelry. "She knows my handwriting. She will know if someone else wrote it."

"I don't mean to cast doubt..." Helene stated.

"But?" Elizabeth asked in anticipation.

"Are you sure she will answer your summons?" Helene asked. "The others too?"

"I am," Elizabeth replied, a smile growing over her lips. "I am still the Queen after all."

"I didn't mean—" Helene quickly explained.

"I know," Elizabeth interrupted. "Just trying to flutter your heart. So, what do you think?"

"Other than your mistake?" Helene asked with a smile of her own.

"Other than that," Elizabeth replied.

Helene glanced at the piece of work once again, as she reread each of the inked scratches. With each completed line, she nodded in consent, until finally, she looked back to her company. "I approve."

"Can you take care of the wax?" Elizabeth asked.

"Of course," Helene replied, rummaging through the table drawer and pulling it forth. It stood no longer or thicker than a finger, though its value lay in its malleable nature. Holding the red stick of wax over the flame, she turned it over from side to side, as it grew more pliable to the point of collapse.

"Can you have them sent out too?" Elizabeth asked.

"Of course," Helene replied. "We can use that man again. He can get anything to anyone without getting much attention. No one really pays attention to a pilgrim. As much of one as he claims to be."

"See that it is done," Elizabeth ordered, moving over to the far side of the room and plucking forth an item, before returning to her company.

Helene quickly moved the hot dripping wax onto the folded crossroads of the parchment and leaving a red oasis. Quickly, the item the Queen had procured and kept behind her back was pressed firmly against it, sealing it with her royal mark.

"Well that completes that," Helene said smiling, admiring the seal that bore an eagle with a shield over its breastplate and a lion beside it. "The easy part. And you even managed to get the seal on strait this time."

"The easy part is done," Elizabeth stated with a smile of her own. "Now onto the next stage. We will have to move quickly. I will keep them distracted for a while. I trust that you will be able to do what we discussed."

"Of course," Helene quickly assured her. "I know the route. Know the man to look for. Know what to say. There is only one thing."

"One thing?" Elizabeth asked with a slight tilt to her head.

Helene leaned closer, sharing a soft whisper, careful so that no others would hear had they been listening through the walls. "Do you have the purse?"

"Oh, right," Elizabeth stated, her eyebrows leaping up. "I completely forgot." She pointed down towards the desk she had labored over, revealing a treasure wrapped in leather. "You will find everything you need in there."

"Will it be enough?" Helene asked sarcastically, shaking the heavy purse with a laugh.

"It should be," Elizabeth replied, sharing a chuckle, though she continued to prepare the last of her appearance with a somber expression. "Do you have everything you need?"

"I do," Helene stated, reaching for her cloak and throwing it on, the secrets of what she held, nestled beneath it. "Do you?"

"I do," Elizabeth stated, taking a deep breath and brushing the last creases of her attire off. She turned her eyes a final time to her mirror and tended to the details of her appearance. "Time to start the ceremonies and move towards what must come. Shall we go and do what we need to do?"

"Ready when you are," Helene replied.

"I will leave you to decide for yourself which destination you wish to visit first," Elizabeth said, making her way for the door with a stern expression. "Just make sure no one is following you."

"Understood," Helene replied, just as the lock to the door was released. "One last thing," she said before the hinges could whine. "Good luck, my Queen."

"I told you that you don't have to call me that," Elizabeth said, a smile returning to her face. "But, good luck to you as well, my friend."

Chapter 14

A Bribe at the Door

The sun was in the process of its late fall, as the days grew darker and shorter with each one that slipped away. Its rays fell short, no longer reaching into the alleys and streets with the warmth of its gentle touch, but rather, giving way to the night. Most had already fled with hurried steps, as their bundled selves rushed to warmth and shelter. Though, in the encroach of the dark and the bitter cold, there were a few who still remained in the streets.

"Hurry up men," Andreas ordered, waiting in the threshold of a splintered door for those who followed him to enter. "Get in and go deal with the ones we need to. Get it done fast and we will get to have a calm night. No need for anyone to wait outside the door tonight. Cold tends to keep trouble away. So, you can thank God for the cold and maybe even some mist in a little. Now, focus on those we already have. And bring me some wine."

One after another, the armed guards crossed through the threshold and quickly vanished within the structure of stone that held the criminals of the city. Though, as the last one entered and Andreas pulled the door shut, a figure moved over the desolate streets, as the objective of her sight beckoned her forward.

Barely had Andreas taken a seat and released a loud yawn, before a series of knocks called for his attention. With a grumble and a sigh, he turned his eyes back to the door, though he did not move to answer, remaining seated with still limbs and a look of annoyance. The one who knocked, did so again, the call of their knuckles echoing loudly. With a twitch that pulled his eye and forced wrinkles to grow, he advanced back towards the door.

"Who are you?" Andreas demanded, throwing the flap to the door open, and the faint remnants of his joy vanished with a heavy sigh. "Other than my problem?"

"Open this door for me, now," the cloaked woman at the door ordered.

"Under whose authority, love?" Andreas asked with a laugh.

In silence, she held up a purse towards the flap and shook it until it jingled. The metal held within its place by the leather, strained the straps in a tantalizing dance, as the beholder was left to imagine its contents.

"Under this authority."

Andreas' eyes grew wide and his eyebrows high, as he watched and listened to the sound. Finally, though, with a scoff and laugh rolled together, he slapped the flap to the door closed and left the woman to the solitude of her wealth.

There she stood like a statue holding the purse of coins, though not for long.

The sound of metal and timber clacked and banged against one another, as the teeth of the door let loose and swung open. The touch of warmth left through the opening, and the light that had been kept within was set free, save for the figure that guarded it.

"Coin," Andreas demand, holding his hand out. "And that way I will care."

"When I get what I want," she replied, throwing her eyes up and revealing her beauty to the man before her, though it did little to reveal her identity as the Queen's friend. "Then and only then can you have this."

"Which would be?" Andreas asked with a grumble, his eyes following the metal, although he was quickly made to walk with a lit candle.

"I'm looking for someone," Helene said to Andreas, as they marched down the hall. "Someone who would be skilled in criminal activities."

"You're both in the right and wrong place," he replied with a loud laugh that echoed down the dark halls. "This has criminals, but they all got caught. Don't know how good they will be to you."

"And would you know where to find better ones then?" Helene asked, her tone stoic and calm.

I mean…" Andreas said, his smile slowly vanishing, as the rendition of his own joy was stripped away and replaced by a stoic expression. "If I knew, they would be here. Sitting in a cell. Waiting to be branded like the rest of them. But, I don't know for certain. You could try the taverns and inns, but they would probably cheat you out of that heavy purse of yours. Better that you stay here. Better if you let me carry it."

Helene seemed undeterred by his words, as her pace did not falter, and she continued to move through the structure. "Then who here are worth taking?"

"Depends what you have in mind," Andreas replied. "I doubt you want any of the men who have failed to pay their debts. Not much they can do… besides spend what isn't theirs. Got a few who assaulted a woman, if that's your thing, but they will soon be made useless in that department." He explained, holding two fingers up and moving them like scissors. "Got some who were drunk and heretics. And another that did some crimes with a knife."

"Do you know of any who can work with locks?" Helene asked, turning her eyes into a cell, only to quickly pull back and cover her mouth. "And any who are not so… rotten."

Andreas turned his eyes up and down the hall, his expression showing one consumed by thoughts. With a slow nod he turned his gaze down beyond any sight. "You're in luck. Caught two beggars just the other day."

Helene's feet fell still, as she stood in the hall and the light of the candle fell a few steps away. "I asked you if you had anyone who knew locks. I didn't ask you for a beggar."

"Come on," Andreas said, waving at her to follow, while doing little to slow his limping gait. "You didn't let me finish. You see, these two beggars were caught after they got into a brawl."

"What did they get into a brawl over?" Helene asked.

"The hell do I know?" Andreas asked back with a laugh. "I just caught them fighting. And like any beggar I come across, I put them in the pillory for a day and a night and then kick them out of the city. Like we're supposed to. Well, my wife, a bit like you, tells me I should be nice to them, seeing how it's almost the day of Christ's birth and all. So, being a good husband and not wanting to get on her bad side, I do as she wants and leave early to set them free. But, guess what?"

"What?" Helene questioned, playing along, the hint of sarcasm on her lips.

"The beggars were in the middle of escaping," Andreas continued, shaking his head. "And I don't mean trying to escape. Like so many fools, shaking back and forth, or trying to use strength they don't have to move the timber. Or having some other fool come over and help them. I mean, one of them was out of his punishment. He had actually gotten himself free of his bonds. I almost didn't believe it myself, would have sworn it was someone else who had set him free, but no it was him alone. And I am sure that if I had arrived a moment later, he would have set the other one free."

"Sounds like I should thank your wife then," Helene said with a smile. "Weren't for her, they might have gotten away. Might not have my man."

"Well, anyway, after I caught them, I knew that they were more than just your typical beggars passing through the city."

Andreas continued, seeming to ignore her words. "I figured anyone who could escape from the pillory, was someone worth taking a closer look at. Haven't had the chance to get to them yet, too many other 'visitors' who need attention first. So that's why they are still beggars. Want to get a look at them before my men do?"

"Show me to them," Helene ordered.

Chapter 15
The Cracks of a Foundation

The faint chatter of a few dozen echoed in the open hall, as groups of self-interested men formed and gossiped with each other. Some flowed like leaves in a stream, shifting from pool to pool, as if searching for something. All the while, others stood frozen where they were, content by those they stood beside. They whispered and plotted with each other, as the rendition of the world lay gripped in their fat fingers and the ambitions that drove them.

Benches and tables filled the space, though they all faced the same direction, to the empty thrones that stood before them. Yet, there were those that stood disregarded within the hall like pieces of furniture; the guards. They stood by the doors, still as statues, save for their eyes which subtly moved from one group to the next.

However, while the conversations of men dominated, and their individual agendas pushed forth, the Queen moved to join them with an agenda not limited to that of her own, but for those who would follow.

Down the hall she went, with only the company of her unborn child, as the green gown she wore fluttered with each step. Her pace was like her demeanor, calm and reserved, only the faintest hints of any ripples to shimmer in her eyes. Yet, before she could reach the whispers of the hall, a figure that cast a shifting shadow leaped in front of her with a dagger behind his smile.

"Ah, fair Queen, Elizabeth," Fodor said making his presence known. "And where are you off to with a pace like that?"

Elizabeth was unstartled, staring at him with little emotion. "Shouldn't you be with the others in the hall?"

"Perhaps," Fodor replied. "I was in fact already with them. I was with them for so long that I decided to go and look for you. And as luck would have it, here you are. I could almost call myself blessed."

"Almost but not quite," Elizabeth said, moving to step past him.

Yet, before she could, Fodor leaned his body and head into her path and as subtly as the sun rises, blocked her.

"My Queen, if I could just have a moment of your time, I would like to have a chat with you."

The light from the nearest flames fluttered and danced, as the two stared at one another. There they stayed, each forced to wait on the attention of the other, as the shadows tried in vain to pull their eyes.

"And what would you like to chat about?" Elizabeth finally asked.

Fodor seemed to grow ever more content, his eyes glistening with excitement and hunger. "A great many things, a great many things."

Elizabeth was far from impressed with his cryptic reply and took rest leaning against the wall. "You must think highly of me, if you think I can read minds."

"Where is your helper?" Fodor asked, subtly studying her with a narrow gaze. "Does she not follow you around like a lost dog? Like a bitch, or a pup from one?"

"Why the concern?" Elizabeth asked back calmly and coolly, indifferent to the words or tone while leading her company forward with slow steps.

"I did not see her at the funeral," Fodor replied. "I was thinking—"

Elizabeth interrupted him with a laugh, her smile growing. "I have already told Istvan that she is already married. Funny that you both would have an interest. I wonder if she would be pleased? I wonder if Istvan will be concerned of the competition?"

"Funny," Fodor said with a false sense of amusement thinly masked. "You know you never answered my question."

"Do you enjoy having enemies?" Elizabeth asked serenely, her words forcing her companion's steps to falter.

"Enemies…" Fodor said, seeming to reflect on those words, before quickening his pace to catch up. "Your former husband, the late King, he once told me that anyone who makes a deal will always soon find an enemy. Now I enjoy making deals—"

"Everyone in the Kingdom knows that," Elizabeth interrupted with a laugh.

"Indeed, some are so bold as to say, that many outside the Kingdom know that as well," Fodor replied.

"And is there truth to what such people say?" Elizabeth asked, her eye fixated on him from the corner of her vision.

"I'm sure you know what they say about rumors," Fodor replied with a slight upwards curve to his lips.

Elizabeth maintained the pace they walked at for a moment, turning her gaze forward. There she strayed with her thoughts, until finally, with a smile of her own she spoke. "You like to quote my husband, the King, and he did always say there was truth in the rumors people spoke."

"Humph, I suppose he did," Fodor replied, his smile vanishing, leaving the two to stare at each other in silence.

The whispers of the hall now reached them, as well as the light from the many flames and the first of the guards who stood at their posts.

"You do know you are late," Fodor stated with a grin that ran from ear to ear. "A word from the wise. I would tell you that that was a mistake. Many, myself included, have had the luxury of talking amongst each other about a great many things. Being late gives men that opportunity."

Elizabeth grew a smile turning back and looking at the man. "Maybe I had meant to be late. Did you not think of that?"

"What?" The grin that had reached from Fodor's ear to ear quickly vanish, as a look of concern gripped his face. "What?" He echoed with a tone that seemed more of a plea.

"You know, I am well aware of the meetings that go on outside of the council, and those that are planned," Elizabeth explained. "I am also well aware of what some of the worms that would eat this Kingdom have in mind, yourself included. Along with those who would call themselves wise. But, I do not know who stands with who. Well, I did not before tonight. Not before my men studied each and every one of you." Her feet carried her forward, advancing once more towards the hall, though again, she turned her sights back to her company. "Shall we? There is much to discuss in this ceremonial meeting."

Chapter 16

The First Encounter

The solitude of the night echoed loudly in the prison that was their home, as the suffocating entrapment whispered the fear and anger of a thousand souls. They sulked with tears, besieged by the smell and tormented by the imagination that manifested within their minds. Though within a solitary room that held only two, the night seemed to finally pass with a docile calm that could be found on a warm day below the stars. However, as the sound of keys and locks banged, and the door began to rattle, the tranquility that was, vanished.

"Company," Lucas said, propping himself up and pulling his head from its slumber. "Are they coming to get us, or are they going to feed us? I hope it's some food."

Paulus said nothing and did little to move while his eyes sat subtly opened watching the door, long aware of those that came.

Once more the door rattled, as a key was turned beyond their sight and a shoulder hardly pressed against it. The faint mumbles of a complaint could be heard on its other side, though the words were inaudible and swallowed by the prison's echoes.

"You two, get up," Andreas ordered with a bark, opening the door. "Get against the wall over there!"

"Finally," Lucas said to Paulus with a smile, as they both did as they were told. "We are finally getting some food. I hope the food is good. I have not eaten since they threw me in here—threw us in here. Told you we didn't have to escape."

With a smile that seemed sinister in nature, Andreas stepped into the cell. "What was that about escaping?" he asked, towering over those in his presence. "You two been plotting something? Is that it?"

"Nothing," Paulus quickly replied. "He was just making a joke. A really stupid bad joke."

"Ugh-hum," Andreas said with his sight on the two, before finally calling to the one at the threshold of the door to come forth. "This woman wants to speak to you, and I expect you to listen. If you don't, you will cost me and if you do that, there will be trouble! You got that?"

"Why?" Paulus asked, keeping his sight forward and on his own shadow.

"I'm only going to say this once more," Andreas warned. "This woman wants to speak to you. You both had better listen. You got that?"

"Yes," Paulus and Lucas replied in union.

"Good," Andreas stated, turning to Helene before making for the door. "Say what you want."

"I'm looking for men who have certain skills," Helene said, stepping towards them as Andreas stepped out and closed the door.

"Skills? Let me do the talking. I know just what to say." Lucas said with a whisper and a wide grin from cheek to cheek, as he stole a glance and ran his eyes all over Helene. "Hello, my lady, you're looking beautiful this evening..."

"Why do I feel like that's a bad idea?" Paulus asked himself with a sigh under his breath and a roll of his eyes.

"I hear you have asked for the best," Lucas continued. "Then I can finally tell you that you have chosen to talk to the right person. I am known far and wide for my skills. Skills that cannot be matched by any. Some call me a saint, others a sinner, but you, my lady can call me your master thief."

Helene was silent for a moment watching the man before her, though it was not until she turned her eyes to Paulus with a slow glance, that sound finally left her lips. "I take it you're the one in charge then?"

"Yeah, I guess you could say that," Paulus replied, with just the faintest hint of a curve to his lips.

"What, what?" Lucas asked baffled by the two.

"Turn around," Helene ordered. "I don't want to talk to your back."

"Let me do the talking," Paulus said to Lucas as he did as he was told. "I know just what to say."

"I was sure that would have worked," Lucas said stepping back to the wall.

"It might have," Helene commented. "I mean, not on me. But it might have worked on someone else."

"Someone more gullible," Paulus added, his words salt to Lucas' already wounded ego. "Or, maybe someone drunk. God I could use a drink…"

"Precisely," Helene agreed.

"So, what do you want?" Paulus asked.

"You're the one who escaped the pillory, is that right?" Helene asked, ignoring his question and answering it at the same time.

"And what if I am?" Paulus asked back suspiciously.

"He definitely is," Lucas said chiming in. "And can you believe he didn't let me out?"

"What is that smell?" Helene asked back, holding her scented cloth over her nose and mouth.

"It isn't me, my beautiful lady," Lucas replied with a semblance of pride, though he stole a quick smell of his armpit when eyes pulled away from him.

"It's this place," Paulus said chiming in. "Not exactly the finest inn."

Helene stared at him for a moment, giving a faint nod and quickly moving her scented cloth back into hiding. "I think then, the best thing would be to get out of this place and continue this conversation at an inn."

"If only it were that simple," Paulus replied.

"It could be, if we would have tried the escape plan," Lucas added.

"I have an offer for you, for the both of you," Helene explained. "If you wish to hear, you will be released. If not, you will serve your punishment, which from what I hear, will be determined after some questioning."

"That does sound pretty good…" Lucas mumbled to himself, though the one who shared his company in the confines of their prison was far from impressed.

"What if we hear what you have to say but don't want to join?" Paulus asked bluntly. "What do you have to say about that?"

"I will only tell you the most basic of details and nothing else," Helene explained. "What do you say to that?"

With a silent nod Paulus gave his agreement.

"We are both in," Lucas added with a hard clap.

"Good," Helene said. "Guard," she called, turning towards the door. "They are coming with me."

With a grumble, Andreas threw open the door and waved them out. "Follow me then."

Back the way they had come, he guided them, as the wails and cries of his men's labor called out to all those that could hear. Through a few open doors they stole a few glances, as men carried out punishments befitting the crimes.

"Just so you know…" Andreas explained over his shoulder leading them all towards the entrance. "There are no exceptions from any other crimes. They get caught, you're going to have to come back and pay again. Probably more than you have in that purse."

"If they get caught, there won't be anything to come back to pay for," Helene replied, as the two men shared a brief look of uncertainty.

In a silence that consumed them, they marched the rest of the way, until before them loomed the worn door to their freedom.

"You can all go, once I get what is mine," Andreas said, holding his empty hand out to Helene. "No more delays."

"Wait," Paulus ordered calling attention to himself. "Wait."

All eyes fell on him with baffled and unsure expressions.

"Sounds like he wants to go back," Andreas said with a laugh, reaching for him with one arm, and with the other gesturing to the way back down the hall and towards their former place of slumber. "Go on. One of my men will take care of you until I finish here."

"No," Paulus replied, staring Andreas down. "I'm not going back and I'm not leaving. I'm not leaving until I get back what you took from me."

Helene and Lucas shared a quick glance, both searching for an answer they hoped the other had.

"And what would that be, huh?" Andreas asked with a roll of his shoulders.

"You know what," Paulus said, holding out his hand. "Give it back."

Andreas and Paulus continued to stare each other down, their resolve gleaming in their eyes. Neither man dared to blink, as if it would be to admit defeat and surrender what was at stake.

"What's he talking about?" Helene finally asked Lucas with a whisper.

"He has this thing with his purse, I don't know why," Lucas explained. "Don't think he will leave without it… But you know if you want, I don't mind going with you alone."

"Are you going to give it to him?" Helene asked, summoning both men's busy eyes.

"I think I'm going to give him something," Andreas replied, rolling his fingers into a fist. "Just not what he wants. What do you think, beggar?"

Paulus took a long deep breath and held it for a moment, before he let the warm air out of his lungs with an equally long exhale. His fingers rolled as well, just as his jaw began to tighten and his lips parted. Yet, before he uttered a word, he was held back by the words of another.

"Well, I guess we don't have a deal then," Helene suddenly said, causing each man to gasp before her. "Good thing I didn't give you this then," she added holding out the sack filled with coins and making it chime. "You can show me out."

"You are going to throw away the deal, for this guy's purse?" Andreas asked with a loud scoff, before raising his eyebrows. "Really?"

"No, no, no," Lucas quickly said, chiming in. "Of course not. I mean, we are already at the door."

"Me?" Helene asked, continuing to ignore Lucas. "No. But, I think you are. That's the way I see it. So, let me ask you, are you willing to throw away a deal for that man's purse? Even when I'm going to give you one? Because, if you are, you can just take them right on back."

Once more the resolve of Andreas was tested in the form of a stare, though unlike before, she mirrored his gaze.

"Fine," Andreas finally said, following his wiggling tongue with a pinch between his teeth. "Fine. Wait here."

Andreas turned and left the others to their company and the opportunity that the silence would bring, though there were no words that could be brought forth between them, as Paulus simply stared after where Andreas had gone.

"I don't know about you, but I think we could make a run for it," Lucas said, turning his eyes to the door. "I'm just saying—" Yet, before his plan could take shape, Andreas returned and reduced him to whistling in a corner.

With a hard toss, Andreas threw the purse right at Paulus.

"There," he said, turning his sight on Helene. "Happy now? Even has his two pieces of rust."

Helene stole a glance at Paulus who held a tight grip of the purse, with the hint of sorrow in his eyes and the faintest indication of a smile. With a satisfied nod, she moved her limbs below her cloak and pulled the sac of coins forth and into Andreas' hand, but refused to release her grip, as she stared him down. "Not a word. Of me, of them, or of this."

"Of course," Andreas replied with a grin. "Would be bad for everyone. But, if you think of anyone else you want to get for whatever thing, you don't have to look further than me. My wife could always use more of a jingle."

"I won't forget," Helene said as she continued to hold his stare. "This is the place where men who break the law can be found," with that, what grip she had of the coins was released to the one before her. "Open the door."

With a final nod, a smile, and a jingle of the purse, he pressed past the three, opened the door and allowed them to depart.

Helene led them away through the quiet streets in silence, as a mist slowly descended upon the city. Its eerie encroachment melded with the cold, swallowing what few souls braved its consumption in silence. Though, the group that was being led was not without its voice.

"Thanks," Paulus mumbled to Helene, following her shadow in the night. "Thank you."

Chapter 17

The Rejection

The cold of the night accompanied the light of the countless stars, as they shined down on the otherwise still scene. Their unobstructed beauty lay for a seemingly rare change unbothered by the veil of the clouds, or the opulence of the self-important moon. They glimmered with a beauty that demanded attention, though for those that did not sleep, the chance to lull in the embrace of such a spectacle was unknowingly fleeting. Yet, for most, as they focused on their closed eyes or the distractions of being awake, they soon found themselves too close to the ground to appreciate the beauty that lay covered by the ever-thickening mist.

Three such souls made their way through the veil of water, as they advanced with speed towards the light of a great deal of candles.

"You weren't joking about an inn," Lucas said with a smile on his face, catching sight of a hanging empty barrel. He wasted little time and rushed forward through the door, the other two following at their own pace.

The inn was crowded with the rowdy spirit of men who had had too much to drink. Worn tables and long benches filled the space, as drink and food were called to be consumed. A man who seemed more of a guard stood behind a counter, as he restricted the quantity of inebriating nectar that flowed passed him, though the only restraint was the demand of payment.

"Sit there," Helene ordered to Lucas and Paulus, pointing to an empty table at the far end of the room.

"What about you?" Lucas asked.

"Drinks, food," Helene replied, leaving their side and beginning to speak to the owner.

With a nod that called Lucas to follow, Paulus led the way. He pressed past the crowds, as the sights and smells distracted him, though he fought to ignore them.

"This place is great," Lucas said, as every distraction caught his eye. He waved to the women with a smile, though was quickly drawn to the food and drink that moved just out of reach. "I can't wait to fill my belly." He slid onto the far side of the bench and drummed his hands over the scattered red of the table.

Paulus was silent on his chosen seat, right on the edge of the bench and table, as if at a moment's notice he would rush forth and depart.

"What are you going to eat?" Lucas asked.

"You should be taking this more seriously," Paulus replied.

"What do you mean?" Lucas questioned, continuing to follow each distraction that called to him.

"I mean, don't you think that it's a bit suspicious that we are here?" Paulus asked. "Don't you think it's all a little too good to be true? Don't you think we are in a situation that could put us in a worse place than the place we were?"

"So, do you think we should try and leave the city?" Lucas asked, leaning in closely. "Make a run for it, after we are given our meal? What do you think? I could pickpocket a few people before we do, you know. The inn is pretty crowded. Could make a good getaway. What do you say? We could get away from whatever it is that woman wants with us. Remember what she said? If we get caught doing whatever she wants us to do, there won't be anything we can do to get out of that cell."

Paulus opened his mouth to reply, though before he could, he was silenced by the approaching presence that shifted his fate.

"I ordered us some food and drink," Helene explained, taking a seat in front of the two. "Should be here in a moment. You both can—"

"You got us out a few moments ago," Paulus interrupted. "You got us here now. I think I can speak for both of us when I ask, what is it you want?"

"Yeah," Lucas added. "What is it you want? Not that we are not happy with you getting us out of that place, and for getting him his purse back, but it would be nice to know what's going on. Maybe we had some connection that you noticed at the King's mourning? I do have that affect. Would not be the first time."

"No, just no," Helene replied, softly shaking her head. "Let's begin by me saying, thank you. I appreciate you coming, both of you."

"Well, you did threaten to have us thrown back in a worse place than the pillory," Paulus commented, under his breath.

Helene ignored the comment, simply letting it be swallowed by the noise of the inn. "If you both do not want the pleasantries, fine. We can delve right into the thick of it."

"So, what do you need?" Paulus asked, leaning closer and keeping his words between only their ears.

"Like I said," Helene explained. "I need you for a task."

"What task?" Paulus asked.

"I will tell you about that after I decide whether or not you are both the right men for the task I have," Helene explained.

The two turned to one another with a look of confusion, unsure of what to say.

"Then why did you get us out?" Paulus finally asked.

"Wait," Lucas added, struggling to grasp the complication of what he had been told. "Yeah, why did you give that sac of coins for us? Not that I'm complaining or anything. But, why do that?"

"For once he has a point," Paulus added pointing to him with his thumb.

Helene leaned forward with a serious expression and rested there with her eyes on both men. "What he says only has merit, if you consider that the price I paid to set you free was a thing of substantial value. If, however, you see it the way I do, the way the one I serve does, then you know that the cost was at most a drop in a far larger bucket. One of such small proportions, that should we succeed with what we need doing, I can promise each of you far more."

A lull hung between them all, as the hustle of the inn tried to reach out to them, like a child that pulled on their sleeves again and again, but was cast down at every seeming opportunity, until unexpected company joined them.

With a hard thump, a woman as appealing as she was unappealing, placed filled cups of wine and water before them all, a few drops spilling onto the already stained table. "I will bring the food out in a bit," she said as she departed just as suddenly as she had appeared. "Might be a while."

A heavy sigh left Paulus when he reached for the cup in front of him and filled his mouth with as large a portion as he could.

"He knowns what to do," Lucas stated.

"What do you want to know?" Paulus asked his host.

"Let's start with you," Helene said, turning her undivided attention to Paulus. "You have a brand on your hand, do you not? Below that rag, yes?"

Paulus was silent, trying to subtly move his hand to the cover that was his rag, though such a reaction only drew his companion's eyes. "What does that have to do with anything?"

"They allow branded men into the city?" Helene asked, as she pressed softly and calmly for an answer.

"No, they don't," Paulus commented cautiously watching the walls and any shadows that lingered. "Is that what this is about?"

"No, I only want to know what I have asked," Helene replied.

"So, what, you want to know how I got into the city and close up the holes?" Paulus asked. "Keep others from finding their way in?"

"Wait, then why am I here?" Lucas asked, pointing to himself. "I don't have any brands. See," he held his hands out and showed his wiggling fingers. "Not as nice as a nobleman, but nice enough to hold a noblewoman."

"You want to get rid of the beggars?" Paulus pressed, ignoring his company. "Is that it?"

"I'm not a beggar," Lucas said, his eyes still on Helene. "In case you were confused. I mean, not that you would be." He said as he gestured down at his attire. "I just needed to make sure your pretty eyes could tell."

Paulus turned to the man, with a look that appeared strained and the last bit of his patience running short. "You done?"

"Yeah, alright," Lucas quickly replied, his voice made weak.

"You haven't answered my question," Helene said, her eyes sitting on Paulus.

"You haven't answered mine either..." Paulus replied under a muffled breath.

The small company was left in a momentary silence.

"Let's just say that your mumble was a yes and move on, alright?" Helene asked.

A slow nod followed her words.

"So, let's say you know how to get into places you aren't supposed to be, would that be an accurate statement?" Helene continued.

"I can," Paulus replied cautiously. "But—"

"But he has other skills," Lucas interrupted with excitement.

"Such as?" Helene asked with only a slight inclination of genuine suspicion seeping forward. "Escaping from the pillory in the middle of the night? The guard that was watching you told me. He seemed quite taken to you. Could only image what would have happened if I hadn't shown up."

"I already thanked you for that," Paulus replied. "As well as the—"

"They don't brand beggars," Helene interrupted firmly. "They flog them and kick them out. The only ones to get a brand are criminals, at least on the hand. They do brand some on the face, makes it harder to hide. But you have to have done something bad to get that."

"How do you know all this?" Lucas asked, his eyes going from her to Paulus.

"That's not important," Helene replied. "What is important, is that you tell me why you got it, that brand."

Paulus held her stare, seeming to wait for something that was not coming. "Why?" he finally asked.

"I have to be sure you are the right person." Helene replied.

"Right for what?" Paulus asked back, holding her stare. "What do you want to know?"

"Let me ask you a final time," Helene said crossing her arms and leaning in. "What did you do to earn that brand?"

Paulus stared at her for a moment, feeling the hungry eyes of her and the young man at his side as they waiting to see what secrets he would reveal.

"I used to work with locks," Paulus finally replied. "I used my knowledge of them to take what I needed once. The guild took notice and with them the city watch. Rest is history. I take it that is enough to keep you happy."

A long lull held the air between them.

"You know how to pick locks?" Lucas demanded, bounced his eyes back and forth between his company. "Is that how you got out of the pillory? That's awesome. Can you teach me? I think I could—"

"Good," Helene interrupted with a nod, covering her smile. "You will be perfect. Simply perfect. And you still have your skill with them? I mean, more than is needed to escape where you did?"

A pause gripped the conversation, as Paulus was hushed and seemed to be lost in his head. He grasped his drink once again and swallowed a large mouthful, before speaking. "Yeah."

"Of course, he does," Lucas said, with a slap on the table. "That is why I spend my time with him. Why else would I spend time with an old bag like him? And that's why we deserve the good stuff."

"Excellent," Helene replied.

"So, what's next?" Lucas asked in confusion. "Other than waiting for the food? Got some questions for me? Remember, you can't have him without me."

"Next, you are going to meet the one I serve," Helene explained.

"And is he going to tell us what we need to do?" Lucas asked.

"She," Helene replied with a faint smile. "She will tell you what she wants of you."

"She?" Lucas asked. "I never say no to meeting a woman. Especially one who wants my skills."

"That reminds me," Helene added. "You're a pickpocket, right?"

"You know of my reputation?" Lucas asked with the excitement of a child. "You have heard of my amazing skills?"

"No," Helene replied bluntly. "I just heard you talking about it earlier. But, it's a good thing. I think there will be a role for you in what we have planned."

"I think I have heard enough," Paulus suddenly stated, pressing his hands against the table and rising. From his treasured purse, he plucked his two green copper coins and threw them onto the table. "I am grateful to you for getting me out of that imprisonment, but I will not trade one for another. I have places I have to be."

Chapter 18
The Acceptance

Loud voices filled the air, as the flames of a thousand candles painted the walls with their silent dance. Though, in the sea of pleasure and comfort, there was one who pressed past them making his way to depart. No distraction called his eyes, no scent pulled his attention, only the door stood in his sight, the only escape from his past, present, and future.

With a hard press of his shoulder that struck a passerby, Paulus swung open the door and took a few steps beyond the comfort of the warmth and light, lingering there as the cold reached into him. Yet, before the temptation of the sanctuary he had turned his back to could grasp a hold of him, he began to walk away, though not far. Moving over the mud and ice, he crossed beyond the reach of the warmth and of light.

For a moment he paced back and forth, before finally throwing his back against a wall and slumping down. In a still state that left his eyes staring down at the ground, he saw to pass his time.

A light snow fell over the slated roofs, slowly sticking with a fervent cold that forced those outside of shelter to shiver. Puddles froze, and cracks grew over their surface, as the dark of the night lay veiled by the mist, which only grew more pronounced with each moment that passed.

With slow movements that forced a few flakes from his head, Paulus extended his hand into the night. His branded limb was only sheltered by the warmth of a stained rag, and he silently pleaded for some measure of wealth that would fill his precious purse. Though, the company that was coin did not join him, but rather that of a woman who had also abandoned the warmth of the inn.

"Is this really where you want to be?" Helene asked, standing before him.

"It is," Paulus replied.

"Fine," Helene said, as she sat down beside him.

Paulus turned his attention to her and stole a glance, raising his eyebrow before turning his sight back to the inn. "You know you just sat in something I would not want on me."

Helene looked down for a moment, though quickly returned her sight to him. "Still a good seat," she said with a smile.

"You ruined your clothes," Paulus said keeping his eyes forward.

"Worth it," Helene replied with an indifferent shrug. "It's a good view from here. The place you were in a moment ago was better wasn't it? With the light. With the warmth. With the company and food, drink, and your friend."

"He's not my friend," Paulus mumbled.

"Partner then," Helene replied. "Also, that is not all. It is the support of the one whom I serve. That is really all I need."

A lull hung between them, as the sounds of the inn called to them. They watched as the world passed them by, comical joys beyond them. Helene watched with the hint of content, as the sight of happiness forced a smile on her face.

"So, that's your answer?" Helene asked.

"Look," Paulus stated with a sigh. "You came to me with a thing in mind that is so drenched with trouble I don't want to be even near you when you do finally get the courage to tell me. As it stands, I know better than to chase something like what you're offering. I'm many things, but not stupid. I won't tell anyone what you have planned or what you plan on doing.

"You know you're not the first man I tried to recruit for this," Helene explained with a smile. "No. I found another. A man who knows locks, like you. And I told him the same things I have told you. You know what he did? He ran faster than anyone I have ever seen. I could have sworn he managed to escape his own shadow. So, I'm not worried about that. If you told anyone, it would not be enough to figure anything out. That is, if you could get anyone to listen. And besides, you don't even know my name."

Paulus shook his head slowly, the words on his tongue trying to force his teeth to part. There he sat as his breaths grew louder and his heart drummed. "So why are you here? Why are you in the dark? And sitting in what you can only pray is mud? Can't find someone else? Too short on time?"

"No," Helene calmly replied. "Honestly, I see potential with you. I think you're just someone who lost his way. Just like I did after my husband died. My first husband."

Paulus said nothing for a moment, as he stared out into the misty night lost in his thoughts. "I'm sorry."

"Thank you, it was a long time ago," Helene explained, as the calm of the night washed over them.

"Did you love him?" Paulus finally asked, staring at his purse. "I know of a lot of people who end in marriage without the inclination of love. Only a few are so lucky. Did you love him?"

"I did," Helene replied with a soft smile. "And if it wasn't for an opportunity by a kind woman, I would have been lost because of it." A pause permeated for a moment, as the sound of the night and inn toiled with one another. "So, do you want to sit here all alone, waiting for someone that isn't coming? Do you want to wait in the cold for a few pieces of copper? Or do you want to come back inside and hear what I have to say and maybe earn enough to fill that purse you were so desperate to get your hands back on with gold? And while you're at it, get something worth far more, for yourself and the Kingdom. What do you say? Do you want to try to have a meal with me? Do you want to try to listen to what I have to say?"

Paulus grumbled, pulling his extended hand back inside the shelter of his cloak. "Food should be ready."

Chapter 19
The Viper's Nest

The sound of a fire crackled, as sparks jumped out only to be swallowed by the cold, though from its light so too came shadows. Its sound was no vestige of a melody to aide those who waited in their company, but rather one that seemed to boil nothing but the blood of those that found themselves in its embrace. They reached far and swallowed one another, as the figures that cast them watched one another with suspicion and doubt, until finally one of them spoke.

"This is getting ridiculous," a man by the name of John Hunyadi grumbled to the other half dozen, shifting his weight in his chair and letting an already unpleasant face grow worse with a scowl. He scratched his mustache, running his chewed nails through the curly hair that was his facial feature.

With a loud crank, the lock loosened its teeth and the hinges of the door gave way to the figure that stood on the other side. Steps quickly drew the attention of the room, as the host made his entrance with a smile.

"My fellow noblemen," Istvan said, moving to the empty chair that awaited him. "I thank you for your patience."

"So, why have you brought us here, Istvan?" Fodor pretended to demand, before his host could take his seat.

"I want to know why you have kept us waiting." John added as he chimed in, the drum of his fat fingers sounding loudly against the table. "I want to know, what kind of a man does not even greet his guests' when they arrive? That's what I want to know."

"You seem to want to know a lot of things," Istvan stated with a grin, as the obviously practiced speech he had memorized left his lips with confidence. "You want to know a lot of things, but you don't seem to want to ask the right question."

The men at the table turned to one another with suspicion. A few whispers could be heard, as the ones that made them tried in vain to hide the wiggle of their tongues. Yet, there was one among them that was unimpressed with the rehearsed dialogue.

"Quit the act and just tell us," John ordered with a tempered voice.

Istvan looked to him with a heavy glare that hid little of his contempt. "We are going to force the Queen to submit to the King of our choice."

A faint laugh echoed in the room, as the nobles were left once again to look to one another.

"You're serious?" John asked.

"You're thinking about calling the council to vote, on that?" Fodor asked, once again playing his part. "That is a novel idea."

"Indeed," Istvan replied. "These are trying times gentlemen. We have the Ottomans to the south to contend with. They who are actively trying to swallow us whole. We are surrounded. And at any moment, they could advance upon us. If we do not have them dealt with and we do not have the strength of a capable leader on the throne, we might as well leave an invitation for the wolf to come and devour us." He paused only to study the faces of those who hung on his words and buried his smile. "Currently, the council is assembled, and we have plenty of time to deliberate whether or not we want to be the voice for the Kingdom. Whether we wish to be the deciding force."

"Individually our power is strong, when compared to those below us," Fodor explained, with words that drew anger from those whose ears were filled with them. Yet, he did not give them the opportunity to leap at his pause. "That is what you are saying. But, when our authority is held in unison, not even royal blood can contend with us. Not in this Kingdom, or those of our neighbors."

Slow nods of agreement spread, as the anger evaporated and the mood was replaced with a hint of joy and the stench of ambition. Nearly each man's eyes shone with a silent desire, as the faint mumble of words of power and wealth echoed and reverberated. Though, there was one who did not seem to share the direction of the room, and who sat like a boulder against the tide of the encroaching storm.

"So, you wish to force the Queen, is that it?" Count Ulrich Cillei asked, finally releasing his thought. "You wish to have her made a puppet?"

"You finally speak, Ulrich," Istvan said, leaning forward and shifting his weight onto the table. "The last time I think I heard your voice was at the King's funeral. You were with the Queen, were you not? Chatting with her? Gossiping. Wiggling your tongue."

"I was consoling her," Ulrich replied with a tone that was defensive and harsh. "She had lost her husband, in case you had forgotten. You know, the man who was the father to her children."

"And do you still console her?" Istvan asked with a devilish grin. "Still giving her company?"

"How dare you?" Ulrich growled, pushing back the chair he sat on and quickly rising. "You would dare speak that way about the Queen?"

"Calm down, Ulrich," Fodor said. "We are only talking about a woman."

"She is the Queen," Ulrich said.

"She is a woman," Fodor replied, as he echoed his own words.

"Exactly," Istvan said. "She is a woman. She is a woman, a woman who happens to be a Queen. It does nothing to change the fact that she is not worthy to hold the throne alone."

"She does not want to hold the throne," Ulrich replied, his tone made evermore harsh. "She only wants what is best for her children. For her unborn son. And she is more than capable to sit on the throne."

"Are you to say she is more capable than any of us?" Fodor demanded, as the tension in the room continued to rise.

"I can't speak for everyone, but I can certainly say for you!" Ulrich shouted back, forcing the man to leap up in anger with his words. "I can certainly say more than most of you!"

The rambles of wise men soaked the walls, as they waved their limbs and turned their faces red, in a savage display that tried to dominate those before them. Yet, as they did, there were a few who remained silent, watching and waiting, if only for a moment longer.

"So, where do you stand?" Istvan suddenly demanded to know, laying his ultimatum down and shrouding the room in silence. "Ulrich, will you be with us in the room, or will you go and stand by the Queen?"

One after another, the men's red faces faded back to the calm demeanor they had been before. They stared at him in a seemingly patient manner, the last semblances of the turbulence passing like the trickle of dew following a storm.

"What do you say?" Fodor added, pressing the question.

Ulrich was silent as he stared at those in his company. "I chose what is best for the Kingdom and I choose what is best for the Queen." He finally replied. With a nod, he pushed himself away from the table and that of the company and without another word, moved to the door.

"Hey," the others protested at his departure, though they were subdued by their apparent ringleader.

"Let him go," Istvan ordered with a wave, as the door was slammed closed. "We don't need him. And we don't even have to worry about him, or the Queen for that matter, saying anything to anyone. Let him run to the Queen. We have all the information we need. We just need to acquire the majority of the council and force our will onto the others. No one, and I mean no one, will be able to stand against us."

Chapter 20
The Second Stage

In the faintest light of the early dawn, where shadows sat still and the deep thoughts of dreams still had authority, the cold of the morning gripped the city and left those who lingered on the cusp of awakening, to cling tightly to their covers for warmth. Though, while the city lulled in those final moments before the hustle of the day would awaken its streets, there was within shelter movement that already took place.

Grains of sand poured through the narrow curves of the hourglass in near silence, their weight betraying them. While in the embrace of the room, two other pair of shadows shifted their weight about turning their attention back and forth.

"What's taking so long?" Lucas asked, pacing back and forth. "I don't like this. I don't like this at all. First having to wake up so early and now this. I feel like I'm being watched... I feel like I'm being trapped."

"I guess that makes two of us," Paulus replied watching the man in his company move back and forth. "I need you to stop doing all of that. I don't like the pacing or the complaining. It's making me nervous. So, why don't you just stop?"

"Don't you think it's odd that we are in this place?" Lucas asked, gesturing to the wealth that was on full display all around them. He gestured to the fine tapestries and painted walls, to the ornate furniture and the wealth in the form of items and books. "I mean look at all this... Isn't she afraid we're going to steal all of this?"

"It means they trust us, at least to some degree," Paulus replied running his eyes over the decor. "Or that we said something that got her attention. Probably at the inn. Or they just need us. Or they are testing us. Or they—"

"All I am hearing from you is that you don't have a clue about what's going on," Lucas interrupted with a nervous demeanor, as he continued to pace back and forth. "I don't like this. I don't like this one bit. I feel like a rat."

Paulus's grew a look of annoyance as he blew out a warm stream of air and rolled his eyes. "A rat?"

"Yeah, you know, a rat," Lucas explained, as he finally fell still. "The ones you see at night. In the streets. They got those eyes, and those teeth."

"Are you really explaining what a rat is to me?" Paulus asked.

"Well, you know, a rat," Lucas continued. "Think about this. How do you think they feel being watched when a cat is around? The hairs on the back of their necks must be raised when they are. That's how I feel right now."

Paulus stared at him for a moment, with the hint of humor behind a faint smile. "Do you think rats have necks?"

"They must have," Lucas quickly replied. "Right? I mean, how else can they look up? They do look up, right?" His words faded away and one could only imagine what thoughts echoed in his mind.

"Look, what are you so worried about?" Paulus inquired, the smile still on his lips. "Worst case is we lose a little bit of time is all. Better than getting hit in the face with a shovel."

"The hell you talking about?" Lucas demanded to know, casting away all semblance of his former thoughts and stricken by panic. "You think we're going to get hit by a shovel?"

Paulus squeezed the bridge of his nose pressing his eyes closed and letting out a slow, but loud sigh. "I didn't say that."

"Look, this is what I think, I say we just grab a few trinkets and go on our own way," Lucas suddenly announced, plucking the practically empty hourglass into his hand along with whatever he could find. "Grab some of this, and some of that. What do you say, are you with me? I know a guy who will take this. Give us a few coins. And for all this, I'm talking silver. We could even go back to the inn we were in when we got set free. The food was good there. Real good. Drinks watered down. But the food—"

"Stop it," Paulus ordered, stomping over to him. "This is not the time for your... Whatever it is you do to get into trouble. Just sit down and wait."

Lucas stared at him for a moment with a still expression. His mouth opened and closed, searching for the right words as reason tried to burrow its way forth, though to no avail.

"No," he finally said, stepping past him and proceeding on a path to leave the room.

"Fine, but you're not taking that," Paulus ordered, quickly catching up and trying to pluck the hourglass from his once condemned accomplice. "Give the rest here."

"No," Lucas replied, tightening his grip on what he held. "It's mine."

The two men grabbed at one another, struggling to dominate the other. They pushed and pulled as they both tried to keep their hands on the items in the room. Though, as they fought, they were oblivious to the door and the well-kept hinges that turned without so much as a whine.

"Thank you for waiting," Helene said, entering the room as the two men leaped apart in startled shock. "We didn't mean to have you wait for so long... What are you—?"

The two men stared in surprise at Helene, quickly shaking their heads in silent defense at what they could only guess was pressing its way through their recruiter's mind. Before a word could be uttered, they leapt even further apart leaving a gap of space between them.

"We were... we were..." Lucas mumbled putting down what he carried on the nearest ledge. "I think they look better like this."

"Moving things around," Paulus added, as he too did the same thing. "That's right, moving things around."

Helene watched the two men for a moment in silence, as she seemed to struggle to draw forth the right words. "Well, I suppose they could have been in different places," she finally replied, still taken aback, and trying to collect herself. "Well, I suppose if nothing is missing... No, that doesn't matter. I am about to present someone to you. Someone that I am sure you have no knowledge of how to greet. So, that being said, please stand over there," she ordered calmly, pointing to the far side of the room.

The two men did not even share a nod, moving as they were told. They stood on the far side of the room, waiting for Helene to open the door fully and reveal the one they had come to see.

"So, who are we going to meet?" Lucas finally asked, before he turned his attention to Paulus with a grin. "It's a woman. You think she's pretty?"

His question however, was left unanswered, as Paulus paid him little attention and Helene swung the door open once again.

There in the threshold, stood a still and tall figure whose appearance was shrouded by shadows and draped in secrecy, except for the fact that she was a woman. She dawdled in the doorway for a moment, her eyes peering through her own cast shadows and onto the two who stared back.

Helene was quick to bow, holding the door for the cloaked Queen. Yet, for the other two who waited in the room, there was little movement, beyond their raised eyebrows.

"Do you know who this is?" Helene demanded, closing the door and gesturing politely to Elizabeth, who still hid below her dark cloak.

The two men looked at one another, blank stares on both their faces. "Should we?" they finally asked in unison with a roll of their shoulders.

"Should we care?" Lucas added, trying to see through the shadows that swallowed her face, much to no effect.

"Then it is better that way," Elizabeth stated with a smile, as she subtly requested with a wave to Helene that the issue should be left at that. "Until I can trust them."

"What makes you think you can't trust us?" Lucas asked.

"Most of the things in the room seem out of place," Helene replied with an eyebrow raised and a point of her nose.

With a grin and a scratch to the back of his head, Lucas released a faint laugh. "Yeah, that makes sense."

"There was a rat," Paulus stated with his usual demeanor, that screamed the need for more sleep. "So, what do you want from us? I hope you know though, that when we spoke to your lady here, I was clear that I would not do anything that involved getting blood on my hands."

"A rat?" Helene asked under her breath, her words going unnoticed.

"I want you to precure something for me, so that I may bestow it upon my unborn son's head," Elizabeth explained revealing her abdomen and stroking her belly. "And yes, she has explained that to me, though I am glad at your conviction. There was never a need or even a thought for you to do such things."

Lucas nodded slowly lost in the labyrinth that was his mind. "Like a cap? You do know they sell them at the market? I mean, I could try and steal one for you, if that is what you want. Your lady friend who took us to the inn, yeah, there, saw a few people drink themselves to sleep. I could run and grab one off of them."

Elizabeth's smile grew releasing a light laugh, as Helene joined in the levity of it.

"She's saying she wants us to get her something that isn't so easy to get our hands on," Paulus explained, keeping his eyes on the woman before him. "Something kept beyond the reach of your average man. That about right?"

"Acutely," Elizabeth replied.

"What?" Lucas asked back.

"It means right," Paulus replied before the others could. "So, what would this thing be that we need to get for you? And why is it so hard to get our hands on?"

"I know what 'right' means…" Lucas mumbled to himself under his breath.

Elizabeth opened her mouth to reply, though before the words could escape her lips, she was rendered silent by her smile, if for only a moment. "It's something that only those of royal blood can acquire. At least, until recently only they could."

"Lady…" Paulus said with a heavy sigh. "I don't know who you are. And honestly, I don't much care. What I need to know, is what your plan is. I need to know if you actually have one. I need to know the details of everything, if you want me to be a part of this… let's call it, venture of yours. And I definitely need more than just a line about royal blood. You don't need to sell us some lie, we are here."

"Are you from this Kingdom?" Elizabeth asked, her tone undeterred by the words spoken.

"I am," Paulus replied, his eyes narrowing and a semblance of suspicion growing in the back of his mind.

"Allow me to formally introduce myself then," Elizabeth stated, removing her cloak and the hood that covered her head, revealing her existence to the world before her. "I am Elizabeth, Elizabeth of Luxembourg. I am the sole child of The Holy Roman Emperor Sigismund. And I am the Queen to the throne of Hungary. I am your Queen."

The two men stared at her in frozen disbelief, not even a gasp leaving their lips or a blink obstructing their vision. Time seemed to pass at a pace that could not be measured, as the grains of sand in the hourglass were still and all together on one side.

"Wait, what?" Lucas finally asked with a shake of his head.

"She said she was the Queen," Paulus whispered a reply. "The Queen of Hungary... The Queen..."

"Yeah, I heard that," Lucas said with a whisper. "But, how do we know that? Aren't royal blood people supposed to be taller or something?"

"Only a few of us," Elizabeth replied with a laugh. "My uncle was at least."

"She is the Queen," Helene said, her voice holding the authority she was used to. "She is the one I serve."

"So..." Lucas said, beginning to lower his head and starting to bow. "Are we like supposed to bow? Queen...?"

"Maybe—" Paulus said simultaneously as another gave a more fervent answer.

"Yes—" Helene said alongside him.

The two stared at one another with a gaze that seemed to challenge one another's authority.

"You do not," Elizabeth suddenly said, with a soft and calm whisper that left a tingle to climb up the spines of both men. "In fact, allow me the honor," she added closing her eyes and bowing before the two of them.

"My Queen," Helene said in disbelief. "You can't lower yourself!"

"These men are worthy to bow to," Elizabeth explained, standing upright and stepping closer to them. "They may hold the very fate of the Kingdom, of myself, and that of my unborn son in their hands. That is worthy to bow to. That is worthy to stand beside them for."

The slow light from the rising sun reached into the solitude of the room, as those that had the haunting words in their ears, stared in disbelief. Their eyes were nailed to the one before them, as she stepped closer and the faint details of her beauty could be seen.

"Lady..." Paulus finally managed to mumble. "You didn't need to... Even if you aren't... the Queen. I mean—"

"You wanted to know the plan, did you not?" Elizabeth asked, stopping his mumble in its tracks. "I will tell you it. The next time we meet. Let us say, in one week we will discuss it. Until then, I am sure you can both keep your discretion about meeting me. The fate of the Kingdom and every soul within her may very well rest upon it."

Chapter 21
The Pieces in Movement

The high sun shone bright and warm with rays that reminded those who sat in their embrace about the distant relations that was the summer. Were it not for the crisp air that left breaths growing into clouds of mist and the lack of song from those with wings, one who had awoken from a long slumber might have thought winter was as far away as the memories of their dreams.

"It's a nice day," Fodor said, staring out the open window, the once imbedded ice beside the window dripping and running away. "Makes you wonder what everyone is doing out in the bright world. Makes me wonder what those like the Queen are doing. Probably still in bed sleeping, right?"

"You trying to distract me or something?" Istvan asked, keeping his eyes on a piece of parchment and the ink that lay scratched upon it. "Or are you trying to waste all the heat with the open window?"

"So, what did you think of the meeting?" Fodor asked. "I think it was a success."

"We were forced to react to the Queen's agenda," Istvan explained with a grunt, as he stood up, walked to the fire, and threw the piece of parchment into the fire. "You do know that, right? You do know that we were outplayed by the Queen to an overwhelming degree, right? Everything has been reacting to her actions. To her."

Fodor held an air of contempt, considering the words that burrowed into his ego. "Everything until now. I think the Queen is the one who made a mistake. I think it was her that might have made us react, it was her boldness, no, I should say, it was her arrogance that revealed what it was she was doing. It was either that, or it was my own skill with rhetoric and words that drew her out, much like the poison from a wound."

"Spying on us," Istvan said with a harsh tone of voice, and ignoring the self-praise. "Watching us, while we were going through the rhythms of those ceremonies."

"I would have done the same," Fodor mumbled to himself.

"She has no sense of honor, does she?" Istvan continued with his harsh voice. "What we are doing, we are doing for the benefit of the Kingdom. We may get a little bit of an advantage from it, but our goal has always been to secure the Kingdom. That is what history will remember, nothing else. She only wants to put herself on the throne. Or that failed excuse of an unborn son. Assuring us that her physician is right when he claims a boy is on the way… Probably been paid off… Probably even let the King die so he could get close to the Queen… We can only hope she passes while giving birth. That would solve my problems."

"I think things are going quite well," Fodor finally said, his smile drawing levity into the room. "I think things are going to work well. We have the numbers. We have the majority we need. We have the authority to bend her to our will. We have everything we want. I say we should celebrate the victory. Stop burning parchment as if you were some sort of witch. We both know you are too cheap a man. We should arrange a feast. Invite the people who have given us their support. Invite those who still are on the border."

Istvan stared at him with such a gaze, that malice alone would have been pleasant by comparison. With slow steps, he began to approach, as each thump was followed by another and his shadow grew. "You want me to be less cautious? You want to celebrate? You want to claim victory? You want to say that we have won?"

"Well..." Fodor tried to reply, though could not, as his steps were driven back with his companion's advance.

"There is nothing to celebrate," Istvan continued. "Nothing. I want you to understand that. That woman, she can still be a threat to me. She can still find a way to wiggle free from me. Not until the vote is cast and her lips and tongue bow to me will there be anything to celebrate. Understand? Not until the vote. Until then, there is nothing. So, I will continue to burn and purge all evidence of what we are doing. Because, unlike you, I know what will happen if the vote fails. Because, unlike you, I know what will be waiting for us and every other man that casts a vote against that woman. I know, it is about time that you did too."

Fodor held a long stare at the man before him, as the rant of a lecture died out. With a sudden burst of laughter, he spoke between chocking gasps of hysteria. "Is this a God damned church? I had no idea I was in the company of the Archbishop himself. Do you hear what you are saying? You're making the Queen into some kind of master conspirator. Some sort of shadow inside a shadow. Was it not you that said, she is just a woman? Was it not you that assured alongside me that there was nothing to fear from her, as long as we had the majority?"

"You need to be more vigilant until the vote is cast," Istvan ordered, turning his attention back to his work. "You need to have more doubt in the world around you. Until then, the Queen, that woman, has authority. But, once we have our way, she will be under our thumbs, like all women are supposed to be. Then and only then, can we celebrate."

With another long stare, Fodor turned his attention towards the window once again. He held his eyes at the beauty of the city and the faint sight of smoke that rose from the chimneys. There he remained in solitude, as the world beyond whispered in tranquility once again.

"We've already won," he finally mumbled to the city, as the warmth of his breath met the cold.

Chapter 22

Beggars Return

The light of the sun's early rise shone brightly against the snow, as the extended grip that had held the warmth of the day at bay was finally released. The faint trickle of drops fell to the ground, as the trees cast off what snow lingered on them and moved to restore their limbs to a barren state. The remnants of fallen leaves permeated through the ice and snow, its purity rendered stained. Though, in the serenity of nature, there was an intrusion that broke the scene.

With a whine of an old rusty hinge, the door to a quaint home swung open as Mathias pressed his hand against it and yawned wide. His arms stretched wide, as his jaw cracked before finally being allowed to settle. His head tilted from side to side, the cracks of his neck sounding loudly. His eyes were pressed tightly closed, as he brought his hands to rub them and remove the morning grime. Yet, as he finally finished and his eyes opened, a sight instantly caught his attention and made his heart flutter.

Eyes growing wide, he watched the open door to his barn flutter ever so slightly in the wind, as the small window was once again left open. With limbs that moved as fast as the heart pumped blood through them, Mathias rushed over to the barn. He stormed in, his hands in fist, ready to deliver a blow against any who might have been doing anything nefarious. Though, before he could, the wind in his sail was robbed from him, as he caught a familiar sight.

"Don't start," a figure warned, laying just beyond the reach of light.

"Where the hell have you been?" Mathias demanded to know, the words echoing through Paulus who had left the structure open to the cold's breath. "When the hell did you get back? We have been worried sick! Paulus!"

"Who, you and the shovel, Mathias?" Paulus asked back with a faint snicker under his breath while wrapped in his cloak on the ground. His voice fell even softer, his mouth muffled as he whispered an added thought. "Could not have been that boar of a wife…"

"What was that?" Mathias demanded to know, stepping closer. "You say something? Speak up! Where have you been?"

Paulus was silent and still from beneath his cover, ignoring his company for a moment. "I'm trying to sleep," he finally replied, revealing his face with a yawn.

"You look like shit," Mathias said. "What happened? You get into a fight? Trouble? You know what she says about trouble don't you? She won't have it. She won't let you bring trouble here."

"So, don't tell," Paulus replied, shuffling back under cover. "Don't tell her anything. Better off that way anyway."

Mathias grew visibly angry, his fingers curling, and becoming a fist. "Where did I put my shovel?"

"I hid it," Paulus quickly replied with a laugh. "Don't want you getting hurt."

"Me getting hurt?" Mathias asked with a laugh of his own, as his eyes combed the barn. "Is that what the bruises on your face are? Me being hurt?"

"There are no bruises," Paulus replied, with a grin. "None whatsoever. And those that were there were from a long time ago. And that was unrelated."

"Ugh-huh," Mathias said, obviously unconvinced. "So, why are you suddenly back?"

"Just needed a place to rest for a few days," Paulus explained. "I will be going back to the city soon. Didn't want to stay there, not with the new company I'm forced to be with. Mostly because of that. You don't have to worry about much from me."

"The city?" Mathias asked. "So, that's where you've been? And do tell, what were you doing there? Were you doing something important? Or were you drinking, again? I heard about the King's passing."

"As a matter of fact, I found work," Paulus quickly replied.

"Begging isn't work," Mathias replied. "We've been over this before. You can't just claim an alley, or a corner and say you are working. You need to get back to work. You need to get back to doing some good honest work. Something that will do some good for yourself and everyone else. Work like you used to do."

"I'm not a beggar," Paulus explained. "I found some good work."

"You found some good and honest work?" Mathias asked with a loud laugh. "Did you really?"

Paulus was silent for a moment, as he remained still. He lay there, seemingly ignoring the words that had been spoken to him.

"Paulus," Mathias called. "Did you really?"

"Yeah," he finally replied. "Yeah, I found some work."

"So, what's the work?" Mathias asked with a smile, as he sat down and began cracking his joints. "Good work? Going to become an apprentice of something? Back at work with which guild then?"

Paulus was slow to throw off the cover that was his blanket and look his companion in the eyes. "I'm going to procure something for someone. Probably going to rob something for someone."

Mathias was still, the words echoing in his ears as his eyes glazed over. With a shift of his weight, he leaned in closer and shook his head.

"Maybe rob a vault?" Paulus added. "Something to do with some very important women."

"Oh, grow up!" Mathias stated. "Can you be serious for once in your life? You were already branded for shit like that. It was that… it was that that got you living in my barn! My barn!" he waved his hands, shaking his head in an attempt to calm himself. "Not going to get into this again. Can't afford it…"

"Fine, don't believe me," Paulus replied. "But, I will be leaving, don't know when, but it will be to go back to the city and help my employer. Until then, you can leave my meals at the door."

"So, let me see if I have this straight then," Mathias said as he began. "You disappear after the last time. You come back out of the blue. You have work, but you can't tell me what it is. I'm pretty sure you insulted my wife, again. And what was that about the food?"

"I want you to leave my meals at the door," Paulus explained. "I have had to spend enough time with one annoying thorn in my side… more like a splinter really and in my neck at that. I do not need to deal with another every time I eat… better make that two, if I count you and your… wife. So, seeing as how that is the case, I think it would be best if I eat alone."

"Why did you say wife like that?" Mathias asked.

"Like what?" Paulus asked back.

"Like that," Mathias explained with a wagging finger. "Like that. That tone. That right there."

"I didn't say anything," Paulus replied with an eyebrow raised and the faint hint of a smile held back. "I think maybe you're finally seeing her for what she is. You know, a few nasty words."

Mathias said nothing and did not so much as even grow a twitch to his eye. "I'm going to find my shovel now," he explained with a voice as soft as a whisper, as he stood up and moved to leave.

"You haven't asked me how much she is going to pay me," Paulus said, calling after him. "Don't you want to know? I'm sure your wife will…"

Only the sound of the dawn whispered in the cold morning air, as Paulus rested with his eyes on the open door. For a while he remained there, though, with a faint chuckle, he turned his attention away and closed his eyes, content to lull to sleep once again. Though, just as he closed his eyes, his ears were filled with a sound that reverberated within him and forced him to stir.

"I found the shovel!"

Chapter 23

The Vote

The whispers of the setting sun pulled the air, as those that remained within its fading warmth were desperate to sway those whose company they desired; if only for the impending night. They called and pulled one after another, as the stars in the heavens grew brighter and more defined. Yet, as the stars that would capture the eye silently shimmered, few paid them any attention, as they rushed to escape the cold.

From the shelter of their homes and places of gathered company, they joined one another beside the warmth and light of many flames. They drank, spilling their drinks and the gossip that they had uncovered, as tales ran long and those that listened were blissfully entertained. Yet, within a structure of stone and authority, the gathered wisdom of the Kingdom congregated in force once again.

Their wealth and attires walked hand and hand with the ostentatious display of the decor of the hall. Though, no eyes were distracted by the display and no thoughts displaced by them. They were all focused on the door that opened for the figure who stood on its other side and the cause for their presence.

With slow steps that sounded like a drum in the deep, a lone figure advanced. An air of confidence surrounded her, as the eyes of the world stared at her with a turbulence that could shake the very foundations of the Kingdom. With a slow seat, she took her place on her throne, casting her eyes on the room before her and returning the stares of those who had the audacity to look back.

All bowed their heads out of respect and tradition, and in unison were made to stand upright. Istvan, Fodor and his gaggle quickly stared at the Queen, as those that opposed them did the same. Silence consumed the room, as all had the singular task of keeping still. Only she, the Queen, could break the suspense she herself had created and return them to their seats.

"I would like to begin by saying to all of you, thank you," Elizabeth said, turning her gaze from one to the next and watching as looks of adoration and impertinence gazed back at her. "I would like to thank you all for the time and dedication you have given this Kingdom, her people, and the very post you occupy. And I say that regardless of the choice you have each decided on. Just as I hope you see me the same way with the choice I have made."

The whispers of all present flowed from one to the next, as they turned their eyes to one another in a brief unofficial respite.

"I know that you have all voted over the past few days," Elizabeth continued. "I know that you have had to contend with the noise of each other, myself included. And I know that you would all rather be doing something with people closer to your hearts, just as I would, or for that matter, anyone within the Kingdom. Therefore, I ask now, what are the results of your decision? What was the outcome of the vote? Were you finally able to decide?"

Istvan held his eyes and felt the gaze of all those in the hall stare at him. With a slight grin and a slow rise, he stood up and called to the attention all those present. "Thank you, my Queen. Your words are kind, if simple. We are happy to hear from your heart, as well as the confines of your mind. I think I can say for all of us, that you have touched us."

Elizabeth returned a slight smile and a nod. "So, what would you have of me?"

"We demand a new King take the Crown," Istvan replied, the nods and chatter of agreement followed his words by those beside him. "We demand that you concede yourself to the role of wife to Wladislaus, the King of Poland. We demand—"

"Demand, you say?" Ulrich interrupted, as he stood to attention. "Should I remind you this is the Queen? She is the authority here! And we have still not come to an agreement!"

"Should we remind you that this is the council," Fodor replied chiming into the debate and forcing whispers to blossom and flow. "The authority of the Crown bends to the will of the majority here, as is the law!"

"Do not try and justify it," Ulrich demanded. "You know well and good that you have been coercing those of this council! Violating the laws and customs that you so eagerly claim to uphold as your own. You are treacherous and I along with many here would call you lot traitors!"

"How dare you?" Fodor shouted back. "You would dare insinuate such a thing? We who have stood for the greatness of only the Kingdom! While you and those old men next to you leave us open to invasion!"

"The greatness of the Kingdom, or the greatness of your coffers?" Ulrich commanded.

A fury of shouts filled the air, both sides taking offence to the words. They cast their fists into the air waving their limbs and forcing their voices to rise to greater heights. It seemed as though blows would be reached, as some went so far as to step across the aisle and meet face to face, as they continued to shout, of which only a few could be heard.

"And let us not forget, that she is our Queen!" Ulrich added, as those on his side of the room agreed fervently with him and the turbulence in the room only blossomed. "And she holds the authority that surpasses each and every one of us!"

"Only individually!" Istvan replied, rousing his side of the room to greater heights and forcing a confrontation of words to fly back and forth in greater anger, and disagreement. "Not when we collectively come together and make our voice heard!"

For a hundred rushed heart beats, the room held its chaos as all followed their passion, though like a hellfire its existence was only short lived, and it eventually simmered and burned away into embers and ash. With panted breaths and tears of sweat falling from them, the councilmen loitered in a calmer state. No longer did shouts leave their lips, no longer did the spouts of wisdom and division shake the air.

"Well, that was an interesting display," Elizabeth said with a smile, letting out a faint laugh, only accentuated by the silence in the hall. "I have not heard such determination in quite some time. I think it was when my husband was still here. That was quite an evening, was it not? My guards had to escort everyone out before we were even done. And the last time I had so many people fighting for my hand, I was a young woman, one with a figure that did not show the birth of two children and a third on the way."

"This is no laughing matter, Queen," Istvan hissed, wiping the last of the glistening perspiration from his brow.

"If you were sitting where I was, I think you would find it to be so," Elizabeth replied with another faint laugh. "Especially if it was you who had to marry that man, Wladislaus."

A few snickers filled the air.

"The Kingdom requires a King," Istvan stated, trying to suppress the anger from his face, but failing. "Not a woman. Not a Queen. A King. We need one who will be loyal to the cause of stopping the Ottomans. I think we can all agree to that, yes?"

"Loyal to the struggle against the Ottomans, or loyal to the one who got him a new throne?" Ulrich demand.

His words once again riled the spirits of those in the room and forced their hearts and voices to flutter like thunder in a storm. Yet, before the chaos could drown out the world, the fire in the men's faces and hearts were extinguished, and all were silenced.

"Gentlemen," Elizabeth said calling for attention with a calm voice. "Can we please proceed to what it is we are supposed to do? Or do you all truly wish to stand to waste what time we have by bickering. I might not hold the wisdom of the world in my mind, but I do know that time is the most precious commodity we possess. Let us not waste anymore of it."

A calm sense of order quickly flourished over the hall as the men looked to one another and nodded in agreement.

"Thank you," Elizabeth continued. "As I was saying, we have been in this situation for quite some time. Let us put it to a vote once again and see what the result may be. If no true majority is reached again, well, there is always tomorrow to try and cast the vote again."

Chapter 24
The Letter and the Duchess of Silezia

The light of the early falling sun shone brightly and warm, so much so, that were it another season, it would have been called the fairest of days. Clouds sailed over the horizon, as the gentle embrace of the wind carried them softly to the world's end. All the while, the ice that had seized the land with its fervent grip was slowly, but surely, made weaker as drops were squeezed one after another in its hold.

Though, while no birds sung their melodies of spring, there was another that filled the air with a sweet tune. The faint hum of an angelic voice occupied the warm air, singing like a siren of old, while lounged in her quarters beyond the sight of all save the light. The notes of her voice hung one after another and should there have been any who could hear or listen, they would have prayed to the heavens to slow down time itself.

"My lady," a voice interrupted at the door, pressing her worn, but thick knuckles gently against the timber. "Duchess, I have a letter for you. Just delivered. A pilgrim brought it. I hope you don't mind, but I gave him a meal and a few copper coins." There she stood and waited, the slight coloring of pink on her plump cheeks.

A silence hung in the air for a moment, the song ending and slow footsteps sounding. With a click, the door's lock pulled away and the barrier was opened. Light came pouring out from the room and into the hall, as the servant was forced to avert her eyes from the gold and red glare.

There in the threshold, stood a woman engulfed by the warmth of rays, hugged by the very sun and suspended by it, which only added to her beauty. Her golden hair shimmered with an elegance, grace and the hint of red that called the eyes to fight the glare and endure the sting, as if they gazed upon a flawless ruby. Green eyes entrapped all souls in their embrace, and as if by a spell, was only broken by their closing. The faint kisses of a few freckles touched her cheeks and might have stolen more attention, had it not been for the lines her body held.

"Did I hear you say you fed a pilgrim?" The Duchess of Silesia asked with her angelic voice, as she lingered in the doorway.

"Ugh, yes, my Lady," she replied. "He was a man. All alone. And he looked a little cold."

"You did well, Berta," the Duchess Barbara said taking the envelop in her hand with a warm smile. "It's bad luck to turn your back on a pilgrim, regardless of what news they bring. I am glad you did. Did the pilgrim say who sent him? Who is it from?"

"The Queen's seal…" Berta said with eyes wide, growing a smile of her own and a flutter of nods. "It's from the Queen. It's from her."

"Is that right?" Barbara asked with a slight tilt of her head, turning the letter onto its back and staring at the etches in the hardened wax.

"It's the Queen's," Berta said again with another smile.

"So, it seems," Barbara replied. "I shall read it in private then. As I am sure she would want. Did you know she always addresses me as Barbara in her letters? She calls me by my first name. Always liked that about her. I shall inform you later of what the letter holds."

"Oh," Berta said, slightly taken aback with the hint of disappointment. "Right, well then, I shall go back to my duty, my Lady." With a slight bow she left and pulled the door closed as she did.

The Duchess Barbara sat at her table, her reflection staring back at her from the mirror, as she toiled once again with her brush and hair. Though, even her own reflection could not keep the silent temptation of the letter's secret at bay for long. Slowly, she lowered the brush and reached for what the pilgrim had brought. She labored with the letter, as it was tuned over again and again, the faint smile already on her lips curving slightly more. Finally, with a pause, she stared at the seal for a moment, watching the red wax stare back at her. With a soft snap, she broke the seal apart releasing it, and with quick yet gentle work, she undid the folds of the parchment, as the secrets it held within were finally left to escape.

Her eyes quickly glanced over each and every curve of ink, studying the words and the meaning they bore. Suddenly rising, she pushed away from her table and made her way back to the door pulling it open.

"Berta," she called, casting her head out of the threshold. "I need you."

"Yes?" she replied, quickly rushing back to where she had been, the glare once again meeting her eyes. "How may I be of service, my lady?"

"I need you to pack up my things," Barbara said. "I will need you to also prepare for my departure."

"Departure?" Berta asked.

"Yes, I have been summoned by the Queen," Barbara explained. "I will be going to Visegrád, and the castle of Fellegvár."

"Fellegvár, the one with that Count?" Berta asked, a nervous fidget to her fingers. "What should I pack? What would you like me to pack?"

Barbara grew a coy smile, tilting her head slightly before letting three notes of a melody leave her lips. "Everything."

"E—everything?" Berta asked in disbelief. "As in…?"

"Everything," Barbara replied again with her smile. "There will be other women in waiting in attendance. I expect to be better dressed than all the rest. And for that to happen, I will need everything."

"But, what about the Queen?" Berta asked back with the hint of fear in her voice.

"Sadly, the Queen will not be in attendance to take me to the capital," Barbara explained, her smile and joy unaffected by the revelation of the letter. With a sudden turn, she left the threshold, and moved back to her quarters and the comfort of her table. "So, I will have to be better dressed than the rest of the women until I am before the Queen. And knowing her, she will have something grand planned. She always has. And when whatever it is, is revealed to the world, and the eyes of the priests and scholars are on her, I will have all other eyes on me."

Berta was still for a slight moment, eyes going wide, though, before much of a lull could blossom, her fingers fidgeted with uncertainty and she was forced to follow. Though, before so much as a few steps could be taken, she fell still again. "I—ugh, I think I—I think I must prepare, my Lady."

"Just one thing," Barbara quickly said, stopping her before she could even move. "I want you to leave the blue gown out for the journey. I wish to wear it when I arrive to Fellegvár."

"The blue one?" Berta asked, raising her hands and gesturing at her own chest.

With a coy smile that only grew, Barbara nodded softly as her attention was stolen by a book she had kept waiting. "That one, yes."

Berta lingered with a conflicted expression on her face, continuing to fidget. "I know it is not my place, my Lady, but… Is it not that Count who has accrued a certain reputation with women there?"

"I will deal with him, just as I have dealt with every other one like him." Barbara replied with a coy smile.

"Right, right, right…" Berta said as the wrinkles on her face seemed to struggle with the tasks. "I will tell the boy to get the other chests ready and a sled for them. And also the carriage. If I may, I will take my leave. I have a lot that must be prepared."

"Let me know when you have completed the tasks," Barbara replied. "My presence has been requested for a very impending date. We will have to hurry with everything."

"Yes, my Lady," Berta replied, closing the door and taking her leave once again.

"I pray it is an adventure," Barbara added to herself, returning to her table and tending to her hair with her brush. "I find it more fun when I travel that way."

Chapter 25

The Consequences and an Opportunity

In the company of silence and shadows, Helene stood alone. She watched whatever could distract her and waited for time to pass, as once again the sands of the hourglass dropped from one side of the curve to the other, and the grains tick-tocked against one another. With a stare that scrutinized and screamed of impatience, she waited, while the sands fell and rendered half of the timekeeper empty and the other half full. Though, the grains did not remain there for long.

With a sudden loud and flustered sigh, she rose from her place and marched with the heavy feet of a charging soldier. In an instant she found herself across the room, her hands on the object that held the secret to the length of her waiting. Her nails scratched the clear glass, to no achievement, other than her print being left behind. Though, as the she waited, the faint sound of approaching company pulled her forward.

Helene rushed to the door, the hourglass still in her hand. Yet, before she could reach to open it, the one she had been waiting for threw it open herself.

"My Queen," Helene said, her expression drawn between joy and concern as she cast her eyes upon her. She opened her mouth to speak again, though there were no words that came forth, only silence.

Elizabeth said nothing, simply walking into her room and finding rest on an empty chair. Her eyes stared out against the wall just as Helene had done moments before. There the two remained, neither able to say a word, as time simply passed them by, unmarked by its passing, unmonitored by an instrument.

"Helene," Elizabeth said with a somber tone, in an instant shifting the weight of her thoughts onto her tongue. "I hope you let me ask you something."

"Anything," Helene quickly replied.

Elizabeth paused for a moment, while the thoughts that lay on the tip of her tongue were held back. "When your husband… Your late husband passed… How did you handle getting married again?"

Helene was quiet, reflecting on the words. She remained in the company of only her mind, her tongue pinched between her teeth, until finally, it was released. "I was never one to think about such things happening. All things must pass. Even as a child we know that. The world can be as cruel as it is beautiful. But, when it did, when cruelty came, the reality of the world fell on me and nearly broke me. I think even you remember that. I think everyone goes through that, if there was love. But, in time, I fell for the man that would be my second husband. And most of all, it was my choice. 'If we have only one thing in life, let it be to have a choice.' My late husband said that."

The winds howled in the dark night; the turbulence of the foul weather stopped only by the barrier of the window. It hollered and scratched at it, though as the glass and its lock shook ever so slightly, it only earned a quick glance.

"The weather has turned foul," Elizabeth said softly, rising from her seat and taking a walk with slow steps from one side of the room to the other. "Thank you, Helene. Thank you, my friend."

"How did it go?" Helene asked softly, the hint of doubt apparent.

Elizabeth was silent for a moment, consumed once again in a still state. "We were outmaneuvered in many ways. It seems the delay that we have been employing has finally come to an end. The majority of the council finally decided that I shall marry. Can't say that I am surprised. Though, I had hoped it would have gone a different way, if only for a little longer. There is still so much that needs to be done... But, that is life. That is life and now I must think of the best plan to implement in response."

"Forced into another marriage so they can profit for themselves, those bastards!" Helene said as anger gripped her and forced her blood to boil. "We have to do something! We can't have you—"

"Helene," Elizabeth said, as she interrupted and silenced her. In an instance, her expression changed, as a familiar smile grew on her face and her tone along with it was uplifted. "I accepted the terms. Well, I accepted it by saying I would rather marry a begging Hungarian peasant before I marry the Polish King. Not the form of submission they wanted."

Helene was silent, her eyes growing wide and mouth hanging open. She stood speechless, the faint gasps of her breath all that she could muster to sound. For a while, the scene persisted, as she continued, unable to face the reality, until finally a faint mumble slipped past her lips. "What... what are we going to do?"

Elizabeth gave her a brief look of confusion, though quickly made her way to her side. "Are you alright, Helene, you don't look well."

"I'm fine..." she replied softly, though quickly roused her spirit and her voice along with it. "But that doesn't matter! The only thing that matters is what we are going to do! What are we going to do? God almighty, I don't know what to do!"

"Helene," Elizabeth said with a light laugh, putting her arm around her. "Breath. Calm down."

"I...I..." she mumbled back as she was led into a seat. "I'm sorry."

"Don't worry," Elizabeth explained.

"It's just, where does that leave you?" Helene asked. "Where does that leave your unborn child?"

"I told them, I would marry a peasant from this great kingdom, before I marry the King of another," Elizabeth replied with a laugh. "And they made the same expression that you are making now."

Helene held a look of horror as her expression only shifted to a worse state. "Why does that sound worse the second time? What about the plan? What about everything else? What about your child?"

"Nothing has changed with anything," Elizabeth calmly replied. "Just means we have something else to contend with."

"Yes, but what about the plan?" Helene asked. "If they want to bring a new King and have voted for it, then what are we going to do about the Crown?"

"We will have to move the plan up, that is all," Elizabeth explained with a subtle roll of indifference from her shoulders. "We will have to secure the Crown before any action is taken by anyone else."

Helene breathed a heavy sigh, as she struggled to contend herself with the news. "Has the council concluded then?" she finally asked.

"They are still debating," Elizabeth explained. "I'm sure they will continue to do so for the time being, if not a little while longer. But, I know what the end result will be, that is why I decided to depart."

"Are you going to go back?" Helene asked.

"I have a few ears that will be listening for me," Elizabeth replied, moving over to her table and finding comfort by it. "And I will go back for the next session. So, for the rest of the day, I will simply plan for the next step. Will you join me?"

"Of course," Helene said, hurrying over to her side. "Is there anything I can do for you?"

"No, I'm fine, but you know…" Elizabeth began, though trailed off to stare out the window. "In many ways, this has given us an opportunity. Quite a good one."

"An opportunity?" Helene asked back. "I'm—I'm sorry, but I still don't see how it could be."

"The men who have voted in favor for the marriage think that they have won," Elizabeth explained. "They think that this matter is over. They think that there is nothing left to contend with from me, or any of my allies." Her smile grew larger. "I think this will work well. I think this is a good opportunity. And I think it was about time that we met with those two men again."

Chapter 26
The Elected King

Heavy steps sounded against the stone floor, which not even the carpets that decorated them could do anything to stop from the man that made them. His shoulders rolled as, a look of distain sat over his face. Without so much as a knock, he pressed his limbs against the closed door and made his presence undeniably known.

"What is all this about now?" John Hunyadi asked with a tone that hinted of anger, as he entered the room. "I have enough things that need doing, so I have to think this must be something important. Because, if it is not… Well, this better not be a waste of my time."

"We have been talking," Fodor quickly explained, taking two cups of wine, presenting one to his guest and bringing the other one to his mouth. "With the vote finally over and our authority made a reality, we will be moving on to the next stage of our plan."

"Stop talking to me as if you are trying to impress me," John grumbled, scratching the hairs on his face and ignoring the cup of wine that was pressed against him. "And before you say you weren't, let me just say, stop wasting my time."

"Fair enough," Istvan said calmly from his chair, waiving Fodor off.

"So, what do you really want?" John demanded to know. "Better be something worth my time."

"Let me get right to it," Istvan explained. "We need someone of substance to go and see Wladislaus, the King of Poland. We thought of you."

"Of me?" John asked with a narrowed gaze, pacing back and forth. "Why do you want me leaving? What's so important about me leaving?"

"It's an important task," Fodor explained. "A very important task."

"If it was so important, you would do it yourself," John quickly replied, growling like a beast that was poked as it slumbered. "Don't waste my time with your lies."

"We have things we need to do," Istvan said, his tone and comportment one of indifference, as he sat unbothered by the beast that lay but another kick from being awoken. "Things that need our undivided attention. I'm sure you understand."

A loud scoff and a roll of John's eyes echoed his displeasure, as those in his company stared at him.

"Everyone has things to do," he stated. "That is not an excuse. Tell me what this is really about, or I will refuse now and leave. I have better things to do anyway. I'm sure you understand."

Istvan and Fodor glanced at one another, holding a silent conversation with each other.

"We need someone to go and work the details of our arrangement out with Wladislaus," Istvan explained. "That is not a lie. That is nothing but the truth. We have documents we want you to carry. We have things that we have that you will use to secure not just your own interests, but that of all the members of the council. I'm sure you are aware of all the potential that such a task can garner for you. Everyone, and I mean everyone from the council will be grateful for your efforts."

A lull settled between the three, as the hollow gateways to their long-vanished souls were left to move and wander.

"With the Queen forced to contend with the vote that we, the council, took, we can now focus our attention to other things," Fodor finally explained, leaping at the pause. "Just so long as the man who we believe in can move the Kingdom in the proper direction and agrees to all the terms we have laid out for him."

John was silent, staring out into the distance, as he studied something only he could see. Finally, with a slow nod he silently agreed.

"You will go?" Fodor quickly asked, as his face wrinkled in disbelief.

"I said I would," John replied, his voice once again gripped with anger as he was forced to repeat himself. "I don't need to answer again. Especially to either of you."

"There we have it, he said he would," Istvan quickly echoed. "No need to press for details. Though, I will advise you to pack well. It is a long journey and the winter does not help make it any shorter. I doubt even in the best of circumstances that you will return in time to be present when that woman gives birth."

"I'm leaving, send what you want me to bring to Wladislaus," John said with a grumble as he made for the door. "I will do what needs to be done." With those words thrown and not another one added, he once again threw his strength against the door and departed.

The two that remained listened as the heavy steps of their guest echoed back the way they had come.

"Well that went well," Istvan finally said with a faint laugh. "I will claim that as a victory."

"Do you trust him?" Fodor asked Istvan softly, listening to the footsteps fade away. "Are we sure he is still the best man for the task? Maybe someone of lower rank? Or with less of a temper?" With a flustered sigh and a faint wave, he swirled the contents of his cup before swallowing it in its entirety. "I don't know, maybe it's nothing, what do you think?"

Chapter 27
The Plan

Four souls lulled in a room without so much as a sound left to flow from one to the next. They sat still, yet far from docile, as a tension called on their very shadows. Though, unlike the four horsemen, there was no such imminent disaster, only the one that lay on the tip of their tongues. One after the other, they waited for the other to speak, though it seemed only the crackle of the flame dared to make a sound; though not from a lack of trying.

Lucas moved to open his mouth and share his thoughts, but each time he sighed in silence, as he filled his mouth with what drink he carried in a cup.

"I have to say something," Paulus suddenly said. "I'm sorry if this comes out wrong, or blunt, especially in your company, Queen Elizabeth... but do we even have a plan? I mean a good one. Or is the plan to just go in there and hope for the best? I'm in the dark here."

"We're," Lucas added, as he chimed in with a nod that left him coughing on his wine. "We're..."

"We're in the dark," Paulus continued. "We are so in the dark, that I can't see my fingers in front of my face. I for one have to say, that just telling us that you just want to commit a robbery would be one thing on its own, but you want us to steal something so impossible to get a hold of and you haven't even told us where we are going to go, who is going to be with us, the window of time we will have, or anything!" He breathed heavily, the rant having stolen the air from his lungs and left him with a hint of red on his cheeks.

"Also, there is the thing about how much we are going to make," Lucas added. "I am a famous thief. I can't just be given a few pieces of copper and have it called a day. That is very important too. I need proper sums of stuff."

No quick reply came to appeal to Paulus's rant or Lucas demands, as Helene and Elizabeth turned their eyes to one another and held a conversation with their gaze alone. There they remained, the two of them ignoring the silence, as the faint expressions and movements rendered their thoughts known to one another.

"Very well," Elizabeth said, turning towards the two men. "Let me start by saying that as for the compensation, I can assure you that you will be well rewarded. So much so, that I can say that you will both be well off after the task we have assigned for you. I can say that I will give you a strong mount and enough weight in silver to make the beast feel the quantity it must pull. And that is for each of you. But, as I have said before, the task that we have is quite a serious one and does carry a great deal of danger."

"No risk, no reward, right?" Lucas stated with a faint laugh, leaning closer.

"So, let me ask, why do I have to do it with him if it's so dangerous?" Paulus added, pointing at Lucas with his thumb. "Better off alone, no?"

"It's dangerous to go alone," Elizabeth replied. "Better to take him, as I have no sword I can give you."

"Am I going to need a sword?" Paulus asked with an eyebrow raised. "I'm not that well versed in using such things."

"If you get caught you might want to change that," Lucas replied. "Either that, or you want to be the fastest in your group.

Did you know that most people are satisfied after catching just one of the thieves? Remember when we first met? Didn't care about my other friend, did you?"

"Huh," Paulus said with a nod. "He's actually right about that."

"It was a joke," Helene explained. "She does like to have some levity. There would be little purpose to bring weapons with us. If anything, it would make the task more difficult."

"You have mentioned the task many times now, are you ready to tell us what it is?" Paulus asked.

Helene and Elizabeth looked at one another, the two sharing another silent conversation.

"So, are you going to tell us?" Paulus asked again, leaning forward and releasing a sigh. "Or is there somewhere else we should be?"

It took a moment, but finally, Elizabeth gave a nod.

"Let's start with where we are going to go," Helene said.

"We?" Paulus asked with an eyebrow raised. "What do you mean we?"

"She will be going with you," Elizabeth replied. "And before you ask, no, it is not negotiable."

"You think they don't trust us?" Lucas asked with a whisper, leaning closer to Paulus, though not close or soft enough.

"That's not it," Helene replied. "The place we need you to reach, will not open its doors to you without me."

"Isn't that why we have a man like this?" Lucas asked, pointing at Paulus.

A smile quickly grew over Elizabeth's face, as a soft laugh left her lips, drawing all eyes upon her. "Forgive me, I don't mean to laugh at you. I merely laugh at the optimism of being able to enter in such a way. You see, it is a castle."

"A castle?" Paulus asked taken aback. "You wish us to enter a castle? What's in the castle?"

"It's more like a fortress," Helene said under her breath, though the flutter of her lips caught Paulus' eyes. "An impenetrable one at that…"

"Helene will get you into the castle," Elizabeth explained. "She will get you through the main gate and all the way you need to go. I have arranged to have some women in waiting who are to come to the city to meet you there and spend the night. With their presence, they will get you into the castle and give you the opportunity to reach the desired destination that is within its walls."

"What castle?" Paulus asked with a calm and stoic expression.

All eyes fell to Elizabeth once again as the words faded away. There they were swallowed into desolation and absolution, as the weight of the pause forced sweat down skin.

"It is in Visegrád," Elizabeth replied calmly. "Do you know it?"

"That is the town's name, is it not?" Paulus asked with a sigh, pressing his fingers against his closed eyes before turning his hands to squeeze his temples. "That is not the name of the castle, is it?"

"Fellegvár," Elizabeth replied once again.

"Fellegvár…" Paulus mumbled, as he echoed the words. "As in the Fellegvár?"

"What's that?" Lucas asked. "Where is that? Is it close by, or will we need to arrange the cost of sleeping somewhere? I don't mind that, just so long as it doesn't come out of our cut."

"The citadel," Paulus explained with another heavy sigh and a shake of his head. "It is one of the most impervious structures the Kingdom has. It has walls upon walls. Gate after gate. Towers upon towers. It sits high above all other structures. And have I said that it has an army of armed men? I would say it is impervious! And you want us to rob it?"

"Yes," Elizabeth replied calmly. "I expect you to get into the vault. Past its locks. And precure the item I need from within."

A look of disbelief fell over Paulus's face, as he stood there, his eyes unmoving and his jaw slack.

"And what are we supposed to take out of the vault?" Lucas asked. "Can I fill my hands with everything I can carry? Will there be gold? Silver? Some treasure with precious stones?" Each question he asked raised his excitement and left him practically salivating. "A young woman I can rescue and call my wife? What is the limit to this vault?"

"There will be all of that," Elizabeth explained. "Well, not the woman to rescue, but…"

"But you can take nothing except for what we have in mind," Helene said firmly, as she finished the Queen's thought. "That is imperative."

"Why don't I like the sound of that?" Paulus asked with another heavy sigh.

"I know right," Lucas added, with the wind taken from his sails. "They want us to break into this place filled with a fortune and not take anything for myself. I mean—"

"That's not what I meant," Paulus interrupted. "You want us to gain access of a citadel and only take an item. What is it you want us to take out of the vault? What is it that is so valuable?"

"An item that rightfully belongs to the Queen," Helene quickly replied. "An item that belongs to her alone."

"Why don't you want to say it?" Paulus pressed. "Why is it—?"

"Wait," Lucas ordered. "If it's yours, why are we going to steal it? Wouldn't it be better if you just got it yourself? Why do you need us to get it? You could just walk in and take it. Right?"

"You do know you would be out of a job if that was the case," Helene replied, as the other two looked at him in confusion.

"Oh," Lucas said, the reality of it dawning on his face. "Ignore what I said."

"What is it you want us to steal?" Paulus asked again.

"The Crown," Elizabeth replied, calmly.

"Is that it?" Lucas said, bringing sound back to their company. "Just a crown?"

"Not just a crown," Helene explained with a heavy exhalation and somber tone. "The Crown of the King. The Crown of Hungary. The Crown that only those who are worthy of ruling the Kingdom are fit to wear."

Once more the silence was cast aside, though, it was not from any words, but rather from a laugh that grew louder and louder; one from Paulus. All eyes fell on him, as he struggled to contain himself and the tears that called upon his eyes. He was quick to wipe them dry, though that did little to halt his laughter, as he began to pace the room. Back and forth he went, and as his laugh slowly faded, he turned to Elizabeth.

"Everything alright?" Helene asked.

"Sorry, I couldn't help myself there," Paulus explained. "I thought I heard you say that you wanted us to steal the royal Crown. The royal Crown of Hungary! The legendary Crown! And not just that, but you want us to steal it from an impenetrable citadel. That has an army of men and horses that could chase us down if they realize at any moment what we have done. And you only want us to do it with just the two—sorry I meant three of us, seeing as how you want us to take your woman with us. Obviously, this is all a joke, because there is no way in the world that it could ever be done even if you could fly! So, if there is nothing else, I think I will be going home."

"It's no joke," Helene said, forcing him to stop.

"You're wrong," Paulus replied. "It is very much a joke. Seeing as how it has not only never been done, let alone can't be done. Now, I for one don't want to be killed trying to steal what can't be stolen, all for some stupid game."

"Hold your tongue!" Helene ordered. "This is no game or joke for that matter! This is—"

"Helene," Elizabeth interrupted, waving her to stop. "It's alright. Give me another moment of your time and I shall explain to you why I must have this done. Will you give me at least that?"

Paulus shifted his weight back and forth, biting his tongue and debating the thoughts in his mind. "Fine…"

With slow movement of her limbs, Elizabeth threw off her cloak and revealed the secret she had kept from them. "I am with child. As I am sure you are now well aware, I will have my child soon. And my physician has assured me that I am to have a boy. I want him to become King. I do not know if you are aware of the politics that dictate succession, but it is a complicated thing. And the reality right now is that my son will not be allowed to claim his inheritance. He will not be so much as anything more than a political tool. Left to be traded and moved under the authority of others. His life made forfeit to the will of others. I cannot allow that. On my life I will not allow that. Would you? For the ones you love? Would you not do everything in your power for them?"

The two would be thieves stared at her with wide eyes, before Paulus turned his gaze down to the ground. None dared to say a word, waiting for an answer from the Queen's question.

"I did everything in my power…" Paulus trailed off, as his voice choked, and his eyes remained fixed on his own feet.

A tension held the air, as they all simply continued to stare at Paulus.

"Then you understand the importance of what I am asking," Elizabeth continued. "Such acts are not for ourselves, but the ones we love."

"But—" Paulus said, though was quickly made silent.

"That makes you think," Lucas interrupted, holding his gaze at no one, but the door.

"I know what you're thinking," Paulus said to Lucas, clearing his throat and rubbing his watery eyes.

"Oh, that's great," Lucas replied with a smile, leaning closer to Paulus and lowering his voice. "I have been trying to figure it out. How do they know it will be a boy? Did they look or something? Maybe, like up there?"

"NO," Paulus said baffled by the man's comments. "About the Crown you fool!"

"Well, there is one thing about that," Lucas replied, turning to the two women. "Do you think I will be able to try it on? The Crown." He gestured at his head, as he mimed putting it on.

"You want to try on the royal Crown of Hungary?" Helene asked in disbelief.

"You know what, don't answer, forget I ever said anything," Lucas replied with a dismissive wave. "Let's just say, we'll wait and see."

"We have a small chance of success and one that is so small that we might not even make it out alive, and you want to play games?" Paulus asked.

"Just forget I ever said anything," Lucas replied with a faint laugh that slowly faded as the room fell silent.

The flame crackled, leaping at the stillness in the conversation and reminding all of its presence. It fluttered and danced, the warmth and light drawing attention for a brief moment, before the severity of the conversation returned.

"Even with what you have said, my Queen, I don't think that this can be done," Paulus mumbled with a heavy sigh, turning his eyes onto his company. "It can't be done… I might not have ever been to the citadel, but I know the rumors and the legend of the place, as well as the Crown. It would take an army of thousands. Tens of thousands to get to that vault…"

Before another moment could extend the silence, or before another word could be spoken, Elizabeth reached for what she had hidden beneath her cloak and threw it forth onto the table between them. It clanked and chimed, as the old black metal slid to a stop and pulled all eyes. Seven shaped pieces sat bound by a loop that held them as neighbors, and seemingly as their twins.

"What's that?" Paulus asked, fully aware of what lay before him.

"I think those are keys," Lucas replied. "I think seven of them—wait, eight—no seven."

"He's right," Elizabeth said.

"Keys to what?" Paulus pressed before biting his tongue.

"What do you think?" Elizabeth asked back.

A heavy sigh left Paulus, as he reached across the table and pulled the keys towards him. He held them in his grip, stared at them and studied each one carefully. Each shaped metal was large enough to fit across the entirety of his palm and the extent of his fingers. "These are not made by some apprentice smith. These have not even been made by an expert. These have been made by a master. These have been crafted by someone of unprecedented skill. I can only imagine what the locks these fit into would be like. But, I think I can guess what it is these unlock."

"A vault of unprecedented strength," Helene replied.

"But, let me guess," Paulus said, as he continued to stare at the keys. "I can assume that these are not the only things that are needed. Am I right? Why else would you recruit a locksmith if the only thing you needed was someone to turn the keys?"

"Those are the only seven we have," Elizabeth explained. "A means of security, if somewhat symbolic. Though, it is one that is very practical. But, you are right. There are more locks than we have keys that will be awaiting your skill."

"Are there more in the castle we can get our hands on?" Lucas asked, as he chimed in.

"There are, but..." Helene explained, searching for the words. "We have reflected on it and don't think it would be wise to peruse that path, unless there is no other way." She turned her eyes onto Paulus, who quickly returned her stare.

"Why not?" Lucas asked.

"It's too much of a risk," Paulus stated, leaning forward and letting out a sigh. "If anyone caught you. If anyone found a key missing before we departed. If anyone caught wind of anything, it would be a disaster. So, if his role is not to do that, what is he for?" he asked as he gestured towards Lucas.

"That is a good question," Lucas added with a slow nod. "I take it you need me to use my skill for something? Maybe seduction of one of the women in waiting?"

"No," the two women replied in unison, as Paulus too shook his head at the thought.

"There are a great deal of guards that watch the citadel," Elizabeth explained. "Some, however, are more vigilant that others."

"Like Demeter," Helene said as she chimed in. "He follows the Count around like a stray dog that has been fed."

"That he does, but that is why he is not much of a threat," Elizabeth continued. "Because he will be following his superior. Each man has a role to play, just like the two of you will. And there is one man there that has a role to watch the vault; the Castilian."

"The what?" Lucas asked.

"It is a man, who is always by the vault," Helene explained. "He is from Castile. Dark hair. Bronze skin."

"Oh," Lucas replied, lost in his thoughts imagining the man.

Elizabeth, however, did not waste more time. "Now, regardless as to whether you can pluck all the keys for the vault, or pick all the locks to gain entrance, the Castilian will be the problem."

"How so?" Paulus asked, leaning closer.

"Because, he practically lives in the vault," Helene replied.

"The Castilian's quarters are right beside the vault," Elizabeth explained, as her words forced those that listened to grow still. "You could even say that he shares a wall with the vault. So, if anyone were to approach the vault, he would certainly know what was happening. Now, imagine if you were going to make any kind of sound."

"He would be upon us within a moment," Paulus replied.

"You don't want us to…?" Lucas began to ask, running his finger across his throat. "You know…"

"No," Elizabeth firmly replied. "I would have none of that. We have come up with a plan on how to deal with him."

"That is the real reason you are here," Helene said, chiming in and pointing to Lucas. "The Castilian enjoys his drink. We will need you to get close to him and put a certain something in his drink." She said, as she pulled from hiding a small pouch and gently slid it across the timber.

"It is not lethal by any means," Elizabeth explained, as Lucas took it in his hand and studied it. "But, consuming it will leave you sick for a day and a night."

"Yeah, I can do that," Lucas said with a nod of his head. "Should I keep this until then?" he asked as he held up the pouch.

"Only if you don't lose it," Helene quickly replied. "It is all we have."

"I haven't lost anything in a long time," Lucas explained with a grin. "I have a safe spot. Will put it there later."

"So that is the plan?" Paulus asked, with a faint laugh to his question. "That is how you plan on stealing a royal artifact from an impenetrable vault?"

"It is," Elizabeth replied.

A silence held the air, as the response rendered the room docile. One again, like it had been before the conversation took hold, a hush, save for a flame, was all that was shared.

"Before I ask you a final question or you ask me yours, let me just say this," Elizabeth pleaded, as she stood up and moved towards the two men. "What we have discussed, is the fate of the Kingdom. It is the fate of myself. It is the fate of my unborn son, who I will give birth to in two months. It is the fate of every man, woman and child that sits bellow the Crow—"

"The Crown you are asking us to steal," Paulus whispered softly.

"No," Elizabeth continued with a soft nod. "No, it is the Crown I am begging you to steal. But, it is for a future where the Kingdom can blossom and all her people with it. Not just a few, who wish to continue to enrich themselves off of those they can exploit. So, I ask you, will you help me achieve my goal by procuring the Crown for my son? Will you help me grasp at a new future?"

"The way I see it, no risk, no reward," Lucas quickly replied with a smile. "You can count me in."

"And what of you?" Helene asked, turning to Paulus.

He stared at the ground, before finally releasing yet another sigh. "My Queen, did you mean what you said earlier?" he finally asked Elizabeth. "Did you really mean it? About love?"

Elizabeth grew a soft smile, moving her hands over her belly. "Yes. Every word."

With a final heavy sigh, Paulus began to slowly move his head, as he got off the seat and kneeled before the Queen. "What skill I have is at your disposal, my Queen."

Chapter 28
The Women in Waiting

In the company of the winter and its emissaries, eyes watched the white landscape high above on the final level of the citadel. Their hands sat with spear and bows at the ready, though their gaze did not stare at the encroach of an army. Rather, they stared past their red noses at the small procession that made its way from the base of the castle's first gate and its ascension to the last.

The highest gate swung open, its thick splinters moving and casting off snow, ice and water, as horses, sleds and a carriage passed by. Through puddles of still water and mud, the procession went until they finally came to a stop. From the sledges, carriages and its shelter, those who helped and tended to service emerged and quickly took their post just before their warm masters. They stood there, their hands at the ready, waiting for the signal.

All eyes were kept on the door to the interior of the citadel for their host to make his appearance. Ripples formed on puddles while all waited, and as the last of the defenses creaked and were thrown open, their host made his presence known. With a nod the servants came alive, and as they offered their hands in assistance, there emerged one woman after another until there were five, or so it seemed.

The men of the watch gazed with hungry eyes, as the fine gowns and clothes of the women who arrived were pressed against their bodies by the wind. The rich vibrant colors of their clothes fluttered and shone in contrast against the white of the snow, ice and mud, and their allure summoned all the men who lingered deep within the structure. Though, for what grip the winter held on them, there was a warmth brought about by the sun that kept shivers at bay, if only against the temperament of the rolling clouds.

"Ah! Fair ladies!" Count Gorge said, stepping beyond the shelter of his warmth with a hungry smile on his face, and his shadow, Demeter, a step behind. "I have been eagerly expecting you, so very eager." His smile grew ever wider, as his eyes were drawn from one woman onto the next. "So very eager indeed. I suspect that after your time here, most of you will not care to leave. And should that be the case, I will assure you now, that you are all welcome to stay. My castle is large, though it is quite comfortable and can accommodate your every desire. I know that it has for me."

The women stood with smiles on their faces, though silent for a moment, until one behind them finally lifted herself up. Moving towards the front, they parted to reveal one amongst them that had remained in hiding.

Suspended in a ray of warmth and light, she advanced with slow steps, as the glow of the sun accentuated her beauty. The blue dress she wore fluttered, and what exposed skin she had was kissed by the sun and the breeze of the wind. Gazes were garnered by the lines of her curves and the deep cut of her dress, as her golden hair shimmered like a halo and left but one emotion within the hearts of all; hope. For all and any who stared upon her could do, was hope she would return their gaze, if not a little more.

"Good afternoon, Count," Barbara said with a coy grin, stepping towards him, her eyes seeing through him and glancing at his shadow. "So, kind of you to offer us such an invitation, though, I would be remiss if I did not say that we are to accompany the Queen's herald and her trusted help to the Queen in a short time. I fear any stay by anyone of us noble women must be short and sweet. It can be nothing more. Though, that does give the opportunity to sow memorable memories."

Count Gorge was at a momentary loss of words, as he could only stare with flustered cheeks. "Well, we can only hope that we create such a memory."

Yet, as Count Gorge's words left his lips and faded, alongside, the presence of his shadow drew attention. Demeter stared at her with wide eyes, jaw hanging down to the ground as the saliva began to fill the space, nearly to the point of being rendered drool. His gaze continued, his expression along with it, until a soft hand reached up and pushed his jaw back into place.

"See something you like?" Barbara asked, her smile made evermore devilish, as she gently caressed his chin. "Or did the cold just get to you? Seems the sun has chosen to depart us for now."

Demeter grew red, struggling to compose himself. Shifting back and forth, he tried to catch his breath and calm his breathing, though all to little avail. "I—ugh… I—umm…"

"Just ignore him," Gorge ordered with a laugh at the blush his company still had on his cheeks, giving the man a hard slap on his back. "He gets that way around… certain women. As I am sure you know, all lesser men do."

Barbara held her hand for a moment longer, though, she pulled it away with a slight tickle to Demeter's cheek and chin.

"A shame," she said. "It would have been nice to have him do more than just stand there. But, as I have said, there are opportunities to sow some memories."

"I can agree to that," Gorge replied with a laugh. "But, I think he stands around too much when he just stands around. I think it would be better to have him earn his keep."

"Pay him little attention," Gorge ordered with a playful laugh, gesturing for the Duchess and other women to follow. "He is always by my side, but he will simply stand there quietly if I make him."

"But there is always time, for him to grow a voice," Barbara added with a wink, as she turned back to Demeter, forcing him to grow an even brighter shade of red than he had been before. "And where may I ask is the Queen's herald?" she asked, tilting her head and looking around slightly. "Is it not customary for them to be here already? Is it not customary for them to be waiting and greeting us?"

"From what I understand they will be here soon," Gorge explained with a nervous demeanor, as he continued to salivate at the close sight of the woman before him. "The last word I received was that they had already made the preparations and would be here in a few days."

"A few days..." Barbara said, as she reflected on the news.

"Duchess," Gorge said, trying to claim her attention and gesturing to her to follow once again. "I hope you will be happy to find that I have paid no expense for a feast, for you, and the other women as well."

"I'm sure that you have, and I will be pleased to see it all," Barbara replied, leading the others towards the entrance to shelter. "Show us the way, Count. We have much to prepare for. I expect the Queen's chosen few to be here soon enough and we have so many memories to make before then."

Chapter 29
Intimidation and Reflection

Whispers and shadows filled the royal structure, as those of rank and those of lesser stature lingered within their circles of company and gossiped away. Yet, while each step of societal norm divided themselves and were far flung from one another, down a corridor, divided by a room, separate from each other's murmurs and ears, the same topic of conversation spewed forth from each one's lips; the Queen.

The murmurs of eager tongues flowed in the air, as those that spoke them expressed a plethora of emotions, their own vested interests at heart. Though, as they spent their time gratified with the gossip they spilled, the one they spoke of moved through the halls, though not alone.

Elizabeth and Helene wound their way through the halls and its shadows, as they avoided the eyes of those that whispered. With each step they took, they exchanged words of their own and moved closer to their departure, until they lay at a junction that forked.

"I am trusting you with this," Elizabeth said with a smile, her limbs falling still as her voice flowed down the halls. "And I am sure you will not let me down."

"Of course," Helene replied giving a bow. "I will not fail you."

With a gentle touch on her arm, Elizabeth sent Helene forward, to tend to the task she had inquired about. Though, as she watched her depart, a shadow crept up towards her. Like a snake that hunted, it curled its way closer, trying to remain unnoticed until it could startle its prey and strike.

"You really should work on your feet," Elizabeth warned, her eyes still drawn forward towards Helene's departure. "They are heavy and loud."

Her words forced a pause on the advance of the would-be snake. "It would seem you caught me," Fodor said with a faint laugh. "Or perhaps I got you?"

"No," Elizabeth replied, her back to him. "No, you did not."

"Was that your little helper, Queen?" Fodor asked with a grin, moving a tiny bit closer. "Is she off preparing your wedding gown? Or is she—?"

"Or is she off doing something else?" Elizabeth interrupted, rendering him silent. "That's what you were going to ask, right? That is what I would have asked. Unless, your only goal was to spend time telling simple jokes. I suppose for you it could be either, you're not Istvan."

Fodor had little to say, trying to collect himself. "Well," he managed to say, striving to grasp a semblance of the confidence he had had just a moment before. "I was going to say, how nice it is to see you again, but it seems that you desire none of it."

"You would be right to think that," Elizabeth replied, her back still to him. "Though, now I am curious what it is you're doing here. Most of the council members have dispersed to their homes. Taken to claim the calm and conformity they are accustomed to. But, still some remain. Still some gossip."

"Some of us take our work quite seriously," Fodor said.

"Do you include yourself in such high standards?" Elizabeth asked, her words striking a nerve making Fodor still, if only for a while.

"Is that bitterness in your voice?" Fodor finally managed to say, forcing his tongue to move as he tried to grasp at a level of bravado.

A faint laugh trickled from the Queen's lips, as a gentle sigh followed. "And what would I be bitter about?" she asked, casting her gaze over her shoulder and revealing her smile to him. "Everything is going quite well."

With wide eyes that lay glazed over in confusion, Fodor stared at the figure before him. "B—because..." he finally mumbled. "Because we made you..."

"Made me what?" Elizabeth asked.

"We elected your new husband," he replied. "We made you submit. We cast your unborn child off the throne. Before he could even be born."

With a silent few nods, Elizabeth gave only the slightest inclination of agreement. Though, what comfort could be found by it, was offset by the weight pressed against it by her smile, which seemed to only grow. "If that is what you want to believe, by all means believe it. Maybe the confidence will help you move with less noise."

Fodor was silent, reflecting on her words. He remained there for a moment, trying to muster himself to speak, only to close his mouth before a sound could permeate and his thoughts leave him.

"I must bid you a good day," Elizabeth finally said with another faint laugh, turning her back to him once again and moving to depart. "Enjoy the rest of your time with your little friends. I can assure you that I will do the same. And enjoy the gossip that seems to have made the halls home. I doubt it will last for much longer."

With those words cast, the Queen's cryptic message echoed away.

Fodor stood in solitude in the hall. Heavy breaths left him, as he struggled to grasp the situation. With a gulp that moved the apple in his throat and forced a bead of sweat that had hung precariously to fall, he finally spoke, "Jesus... I need to... Istvan..."

Chapter 30
The Royal Guard

The sweet scent of fine wine permeated the air, as the heat of the fire melded with the warmth of the sun's light. The two forces of light danced with each other, all the while the gentle lullaby they sang called those in their presence to close their eyes and sleep. Though such luxuries were a rare opportunity, even for those of royal blood.

The faint stain of wine extended beyond the ornate chalice, as the sliver glistened in the sun with a tint of red on it. The one who spilled it brought her fingers to her wiggling tongue and soft lips. With a lick, she stripped the wine that stained her and grew a smile, which only blossomed as the door that separated her from the world shook with a knock.

With a beam she turned to the door and quickly unlocked it. Casting it open herself, and with a wave forward, she gestured for her guest to step within the privacy of her quarters. "Be quick, before someone sees you and gossip blossoms."

With steps that hinted of apprehension, he came forward, as the light before him was quick to devour his shadow's encroach. He stood a tall man, though with shoulders that were narrow for a man in his line of life. His hair was a white that mimicked freshly fallen snow, yet despite the age that gripped his short mane, he was graced from the ravages of time by the lack of deep grooved wrinkles. His nose curved slightly to the side, though his dark eyes pulled the attention of those whose gaze lingered on him. His attire was a mix of metal and leather and a sheathed sword at his hilt. Though it all lay graced with the polish of wealth, the impeccability of being far from battle, and at the service of guarding the Queen.

"Thank you for coming," Elizabeth said, as she took a seat and gestured to the empty one before her. "Would you be so kind as to join me? Please excuse the mess, I spilled some watered-down wine, but there is a cup if you want some."

"I am fine my Queen, but I thank you for your offer though," Viktor replied with a respectful rejection that culminated in a quick, but firm wave. "You have no need to thank me, it is my duty to be at your service."

"Would you be so kind as to join me, even if you do not wish to share a drink?" Elizabeth asked, gesturing to the chair near her.

Viktor gave a silent nod and quickly approached his designed seat. "As you wish, my Queen." His chair creaked beneath him, as the weight of his armor pressed against the ornate timber and forced his eyes to turn their attention down, if only for a glance to inspect that no damage had been done.

"Don't worry," Elizabeth said with a light laugh. "The chair always does that. When my husband… the late King used to sit with me, he took that chair. He was always so comfortable on it, though only after it creaked and whined. If it didn't, he would not have been happy."

A pause in the conversation loitered between them, as both fell prey to their own memory and imagination.

"I am sorry for your loss, my Queen," Viktor finally replied, shifting his weight uncomfortably and struggling with heavy breaths. "I have not had the opportunity to apologize—or better yet, I have not had the chance to speak up… No, if I am being honest, I have not had the desire to speak out of fear of what it would bring…"

The Queen was silent, as she watched and listened. Her gaze sat true, waiting for Viktor's breath to fall and continue his speech.

With a heavy sigh and a scratch to his cheek, Viktor once again shifted his weight, reflecting on the words on the tip of his tongue. "I am sorry my Queen. I am sorry for everything. I am sorry for not being able to protect your husband. I am sorry for not being able to protect the King. It was my failure that he passed. It was because of me that you are a widow. It was me that caused his children to not have a father. It was because of me, that his unborn child will never know his King and father. It is—"

Elizabeth waved her hand in front of her, demanding silence. "Enough," she said with a voice that was firm and commanding, just as it was soft and endearing. "Enough. You have nothing to apologize for. I know you did your best. I know you did your duty. And I know that you desire to continue to serve. Isn't that right?"

"It is, my Queen," Viktor quickly replied, as he bowed his head. "I will dedicate the rest of my life to earn back all the trust that I lost. On my life I will succeed, or on my death I will prove my dedication. I swear it with all that I am."

A smile grew over Elizabeth's lips as she gestured to him to raise his head.

"I know that you will," she said. "And I am sure that you will succeed. Though, I do ask that you do not throw away your life in your quest. Life is short, but precious and should not be wasted."

"I will try, my Queen," Viktor replied, bowing his head. "I will try."

"Good," Elizabeth said with a smile. "Then we can put what has been a long time overdue behind us and move on. You are a good man and I do not want you to become a slave to your own guilt."

Viktor offered no reply other than a silent nod and for a while, all that consumed the room was a lack of sound.

"I must ask," Elizabeth said, pausing only to stare at the man and study his every faint expression. "Did you know that my late husband always thought that I would give birth to a son this time? I ask because I know that the two of you were close."

Viktor stole a quick glance to the Queen's belly, though with what grace he could, pulled his vision away and onto the closest item in the room. "I did not know he said such things, though I have heard some whispers."

"Whispers?" Elizabeth asked.

"Yes," he said with a nod. "Whispers. It is my duty to hear them. The gossip that surrounds you and fills the halls."

"And what other gossip have you heard?" Elizabeth asked. "I'm sure that there has been a lot of it of late."

"I have heard that the council wishes you to marry," Viktor replied. "I have heard from those that are with you, and from those who have determined what is best for the Kingdom's prosperity. They would have it in the hands of foreign rule."

Elizabeth's smile remained, as she tilted her head and stared down for a moment. "I think many guessed that was going to happen," she finally said. "I think if there were any who indulged in gambling, they would have made a few pieces of metal."

"I think many did," Viktor replied. "Myself included. And many expected you to bow to the council. From what they say, that is what you have agreed to do. What you were forced to agree to."

"We all have to make compromises from time to time," Elizabeth explained. "Even if it is something we do not approve of. Even if we have no inclination to follow through with it. Especially should the right opportunity present itself."

"I think we have all been in such a situation," Viktor stated with a stoic expression and long stare. "I doubt that there is anyone who has not been forced into something they have not wanted. Though, an opportunity to escape such a state is often searched for, even if never found."

Elizabeth leaned back, waiting for a moment as she seemed to reflect on what had been said. Finally, though, with another smile, she leaned forward and spoke once again. "And what if such an opportunity was found? What would you advise me to do?"

"From personal experience, I would advise that if a search came with a definitive solution, that it should be taken," Viktor said.

Elizabeth's smile slowly faded, as she leaned closer to her company and spoke so softly, that none could hear, even if the walls had ears. "What do you think will happen if I give birth to a son?"

"I would call that the makings of an opportunity," Viktor replied. "The beginning of one."

"Only the beginning?" Elizabeth asked.

"Yes, only the beginning," Viktor explained. "There would be more needed if success would be had than to temporarily escape a situation such as a forced marriage."

"Let us say that all things fell into place," Elizabeth said. "Let us say that opportunity was present. Would you stand with me? Would you aid me and my unborn son? Would you honor the legacy of my late husband? Or would you advise me to look elsewhere?"

Viktor quickly threw himself out of the chair and kneeled in front of the Queen, lowering his head. "I would advise you to look no further than me, for you honor me with just the question."

"I pray you mean it," Elizabeth said, standing up and offering her hand for him to rise. "For I fear such a day may soon come."

Viktor turned his eyes upon her in a moment of silence, before extending his hand and taking hers, as he rose and abandoned his knee. "If the opportunity ever arises that you shall ever need me, I will, with all of my being, do what must be done for you. That I swear, my Queen. And I speak for all others that serve you when I say that they will surely join when the moment presents itself to you."

Chapter 31
The Departure

The cold of the dimly lit morning touched the air, as those who braved its embrace stayed in the company of the faint and gentle wind. They dawdled as plumes of breath left their mouths like chimneys, and their limbs shivered if they stood still for too long.

With a series of loud caws, black birds as dark as the night began to call to one another. With cries that both taunted and demanded the eye, they watched, as those below them loitered, labored, and talked to one another.

"That a crow or a raven?" Lucas asked, his teeth clamoring, and his arms wrapped around himself.

"A pigeon," Paulus replied with a grunt, putting down the weight he carried on the frozen ground with a thump and a faint chime of metal.

"A pigeon?" Lucas asked back, moving his tired eyes over the sky and trees. "You sure?"

"Why don't you stop worrying about the birds and lend a hand," Paulus said.

"I'm a light packer," Lucas replied, turning his attention to those that labored. Sleds were prepared, as the last of the baggage was secured along with the mounts that would carry those who would lose the means to walk. Goods moved like a current, as every item found its place. With thumps and clanks, timber was pressed and bent, and a carriage was brought forth. "I can fit everything I need in a boot. What's all that anyway?"

Paulus stared at him for a moment, as the morning light left more darkness and shadows than any wanted. With another grunt he lifted back into his arms the weight that he had carried and made his way to a sled. "I think it's better if you didn't worry about it."

"Fine..." Lucas mumbled to himself, shivering in solitude. For a while he stood there, though as the winter's reach extended its grasp on him, he finally moved. "I'm getting cold." He said to himself, as he approached Paulus. "Hey."

"Finally decided to help?" Paulus asked without looking up. "Finally realized you get colder standing still then helping?"

"You think the Queen will come and see us off?" Lucas asked with a whisper. "Maybe she is in the carriage? Maybe let us in? It's probably warm in there."

Paulus turned to him with a blank expression, the cold seeming to fall from him. "You really think that the Queen is going to come and see us?"

"I mean..." Lucas began with a slight tilt of his head. "If you had asked me a month ago if I would have met the Queen, I would have told you, no way. But, if I look at it now, I mean, I already got to meet her. Twice. What's to say there won't be a third time?"

"And?" Paulus asked.

"Well, maybe she likes me," Lucas explained with a smile. "Might want to get to know me a little better."

Paulus held his stare until he washed away his companion's smile. "I would probably ask if you are joking, but I have come to know you well enough to know you might be serious... So, to answer your question, no. She is not coming. And she is certainly not interested in you."

Lucas turned his eyes away and kept them on the preparations. "That's too bad…" he finally mumbled. "I kind of like her."

The winds blew over the cold surface of the land, and those who continued the preparations felt the brunt of the sting. Yet, none dared to slack or seek shelter, as the one who oversaw them all made her presence known.

"We have a difficult journey in front of us," Helene said, commanding every eye to fall on her. "If you slack now, there will be more labor required later and we will be put behind schedule. That is not acceptable. And I assure you, spending the night out on frozen ground is not something you will enjoy. But, if you do your best, I am sure we will all be fine."

Those that had stopped to heed her words returned to their tasks, while those who had already finished went on to help, as Helene made her way towards two particular figures.

"Glad to see you both here," Helene said to both Paulus and Lucas. "I was worried one or both of you would not come."

"I gave my word," Paulus replied.

"And I was promised a fortune," Lucas added. "No way we could turn back. I was so excited I hardly slept."

With an eyebrow raised, Helene watched Lucas.

"You do know it's a long journey," she stated. "And when we arrive, we will all be quite busy."

"Yeah, no worries, I'm fine," Lucas replied. "A little cold, but fine."

"Well, I need to tend to the final preparations," Helene explained, turning her eyes to the noises around them. "See that you have everything you need."

Paulus replied with a silent nod, as Lucas did the same, though with the added expression of a smile.

"One last thing," Helene said stopping and looking back to them. "You both do know how to ride, right? Especially on the ice and snow?"

The two were left to share a glance to one another, before finally, one spoke.

"Of course," Paulus stated first. "I used to own my own horse. That's something you never forget." He replied, as he stepped closer to her.

"Yeah, same," Lucas added with a multitude of nods. "Yeah, we know what to do."

"Alright," Helene said. "The trip will take a bit of time, so we will have to keep a good pace. It doesn't have to be fast, but consistent."

"What about the ice?" Paulus asked. "Snow has been melting everywhere. The river must be losing its strength. Don't want to fall through the ice."

"That's why we have to be consistent with the speed," Helene replied. "We need to cross the ice before it melts any further. It shouldn't be that hard. It's been a cold night and an even colder morning. We will just have to pray the cold has strengthened what the heat has undermined. That is all we can do." With those words said, she turned her back to them once again and quickly began to give orders to those in her sight.

"I'm going to do a final check," Paulus said, moving towards the sled he had put his things. "Make sure we have everything we need to get in."

"Oh, right," Lucas said, following Paulus with a nervous demeanor that forced his numb fingers to abandon their shelter and fidget. "So…About the riding…"

"It's something you don't forget," Paulus quickly replied, as he continued to march. Though, as if some force called to him, he suddenly fell still and looked back to the one who followed. "You do remember, right?"

"Well…" Lucas said, shifting his head from side to side in search of the right words. "It's not so much that I forgot. More that… how do I say this? Oh, right. It's more that I don't actually know how."

Paulus looked at him with a blank expression, as he stood there in silence. Suddenly, with a few shakes of his head and a few heavy blinks, he brought himself to and threw forth a question. "What?"

Lucas grew a nervous smile, before scratching the back of his neck. "I might have… And bear with me. I might have said something that was not true."

"You lied?" Paulus asked.

"I wouldn't say that," Lucas replied. "How about, I stretched the truth."

Paulus shook his head and sighed heavily. "What do you expect me to do about it? You thinking I can teach you? In the few moments we have before we have to depart?"

"What I'm saying is, you should just give me some pointers," Lucas explained. "You know, the basics to get by. So, nobody notices that I don't know how."

"And why didn't you tell, Helene?" Paulus asked. "And don't say what I think you're going to say."

"What is that?" Lucas asked back.

"Don't say you didn't want to embarrass yourself in front of her," Paulus replied.

Lucas was silent, opening his mouth to speak, only to quickly mumble. "Well, I mean…"

"Go back to Helene and tell her that you can't ride," Paulus ordered as he turned and continued to march.

"Wait," Lucas pleaded. "I can't do that."

"Why not?" Paulus asked.

"Well…" Lucas replied, the concern of his voice echoing in his ears. "It's a bit embarrassing. Wouldn't you say?"

Paulus turned to him with a look of indifference. "I wouldn't know," he stated, leaving him behind. "Go and tell her."

With a heavy sigh, Lucas turned his sights back to Helene. He loitered in a still, bleak state reminiscent of the morning weather. Finally, with a kick of snow and a faint rumble of a grunt, he made his way to his employer and superior.

From the distance, Paulus watched, as the two of them chatted away. His gaze followed Helene's arms, observing them point in different directions, though quickly reaching the base of her own temples to press firmly in what could only be frustration. Finally, with a wave and a few gestures she dismissed Lucas, who made use of the time to rush back to him.

"I get to ride in the sled," Lucas said with a smile. "At least until the castle. I can only imagine how the way back will be. Me with the women in waiting. All cozied up next to one another. Oh, by the way, she said we're departing. You should hurry to your horse."

Chapter 32
Doubt and Assurance

Winter's numbing touch besieged the night with the elements of cold and wind, making all recognize its rule. Yet, within the sanctuary of self-importance, there was nothing but festivities that rendered the season a distant fleeting thought.

Faint music filled the air alongside the aroma of an assortment of meats, cheeses, and wine. Drink ran freely, as the smell of meat tickled the senses, and might have succeeded at claiming the hungry, were it not for the company of women. They rendered many men who entered the room dumbfounded, with a newfound hunger in their eyes and a flutter in their hearts. There was no shortage of distractions.

Yet, even in the temporary gilded garden, as the festivities continued to progress and no lack of debauchery existed, there was one who lingered in solitude in a dark corner. Fodor's gaze was hollow, as he stared out into nothing like a husk of his former self. Nonetheless, his presence did not go unnoticed.

"What are you doing here?" Istvan asked with a chuckle approaching his lone guest. "The gossip is in the other room, as are the deals to be made. You not enjoying everything I put together?"

"I was just thinking," Fodor replied, continuing to look beyond the dark window.

"About what?" Istvan asked, as his eyes were pulled towards his other guests, if for only a moment. "It better not be about the same thing again."

"What do you think we should do with the Queen?" Fodor asked, turning towards him. "What do you have planned?"

"Why would you ask that?" Istvan asked back with a laugh. "She is a woman and pregnant at that."

"She is the Queen," Fodor replied. "And I have spoken to her. I told you about it. It was… She is one I would like to—"

"She is a harmless hen dealing with an egg," Istvan said with a louder laugh. "All she can do is cluck at those who pass by too close to her little nest. Trust me. She has already agreed to our terms. Forced by our hand to concede to the will of the council and marry the man we have chosen to be King. And should I remind you, a man who will be very generous to those who have aided in his ascension. All she can do now is play her role as Queen on her back, like the little woman she is. We have nothing to worry about from her. The only thing we have to deal with, is what we're going to do with all the power we are soon going to get."

"Her aide has left her side," Fodor explained, as he tried once again to have his words heard. "I saw when she did. She has gone to—"

"She has gone to fetch some women in waiting," Istvan interrupted once again. "It is not a secret. She has gone to tend with the basic matters of the Queen's wishes. The basic matters of women, right where she belongs. And she is doing what we had hoped she would do. She is surrendering herself to our authority. Nothing more."

"But, what if she is off doing something more?" Fodor asked. "What happens if she is off doing something that is a threat to us? What if she is out there doing—"

"She is a simple woman, not even one of noble birth for that matter," Istvan replied. "Just a simple woman. Trust me."

"Maybe you are right..." Fodor said with a mumble. "Maybe. Maybe I will write a letter..."

With a shake of his head, Istvan turned his eyes back to his other guests. "I will have to go and take care of the others soon... When you come to your senses and wish to join us, there will be a lot of things that should be discussed. Many opportunities. A great deal of fortune to be made."

"Opportunities?" Fodor asked.

"A new King, loyal to us, because of our actions," Istvan explained. "We are already carving out more of the benefits we shall receive from him."

"You are?" Fodor asked, ever so slightly shaking his head.

"Indeed," Istvan replied with a faint laugh. "I have thought of a few things, to those opportunities we have already discussed. You should be thankful I have not told anyone else about them."

"I am," Fodor said. "I have just been trying to think of what to make of—"

"Have you decided what to spend your inevitable fortune on?" Istvan interrupted with a grin, though quickly continued to run his tongue before his company could speak. "I have decided that I will acquire land to the South."

"The South?" Fodor asked with an eyebrow raised. "Why the South? Surely you mean to focus on the North, like the rest of us."

"The South sits near the Ottomans, and while it does sit vulnerable to attack and invasion, it does give something back. Do you know what that is? Opportunity."

"Opportunity?" Fodor echoed.

"It will allow me to attack the Ottoman's lands myself," Istvan explained. "I will be able to pillage and loot more of everything. I will take the opportunity to add to my wealth and power from the spoils of my enemies. I just hope that dumb brute, John Hunyadi, does what we told him to do. I still can't believe how easy it was to get rid of him. Was like dealing with a dropped child."

"Yes," Fodor replied with a faint laugh. "He really didn't take much convincing."

"That's what happens when you deal with a brute," Istvan said with a smile, as he continued to drink. "They are so impatient. They are so eager to just get on with it, that they don't understand the way things have and are supposed to work. They see only the coin in their hand. Not the treasure below their feet."

"You don't think he will be a threat, do you?" Fodor asked. "That he would do something with the Queen, or even with Wladislaus?"

With a grumble of a sigh, Istvan narrowed his eyes and shook his head. "You really are getting paranoid now. First you are sulking over some woman who has already been dealt with, and now you're going on about him. No, he is not a threat. That is why we sent him. And even if he somehow had the knowledge to try and make a deal that would put him above us, he would not succeed. He is incapable of achieving anything like that himself. Just like the Queen. Now I will have no more of this. I want you to abandon what you have been doing here and join the others."

Chapter 33
The Branded Hand

The sound of hooves pressed against the cold yet wet ground, as the sight of scattered snow filled the view, and the faint hum of the sleds and carriage whispered softly swaying from side to side. Trees and mountains painted the scene, as the harsh carvings of stone, timber and the surmountable obstacles they provided, left the heart longing for adventure, solitude and simplicity. Though, such things were fleeting, as those that pressed forward to a distant destination could only steal glances as they passed by.

With eyes focused, Paulus watched as the multitudes of flakes touched the ground, only to fade in an instant and shift into a cold, wet drop to add to the mud. Those that reached his bundled skin, suffered the same fate, as water took hold of his cloak and worked to soak the skin of his shoulders.

"It's not sticking anymore," Lucas noted from the sled, as they came close to one another. He seemed to sway with each bump and ditch in the road, though it did little to stop him from speaking his mind. "You see it too. Been staring at it for a while now. Nothing better to do, other than trying to sleep, and I already did that."

"The views are nice," Paulus replied, his eyes never turning towards him. "The mountains, the trees, the sky. You should try looking at it."

Lucas turned his eyes into the distance for a moment, staring at the wonders that lay around him. Yet, after a few moments, he turned his gaze back to Paulus. "I've seen this so many times it does little to earn my eyes."

Paulus shook his head and rolled his eyes before replying. "You should try sleeping again. It will be a long night, or it should be. If things go as planned."

"And what if they don't?" Lucas asked, rocking back and forth with each sway.

With a heavy sigh that brought forth a scattered plume of fading mist, Paulus continued to ride alongside his partner. "I say we just leave that to the versions of us from tomorrow."

"That's not really an answer," Lucas replied, as he wiped his nose. "Not much of anything really. I don't even know what that really even means."

"Give me something better to answer to," Paulus ordered with a slight glance. "Before I ride away."

Lucas leaned back into the comfort of the sled, and closed his eyes, the rocking seeming to lull him into a slumber. Abruptly though, his eyes sprung open and his eyebrows rose along with them. "You know I heard from a man before we left that he thinks the world will end when it reaches the year fifteen hundred. Makes you think. Gives you something better to answer to, right?"

"About?" Paulus asked.

"How's it going to happen?" Lucas asked back in frustration. "What am I going to do?"

"There is only one thing it makes me think of," Paulus explained. "If people are waiting for the end of the world, what does that say about the world? And what does that say about the people? Something must be making them very unhappy to imagine such a state of things."

"You're no fun," Lucas mumbled.

"Try and find something better to say," Paulus ordered.

"So, what did you think about when we crossed the frozen river?" Lucas asked, though quickly answered the question himself. "I was thinking that we were going to fall right on in. Just fall through the ice. Did you hear it cracking? I could see the water coming through the ice in places. And did you look behind? You know, where we had come from? There were holes in some places. Like big holes. Holes that could eat people."

"We're here now," Paulus replied. "The river is way over there now. And we already talked about this."

"Yeah, but we're going to have to cross it again," Lucas said, bobbing his head from side to side, before turning it back the way they had come. "What happens if it gets warmer? Or it rains?"

Paulus continued to ride; his view unchanged by the world before him. Though the words of his compatriot stuck to him and slowly seeped to his core like the flakes of falling snow. "We will deal with it if that's what happens."

"You do know the other way around is quite far," Lucas whispered, as he leaned out. "Especially if someone is chasing us."

"Quiet," Paulus quickly ordered with a hushed, but firm tone.

Lucas turned his eyes around, quickly watching those whose ears were within range. "Sorry…"

"Last chance," Paulus warned. "Think of something good to say. If not, I will be silent until we get to our destination."

"So, you going to tell me how you got that mark on your hand?" Lucas pleaded, as he tried to break the monotony of the journey with a final gambit that was their conversation.

Paulus was silent as he rode on indifferent, as if the words that had been spoken to him had never been uttered.

"You ignoring me?" Lucas asked cautiously. "Or are you going to ride away? You know that won't work, right? I'm going to keep talking, you know that right? Guess I can sing a song. Do you know the one about the first King? I used to sing it with my friends when we were drunk. Oh, how I remember it. The clouds, the clouds, how they make me remember. I remember it all. Every word, it can go on for hours."

"Shut it," Paulus replied, with annoyance.

"You know how I learned this song?" Lucas asked, raising his voiced and throwing out a melody. "I was but a man, in a land I never had—"

"I used to make locks," Paulus interrupted.

"Locks?" Lucas asked, an eyebrow raised. "It almost sounds like you already told me that before. Oh, wait, you did. I knew about that soon after we met. I remember when you escaped and nearly left me to rot. Almost got me in real trouble, you do realize that, don't you?"

"You don't ever stop do you?" Paulus asked with a heavy sigh. "I think I'm just going to go on alone. You can sleep or something."

"We're partners," Lucas pleaded, stopping him before he could even begin to draw distance. "We should know these things about each other. It might help. It might just save the day. Yeah, think about that."

"It won't, you just want to gossip, and it will make no difference," Paulus replied with an indifferent shrug.

"Well, that's because every time I ask you anything you just ignore it and make that face, that face right there," Lucas explained, waving his finger at Paulus's face. "Like the time Helene asked you about your hand and that scar you have on it. What's up with that? Was like pulling nails."

"I needed coins," Paulus explained with a hefty sigh, holding his tongue between his teeth for a moment. "I was desperate for wealth. And so, I did what I had to do to get more. I was caught, and I was branded so that all would know of what I had done."

Lucas's eyes went wide, as he was left with a slacked jaw and an expression reminiscent of one who was blind, deaf and dumb. "Are you being serious?" he finally muttered. "You? You committed a crime?"

Paulus continued to ride alongside the sled, his eyes following the world before him with a glazed gaze that was hollow.

"Why not ask for charity?" Lucas asked. "I mean, it's not something I would do. Not after what happened when I tried with a friend, but I have heard that it works from time to time. Some people are not without compassion."

"What makes you think I didn't?" Paulus asked back with anger on his tongue. His whispers rose and hissed, as those who had loitered beyond the conversation were suddenly privy to listen in. With a shake of his head and a heavy sigh, he collected himself, and the only turbulence he further released was a loud cough. For a moment he was silent, until those around turned their attention away. "I was not so proud as to not ask for help. Friends helped as they could. And then I turned to the one place that always promised to. A place my love had given a fortune in good faith and nothing else. But, do you know what they said when I asked for some charity? 'It is better to give that to receive. It is better to believe in prayer than that of medicine. Trust in God's plan.' So, what did I do? I got this…" he said as he held his hand up and showed his burnt scar. "She died soon after. Nothing but a fading memory of her… that and this…" he added as he plucked from beneath his cloak his simple purse. "This was hers. I don't deserve it, but I can't live to see it go…It's all I have left of her. It's all I have left."

Lucas silently stared out into the setting sun and watched as the vibrant colors of the inevitable night shifted with a slow dominance. "Sorry," he finally said with a sigh. "Don't think I ever said that after I… well you know."

"Tried to rob me," Paulus said.

"You make it sound so criminal," Lucas mumbled turning his attention back to the view before him. He fell quiet as he watched the snow, the trees, the sky. "You know, I don't really know my mother or my father. I have just a few memories. Not much. Can't really remember what they looked like, or smelled like, or even sounded like. And if I ever did, then that means that I have forgotten them. Don't really know what's worse, never really having them, or having forgotten them."

Paulus looked at him from the corner of his eye, before staring at the ground. "I'm sorry."

With a shrug, Lucas replied with a silent gesture. The snow continued to fall with ever dwindling strength, and the sled continued to rock like a ship at sea. "That's life," he finally said with a tone of truth and remorse.

"You know, I once ate a meal," Paulus explained with a heavy and somber tone. "It was something I hadn't eaten since my wife was alive. It had been a long time since I had tasted such a thing. Such a long time, that the memories I had with her were buried deep. She used to make it for me; it was my favorite. But, one day, the wife of my wife's brother made it, and it brought it all back. All the memories. All the pain. All from a simple bite."

"I do remember that the view was like this," Lucas said, as he gestured to the scenery. "It was like this. The mountains. The trees… Yeah, everything. For all I know it was around here. Maybe I just have to try something from the people here."

A faint laugh left Paulus, as his lips curved. His volume rose with each breath, and as he did Lucas grew a smile and a few chuckles of his own that grew to match his companion's. The two advanced in a semblance of joy that watered their eyes for a little while.

"You ready for what's coming?" Lucas asked, as the last laughs dwindled away.

"No," Paulus replied, rubbing his eyes dry. "Not in the slightest bit. Don't know if we will even get out of there alive. Guess that is why I told you all that. Guess that's why you told me."

Lucas lost the last of his curved lips as his teeth retreated from their shimmering state in the air. "Yeah, maybe I did the same. I never really had a family. Guess I might make one, if this goes well."

"Yeah..." Paulus replied. "Family should stick together. Not that I have been in one for a long time. Or have the right to say."

Lucas stared at him for a moment, a grin growing over his expression. "Are you saying we're family?"

"Wait, what?" Paulus demanded in shock. "No, no, no. We are not family. We are not even friends."

"That sounds like something family would say," Lucas said. "I think I might have a memory of that. Does that make you my big brother or something?"

"Go to sleep," Paulus ordered. "We are done talking."

Chapter 34
The Arrival

The sun dwindled, pulling a shift in the world with it. What few birds had flapped their wings vanished, as they retreated to escape the slow encroach of the cold, and the faint shimmer of the early stars that filled the sky. One by one, the heavens grew to take shape in a mesmerizing splendor, though those who moved under them, did not turn their eyes up in wonder, as with so many things, beauty is so often ignored by the world.

"Have you ever been to Fellegvár before?" Paulus asked Helene, coming alongside her sled as they continued to advance.

"Why do you ask?" She asked back with an eyebrow raised. "Having doubts? Or did you forget that we had this conversation not too long ago? I think it was with someone else, who has a greater status than either of us. Remember?"

"Every day," Paulus replied, ignoring the words of her second and third questions. "But, it might make what we are going to do easier if we know what to expect. You know, hear it yet again. Make it almost second nature. It's either that, or I'm just wasting time and trying to calm my nerves at the same time. Care to indulge me?"

"I have been here a few times," Helene explained with a faint smile. "I know the intricacies of the inside quite well. The number of men that man the walls. The number of guests that will wander the halls. Every difficulty that we are to expect. I can account for most of them. And before you ask, I didn't tell you earlier because I knew that if I told you what awaited you at our destination, I doubt you would have agreed to come. You already ran off once already, remember?"

Paulus stared at her, as they continued to advance, though slowly began to nod. "Fair enough. Good to know that we will be going in with more details. I know we could use it."

"I think that might have been another reason that I was chosen," Helene explained. "Or have you already forgotten? I'm not just here to keep an eye on you and your friend, but to help guide you through the castle. It is quite big."

"Yeah... I remember," Paulus replied.

"Well, you will see for yourself soon enough," Helene explained. "We will be there soon. I think we are just about—"

"Hey," Lucas suddenly shouted, as he leaned out of his sled and waved. "Are we almost there yet? I need to say something."

Paulus and Helene looked back to him, before turning to one another. With a nod, they slowed the procession and brought all to a stop. The momentary respite offered many a chance at shifting their weight and stretching their muscles. Though, such rest and comfort were not for everyone.

"I've been working on our plan," Lucas explained, as the three huddled close while the others tended to themselves or their tasks. "Best way would be to get the key from whoever holds it. Any chance that can be done? We have a pickpocket after all."

"We've been over this," Helene replied. "We've been over this so many times. We have a plan, let's just stick to it for now."

Lucas's mouth moved to protest, as air flowed through it and his tongue wiggled, yet before he could even begin, he rendered his protest silent. "Yeah, alright."

"I have final preparations I need to take care of," Helene stated, turning her back to both and leaving to approach others.

"Let her be," Paulus ordered, leaning closer to him. "She has enough to deal with. She doesn't need your ideas right now."

"Fine," Lucas replied with a shrug. "Just don't get mad when you realize it could have saved the day."

The two were still and silent, as they simply turned their eyes to whatever called to them.

"How much further is it?" Lucas finally asked.

"I think it is close," Paulus replied. "We have been going for some time. I think it's close..."

They turned their sights into the distance and stayed on the desolate tracks they had left in their path, before staring at the road of mud and snow that lay untouched before them.

"Ask her," Paulus finally said, gesturing to Helene who approached once again.

"How much further is it?" Lucas asked.

"We're here," Helene stated, pointing her nose as she nestled her way to a semblance of warmth and comfort in her sled. "Just a little longer. Just one more river and one mountain."

"Wait, so why did we stop?" Lucas asked softly.

"Not because you asked us to," Helene replied. "I needed everyone to remember where to stand and the procession of how to enter. And remember, I told you that you would only be able to ride in the sled until we got there. Almost time to get out. You will have to climb the rest of the way up."

Lucas threw his eyes wide. "Wait, so how am I supposed to get there? Am I supposed to walk? What about the mud?"

"Ask him," Helene replied, as she gestured to Paulus.

"You want to stand there or are you coming?" Paulus asked with a faint smile, as he made for his borrowed mount. "I'm sure it won't be a long climb. Probably not much to worry about. And besides, there are some clothes that were brought."

Once more they advanced, the sounds of hooves, sleds, and the rocking of the carriage filled the air. The landscape consumed them, as they watched the scattered farms and structures in the distance take shape, though eyes were not left to wander for long.

With a sudden glimmer and shine, a mass of frozen water took shape before them, as a bend in the river invited a crossing.

"The Danube," Helene said, abandoning her gaze on it and staring up at what overshadowed it and demanded attention. "And with it... the castle."

There, suspended in a beam of light that glowed with the last of the warmth the sun could spare, stood Fellegvár. At a first glance, its stone blended in with the mountain's, as trees worked their way up high to its base. Though, what stole the eye, even from such a great distance, was the tallest tower that stood in the center and its red roof. It pressed forth with a defiance that scratched the very sky, casting a thousand whispers of doubt to any who approached it with nefarious intentions.

"What, is it behind that mountain?" Lucas asked with a laugh that he alone shared. "That's huge... Anyone else having doubts by the way? No? Nobody? Just me?"

"We will be in the company of a Count, remember your roles," Helene ordered, though quickly lowered her voice and whispered her thoughts to herself. "If not, this will be over very quickly."

Chapter 35

The Welcome

With slacked jaws, virgins of the castle craned their necks to the sight before them, as all were swallowed in its cold shadow sending shivers down each one's back. With each passing moment, the scale of the structure only grew, as each stacked stone consumed even the sky, until one could only see the first gate and those that manned it.

Helene quickly made her presence known, as the walls and gate obstructing her progress did little to delay her. "I am here on behalf of the Queen of Hungary Elizabeth, for the women in waiting. Let me pass."

With creaks and clanks, which were meant to hold the rabbles and armies of the world beyond at bay, the gate was cast open, its defenses inconsequential to the Helene's words.

They moved calmly and slowly, with Helene's sled guiding the way. Under the gateway they went, while armed men stared back at them and the timber of the first gate was closed, before a second was opened on the far side of the courtyard. With only a wave, they departed the first of the defenses, though what lay before them was the mountain and the prize that waited at the top.

The trek was long, each step drawing them up and away from those who had entrapped them within the walls of stone and gates of metal and timber. Climbing the slick ground, mud, snow and ice gave way to the stones buried below, though the faint grip they offered was not enough to spare them all. Those whose appearance were sacrificial were forced to descend from their mounts and aid in the climb, as they pushed and pulled through the muddied snow.

Upwards they pressed, pulling them closer to the sky and the clouds that accompanied the setting sun. Breaths grew heavy, as the air grew colder and sweat began to perforate skin. With grunts and sluggish limbs, they continued to advance. Each step grew weaker, though there was no rest or retrieve from the climb, only the progress of moving slowly forward.

Finally, they made it to the gate of the citadel, and there they all rested, as the ground whispered to them to sit and recover. Though, the momentary delay was short lived, as those that manned the high structure were given the same message those far below them had received.

"I am here on behalf of the Queen of Hungary Elizabeth, for the women in waiting. Let me pass."

Once again, a grand gate built for the turbulences of war was pulled open and the defenses were rendered impotent to the advance of the Queen's herald.

With walls on one side of them and cliffs with even higher walls on the other, they followed the trail forward, as the progressive curve pulled them alongside the entirety of the structure in another ascent. The envelopment of the citadel caught the eye, as the army manned the walls and tended to their tasks. Over timber they went, the bridge and the drop that accompanied it twisting the stomachs of those who looked down, as they were allowed entrance through another gate before progressing further.

The final bend followed the shadow of the high castle, and the spell it cast made its white walls seem like a palace of snow and ice, while its imposing highest tower left knots in the stomachs of the three that drew closer to climbing it. Through a final and off centered gate, they entered the courtyard of the castle, and were left surrounded by more high walls and even taller red roofed towers.

A momentary respite was found, as most of those that had not already descended from their sleds and horses finally touched the mud and snow of the courtyard.

"One way in and one way out," Paulus commented with a sobering tone, as his eyes made their way slowly around before settling on the high tower once again.

"Suppose there is another," Lucas replied softly, a grin growing over his lips. His boots stood drenched, and mud clung all along his cloak and the garments under. "Could always jump."

A light chuckle left Paulus as he whispered to himself, "I guess if we are being chased..."

"Hell of a view," Lucas added with a faint laugh looking back through the open gate and admiring the sight of the river, land, and sky. "This has got to be what a bird sees. Can't believe I had to walk it... Next time I want wings."

Yet, he could not relish in the momentary tranquility or humor, as Helene called them over with a wave. Her eyes were focused on the last of the timber that would swing from its hinges and leave them within the walls of the same structure as those of the royal item they were meant to procure.

"Is it not customary for a host to come out and greet his guests?" Paulus asked, throwing his eyes back and forth in a study of the guards, all the while staying in Helene's shadow.

The Queen's herald was silent along with Lucas who trailed behind, past the watchful eyes of those who gripped spears and stood with sheathed swords.

"Are there always so many guards...?" Lucas finally asked. "I think I have counted more spears than ten times my fingers."

"That is a surprise," Paulus replied with a faint smile. "I didn't know you could count."

Lucas stared at him with a blank stare for a moment, as the words slowly trickled their way through his mind. With a sudden curve of his lips, he released a contagious chuckle. The two held a soft laugh, enjoying the scene, though like an early flower's bloom, their presence was ill suited for the cold company.

"If you knew the Count, then you would not be surprised as to why he does not come out," Helene explained, looking up and down the courtyard in a quick search. "He only comes out when there are women he thinks he can bed. But, he is a Count, so he can do as he wishes."

The two men turned to one another, before staring once more at the highest and most imposing tower.

"Did something happen with her and him?" Lucas asked softly, as he leaned in closely with a grin on his face. "Something she don't want to tell us?" though his words were far from soft or discreet enough.

"Leave it," Paulus ordered Lucas.

Helene scowled at him, her gaze burrowing through his skin and into his soul. Nonetheless, she was not allowed to maintain such a stance, as the shadow of the one they had been waiting for came forth.

"Forgive the delay," a voice suddenly said.

Turning quickly, Helene, Lucas, and Paulus saw Demeter hurrying towards them.

"Let me start by saying it is good to see you again," he stated. "Helene. Forgive Count Gorge, he is currently preoccupied with having his attention given to the ladies in waiting. Though, if you would be so kind as to follow me there, I am sure that he will give you the attention you deserve. Or if you would prefer, I could show your servants where to place your belongings."

"I thank you Demeter," Helene replied with a nod. "It has been a while. I think it would be wise if I were to see the Count first. My servants will just have to accompany me before learning where some of the rooms are. Do you think you could have someone else grab my things?"

"Of course," Demeter said, as he gestured for them to all advance towards a series of stairs that led to the interior of the castle. "There is food and drink in the servant's section, so I don't think they will be disappointed. But we can discuss that within the shelter."

Neither one of them said a word, as they simply nodded from a few steps behind, both long aware of their role in rank and deception.

With clanks their feet abandoned the last of the wet ground and came upon stone, as the warmth from within the castle quickly gave them all a semblance of life, and their cheeks and noses grew red.

"I will go and remind the Count of your arrival," Demeter quickly said, excusing himself down the hall.

For a few moments, there existed a disarmed tension, as the shelter of the structure cast aside all strain along with the cold. Though, as sighs and comfort were found, they were all thrown away when their host made his presence known.

"Ah, Helene," Count Gorge said with arms spread wide and a smile that stretched much the same way. His attire was a fine one and would have made him beyond the reach of any judgement, if not for the stains of food on his chest. "I have missed you and your Queen, though her women have been quite fun. How is she? She give birth yet? Her figure returned?"

"She is good," Helene replied with a soft bow, dismissing the embrace with a polite though affirmative gesture. "She sends her regards and is sorry that she could not greet you in person and spend time with you again. As you most undoubtedly know, she speaks very highly of you. She remembers her time with you and the late King doing some falconry."

"Those were good days," Gorge said with a somber tone and slight nod. "Looking back, there was so much we did together and so much more I would have liked to do with them. But, I suppose that such things are out of our control and in that of God."

"Indeed, they are well beyond our control," Helene replied. "We can simply see how each day progresses and remember the best of those who are not with us."

A pause lingered between them for a moment.

"Well, I am sure we will have opportunities to speak more while you are here, perhaps in the hall tonight." Gorge stated. "But as of now, I must oversee the preparations for the feast tonight. Many of the women you have come to take away still need to be... properly entertained."

With a silent nod that was followed by a bow, Helene gave a silent farewell.

"This way," Demeter gestured, beginning to lead them, though before they could reach their destination, the sound of one who should not speak touched his ear.

"Why were you—?" Lucas commenced to ask Helene with a soft whisper, but was interrupted long before he could finish.

In an instant, his words had pulled Demeter's attention, and with a glancing gaze from over his shoulder, each syllable caused his focus to fall with greater concentration on him.

"Quiet," Paulus interrupted, gripping him tightly, yet subtlety around his arm. "Remember, we are servants. Walk behind her. And don't bother her. We don't want any unwanted eyes."

Nonetheless, as they continued to advance, Demeter's suspicion had been awakened and stroked.

Chapter 36

The Feast

Warmth from a hundred flames filled the room, as the celebrations and entertainment of the feast was well underway. Though, not far from the hall and the excitement, those that were not of rank remained in the place of their labor. Filling their gullets or dawdling in conversation, they let time slip by, as though the abundance of it existed.

Lucas laughed, as he swallowed down the wine in his cup and leaned in closer to the woman before him. His attire was different, as the fine yellow cloth that was appropriate of a servant, replaced the mud stained garments that he had worn on his ascent. "So, you are really unmarried? You're too pretty to be alone, but, I'm sure you hear that all the time."

With a giggle and a laugh, the young dark-haired servant blushed, abandoning her duty, if for only a moment. For as she lingered with the possibility of what the night might hold, beyond the sight of her gaze, or that of her suitor, a man approached with purpose.

"Sorry, but I have to steal him away," Paulus suddenly interrupted, abruptly appearing next to the two and making them leap.

"Paulus," Lucas said taken aback.

"It's time," Paulus replied, beginning to walk away just as abruptly as he had appeared.

"But—" Lucas said, though there was no leniency to his plea.

With a wave, Paulus called him forward and quickly signaled with a nod and a point of his nose that the time had come.

"I would have had her," Lucas stated, rushing to Paulus's side. There their shadows walked on the walls, as they made their way down the passage toward the hall. "And she is not bad, right? Once we're done with whatever it is we need doing now, I will make a move on her. And no need to worry about a husband or father, I call that luck. Why did you have to get me now?"

Paulus said nothing for a moment, as he simply walked on. "This is not the time for that. She has called."

"It's really happening?" Lucas asked with the hint of excitement, his steps progressively speeding up before slowing down. "Like, it's really happening? Happening, happening?"

"Quiet," Paulus ordered with a softly spoken tone. "It is, now quiet and calm."

"It's really happening," Lucas added under his breath, rubbing his hands together. "It's really happening."

Their pace continued down the hall, as they passed the ornate decor and those who rushed for needed supplies, until they reached a grand doorway.

Its timber wall was thrown open, as guards stood at the door in their worn regalia and their spears in hand. The light from all the candles illuminated the scene, as their presence lay accompanied by the warmth of a grand fire.

Tables stood full of both food and drink, as benches sat occupied to the force of bending. Music drowned out the sound of consumption and gluttony, as those that conversed were forced to lean close to one another to be heard. At the head of the room, there stood a grand table where Count Gorge sat with all the women in waiting on both sides of him, and Demeter who stayed behind them like a shadow.

Paulus and Lucas delayed for a moment in the threshold of the open door and the hall, as they stared at the scene.

"Wow," Lucas commented. "This place is nice. Makes where I met you look like an alley. Hey, but think of this, after we finish here, we might have enough to call a place like this our home."

"We did meet in an alley," Paulus replied, surveying one side of the hall to the other. "Come on, she's over there."

They moved through the crowd, making their way to her, each step drawing them further away from the Count and his company.

"Play the part," Helene ordered softly, as the two men she awaited approached her. "Go get me a drink. And you get me a piece of bread. From over there." She pointed to a table.

With only the faint inclination of a delay, the two men quickly went off and tended to the tasks they were assigned, before returning.

"Just take a knee after you put it on the table," Helene ordered softly, "But, do not take part in anything."

"Thought you would be closer," Paulus said, putting the bread down before her and stealing a glance at the Count. "Is this a problem, or a good thing?"

"No," Helene replied, turning her back to the table and stretching her legs between the benches. "It is customary. Not without me accompanying someone of higher status. But, being in the hall is all we need. Besides, being away from his ears and that of his shadow are a good thing."

"So, are we really going to do this?" Lucas asked with a soft whisper, watching the drunken and distracted company that filled the room. "I mean, are we really going do to do this? Guess this really is the last chance."

"Yes," Helene replied softly, as she too turned her eyes to those in the room and studied each and every one of them. "We have come too far, and failure is not an option. We do not turn back."

"Should we wait longer?" Paulus asked, shifting his eyes around the hall and watching the liveliness of it all.

The appearance of slumber could be seen on most, as bags lay nestled tightly under their eyes, though the festivities seemed reluctant to dwindle.

"This is our one and only chance to do this," Helene explained, leaning in closely. She turned her sights on Lucas and fixed him with a long stare. "Do you remember the plan?"

"Should we not wait a little longer?" Paulus questioned. "Your host is still a little bit sober. So is the man behind him."

"I can take care of that," Lucas replied with a laugh, shaking an empty cup in front of himself. "We could get the keys from him. Just like I said earlier."

"Leave him be," Helene ordered, watching Count Gorge continue to try his luck with Barbara, as all the while she stole another glance to Demeter. "I already had his attention for a bit. I would rather not have it again while he searches for someone to join him in his quarters. Besides, he will soon be forced to sit alone, and he will not accept that for long."

"It's a good thing you are here," Paulus replied. "So, do you know who we are looking for?"

"It's him," Helene said with a nod. "There against the wall by the door. You walked right passed him when you walked in. The Castilian."

The three of them turned their eyes to the man that was their obstacle and held their gaze on him, as they searched his manners for something telling. His dark hair mimicked the night, as a touch of bronze painted his skin even in the depths of winter. The only movement he took, was to bring his cup of wine to his lips, refilling it, and doing it all over again.

"You're up," Paulus suddenly said to Lucas. "You got what you need?"

"Yeah," Lucas replied with a series of nods, as he began to burrow his hands beneath his clothes. "Where did I put it? I know I had it here just a while ago. I could have sworn I had it… Maybe with the other clothes…"

"Don't tell me you lost it," Helene said, closing her eyes and slowly shaking her head. "Don't you dare even joke."

Lucas suddenly paused, as his eyebrows leaped up and a grin grew over his lips. "Oh, I remember." He stated, shaking his boot and wiggling it free just enough, so that his hand could burrow down into the depths of it. With a quick pull, he brought forth a small pouch, before he quickly nestled it away in his grip. "Yeah, I have it. A little sweaty, a touch of mud, but I'm sure it will still work." Before a word of protest could be thrown, he stood up and knocked on the table three times as he did. "Well, wish me luck. And watch a master at work."

Helene and Paulus stared at him, as he made his way through the crowd and past all the distractions of food, drink and entertainment.

"Well, if the poison doesn't make him sick, something from inside his boot will definitely do the trick," Paulus said with a sigh, as he watched him make his way casually over.

"I think I'm going to be sick," Helene replied. "How long has that been there?"

"Too long," Paulus said still unable to look away. "Way too long. I mean, just think of the climb up to get here. That's not even counting any of the other days since he put it there. I almost want to warn the man."

"That makes two of us," Helene added, trying to look away, but was drawn in to watch.

Chapter 37
The Feast

"What do you think of the feast?" Count Gorge asked with a grin, leaning closer to Barbara and away from the space before him overloaded with unfished food and drink. "No expenses were spared for this. No expenses were spared for you and the other lovely ladies. But, mostly for you."

"It is quite a fine evening," Barbara replied. "I can see no shortage of joy. Well, except for your man behind us." She looked over her shoulder and held a stare with Demeter, which only rendered him redder with each passing moment.

"That's his work," Gorge quickly replied with a grumble, looking at the man with a glare. "He is supposed to be my shadow and keep out of attention unless requested. But, forget about him. Tell me, what do you think of all the gossip with the Queen?"

"Now that is something that could be discussed all night," Barbara said.

The two continued to chat away, as those in their company joined in and fell out like the tide. Though, like a boulder, there was one who did not move and simply stared out at the ripples and sways in the hall.

With eyes that caught sight of Lucas, Demeter watched him make his way through the hall.

"What is he—?" He began to ask himself with a soft whisper.

"Sir," Barbara suddenly said, turning around and calling for his notice. "I have need of your attention. Would you be so kind as to show me to my quarters?"

"I could go with—" Gorge began to say with excitement and hope, as he jumped to rise from his chair. Though, before he could even finish his offer, he was interrupted.

"I could not accept such an offer," Barbara replied with her coy smile standing up. "I could not be the cause to steal you away from all your guests. There are many here who I can only be sure will want to keep the conversation of the Queen flowing."

"But he is—" Gorge tried to say, beginning to protest, in a desperate need to cling to her company.

"Your loyal man," Barbara interrupted, as she turned to him. "I do believe you have called him, 'your shadow.' I don't think there is anyone I would rather accompany me."

"How could I say, no?" Gorge asked with a forced smile. "But, are you sure you want to leave so soon? This is your last night here. Would you rather not stay a little longer? The night is young, as they say. I am sure we could find something to do." He tried his luck a final time in the hopes of company, seduction, and defilement.

"The night may be young, but I must awaken early," Barbara replied in her usual demeanor. "And if that was all, then I would remain here with all this company, but it will be a long journey and I am in need of rest."

With a soft nod and a lack of hidden disappointment, Gorge stood up and gave his farewell. "I wish you a good night then."

"Until tomorrow," Barbara replied, stepping away.

"Or if you need anything, don't be afraid to ask," Gorge added with a nervous laugh. "My quarters are not far from yours."

"Shall we?" Barbara asked the Count's shadow, leading the way.

Though, as Demeter accompanied her like a loyal pet to her quarters, he stole a glance to Lucas, who was loitering in hesitation, turning one way and then back the other. His pace slowed, and his eyes remained fixed on him, though not for long, as Barbara caught his eyes once more and her smile fluttered his heart.

Chapter 38

The Poison

The dim sound of music drifted into Lucas' ears, as the swarm of the feast weaved its way around him. He moved with a mix of determination and hesitation, the pull of his limbs seeming to draw him back to where he had sat and pushing him forth toward his objective. For a few fluttering heart beats, he paced back and forth, before finally grabbing an unattended cup from a table, and committing to his path.

"Hey, Castilian!" he shouted with a wave, approaching his mark.

The man stared at him with the still gaze reminiscent of the statues of old. He stood there unmoving, his back to the wall, and void of any type of emotion.

"Do I know you?" The Castilian finally asked with an eyebrow raised and a heavy accent reminiscent from a place South of France, but North of the Moorish lands.

Lucas stared back, as his eyes went wide, and a dumb look grew over his face. "Well, not yet you don't," he finally mustered to say, as his usual demeanor returned. "But, if you want a drink, I can promise that you won't forget me, but you will also—"

"Stop," The Castilian ordered with a firm expression, that gave no inclination of change. A smile grew wide on his face, revealing glistening teeth stained red, while those that were missing met the warmth of the fickle light. "You had me at 'drink.' Just tell me it won't make me sick, like the rest of this stuff."

Once more Lucas stared, as the world beyond him seemed to pass him by. "HAHAHAHA! I'm sure you will live. Nothing too bad. Yeah, nothing too bad."

"Good enough for me," The Castilian replied with a laugh of his own. "Just please, tell me you have something to drink from my homeland. I think I might get sick if I drink more of this." He waved his half empty cup across the room spilling a bit of its contents. "I don't know how you can drink this. It tastes like piss-water. And don't ask me how I know that."

Lucas looked into his cup and saw his reflection before swallowing a mouthful and nearly rendering it empty. "I don't know, I think it taste pretty good. I mean, I would pinch a few purses to buy some of this stuff myself."

"You Hungarians," The Castilian replied with a laugh. "That is because you have not tasted the best wine. Grapes from my hometown, squeezed and made into the finest of drinks, there is nothing better. It will make everything else taste like ash."

"Are they really that good?" Lucas asked, an eyebrow raised. "Making me want some of that."

The Castilian stared at him with his brown eyes and a look that cast out the levity from his bones. "To find out which wine was better I took a pilgrimage. I traveled across my homeland just to drink the wine along the way. And do you know what I uncovered along the way there and then again on the way back?"

"What?" Lucas asked.

"That there is no other wine like the one in my hometown," The Castilian replied with a wide smile.

"Wait," Lucas said, his face growing a look of doubt and confusion. "If it's that good, then why are you here?"

"Why is anyone anywhere?" The Castilian quickly asked back. "To make some coin."

A wide grin grew over Lucas's lips as he began to nod in agreement. "I can get that. I spend my life like that."

"Everyone does," The Castilian replied. "And anyone who tells you otherwise is either a fool or just lying to themselves. So, what about that drink? We can talk more after you give it. No point wasting time without a drink."

"Right, well, let's have something different," Lucas said, stepping away from him and making his way to a few untouched cups of wine. Subtly he bent over the cups, as the small pouch he had hidden in his hand was quickly untied and its contents poured into the red nectar of the first cup. "Yeah, this was the wine I was telling you about. It's different from the others." He grabbed them both and made his way back to his company, careful not to spill a drop.

"Which one's mine?" The Castilian asked, extending his hand.

The curved lips on Lucas's face departed quickly, as his eyes fell from one cup to the next. "Oh, I ugh…" he stared at the two, hesitating between pushing one or the other. Finally, with a decision, he moved the cup in his right hand forward and pressed it onto his company's grasp. "Here, take this one, yeah. Yeah, this one's your poison."

The Castilian stared at Lucas and the cup with eyes that were devoid of affection and reminiscent of suspicion, though before sweat could blossom on the brow, his mouth opened wide. No shout emerged, no alarm to gain the attention of the world, merely the sound of a yawn that was quickly subdued.

"Sorry about that," he said, raising his hand to cover his mouth for a moment. "Need more sleep. But as they say back home, we leave that problem for ourselves to solve later." Holding up the cup, he breathed in its aroma, before finally pouring it down his gullet.

"So…" Lucas began, watching The Castilian's throat move with swallow after swallow. "What is a Castilian? Like, is that your name or something?"

With a heavy sigh, The Castilian pushed the drink away from his lips and stared at the dark colored liquid. "This is still not good enough... But it is a little bit better. I can tell the difference, but I would not recommend it to my friends. And Castile is a place far away from here. A land so beautiful that it makes even the most beautiful of women jealous with its distractions."

"So, why are you still here?" Lucas asked. "If it's so great there?"

"Because, that's life," The Castilian replied. "And I need more wealth to live a better life. And for me that is here. Tell me, what is it you do?"

"Me?" Lucas asked, a grin growing over his lips. "I don't want to brag, but I am a master thei—I mean, I am a servant for the Queen."

"Good pay?" The Castilian asked.

"It has some benefits," Lucas replied. "Keeps me out of trouble. I get to travel. Spend time with a friend, more like family. And it keeps the wine in my cup."

"No women?" The Castilian asked.

A grin grew over Lucas's lips. "You know, I almost had this beautiful thing, but then work called.

"That's the problem I have," The Castilian explained, swallowing another mouthful of his tainted cup. "I spend all day staring at a door and then at night, I'm supposed to do the same. And in a tower for that matter. Do you know how much of a climb it is to get there? And the nearest place with women of any beauty, they are always accompanied by their brothers and uncles. That leaves hardly a place to lie down. And I don't pay for company or a bed. That is not the way a man cradles a woman. That is the way a—Oh..." He suddenly said, bringing his hand to his stomach and struggling to hold back a belch.

"You alright?" Lucas asked, an eyebrow raised. "Something you ate, or something...?"

"I'm fine," The Castilian replied with a wrinkled brow. Nonetheless, just as his words faded, a grumble of anger sounded from deep within him making even his Lucas' eyebrows climb. "It's probably nothing."

Chapter 39

Destination

With the faint sound of feet pressing against stone and carpet, a pair of shadows blossomed on the white plastered walls, one following the other, though only a step behind. They moved slowly, going at a leisurely pace, and with each step forward, she moved like a gentle current from side to side relishing the journey.

"Do you always walk behind those you accompany?" Barbara asked with a light giggle.

"I, ugh, I try to, Duchess," Demeter replied. "Being of a lower rank… Your room is just ahead."

"I figured you did it for the view," Barbara said, glancing down the rear of her body and flashing her coy smile.

"Ugh…" Demeter said, raising his hand and gesturing to the door, while the painted blush of red on his cheeks deepened into crimson. "Your—ugh, your room, Duchess."

"Yes, this is me," Barbara replied with a smile, taking a half step towards him. "Thank you for your company. I might have gotten lost without you. But, I thought I told you to call me Barbara."

"Yes…" Demeter said, stealing a glance at Barbara's curves, though it was far from unnoticed, especially with a second longer one.

"See something?" Barbara asked, interrupting the mapping of her pale mountains. "Something you like?"

"Yes… ugh—I mean, no," he mumbled. "No, nothing. I'm fine. Yes. This is your room. Yes."

"Well, thank you for your company," Barbara said.

"You can never be too careful," Demeter replied, his eyes turning up and down the hall.

"Sorry?" Barbara asked.

"I ugh, I was saying you can never be too careful," Demeter replied, turning his eyes onto her and growing red once again. "That's why it's good to have company."

"Do you want to follow me into the room?" Barbara asked, taking another step closer and putting her hand on his chest, "Check it all and be my shadow?"

There the two stood, her warmth pressed with each breath against his skin as she looked up to him, waiting for the last gap to be closed. His heart beat with a forceful fury, as he lay lost in her eyes and was blinded to all things beyond her. Tilting his head and opening his mouth, he was ready to catch her warm breath and share his, but before he could, he released a sigh, along with his answer.

"Go—goodnight, Duchess," Demeter finally said with a mix of regret and nervousness, as he stepped back and let the opportunity slip through his fingers. "I have to go and take care of the Count…"

Barbara watched him for a moment, as she held her smile. Finally, with a turn she moved to open her door, though not before looking back to him.

"A shame," she whispered.

Chapter 40
The Resolve

Winds grew fangs as the cold of winter howled with a furry that was all but ignored. Those within the walls of the castle were oblivious to the world beyond them, though there was one who rushed to escape the warmth and shelter, with a shadow that was not his a step behind; the Castilian.

His steps were a rushed and inconsistent wobble that pulled him in different directions, while his hand perpetually covered his mouth. The rumbles deep within him echoed loudly and a sudden pressure forced its way up his throat and into his mouth.

"Not inside," Lucas shouted, rushing after him.

The Castilian uttered nothing, as he continued forward pressing against the door and stumbling for a moment as the gate gave way and the cold beyond it quickly gripped him. Flakes of snow fell against his clothes as he landed roughly onto the ground.

With a loud heave, and a louder splatter, the ground was dyed red and accentuated by chunks of food.

"You alright?" Lucas asked.

"It's the wine," the Castilian replied, leaning forward, and awaiting the next heave. "It's this God damned Hungarian stuff. Never got this sick from my homeland. Even when I drank—"

But before his rant could continue, the contents of his stomach pushed forth to escape him again.

"You sure you alright?" Lucas pressed. "Maybe you should just go somewhere where you can lie down. You know, let it just run through you."

"I'm going to my quarters," The Castilian replied, as he spat loudly, muttering a few foul words in his native tongue. "Didn't think it could taste any worse. I was wrong... It's worse the second time. I'm going to my tower."

"Your tower?" Lucas asked, turning his eyes up at the tower that housed the vault and its desired content. "You sure about that? Maybe find somewhere else to lie down?"

"I'm going to call it," The Castilian replied, before he held his sides and fought back the force that worked its way up his throat. He stood taking a few steps forward, finding balance with the aid of his arm and a wall.

"Let me get you some help," Lucas said, waving to one of the men that patrolled. "HEY! Some help!" He shouted; his plea carried by the wind.

"What's going on?" The old guard asked, approaching and nearly stepping in one of the scattered puddles. "Sick, or too much drink?"

"Yeah, he drank a lot," Lucas replied. "And then he got sick."

With a heavy heave that seemed to empty his gut yet again, the Castilian spat, as panted breaths followed. "Too much wine... That lousy stuff. Hungarian drink. Help me to my quarters... I need to lie down."

"I think he would do better at the infirmary," Lucas stated, stopping everyone before even a first step could be taken.

"The infirmary?" the two other men asked in unison.

"Well..." Lucas replied, hesitating for a moment in silence in search of words. "Well, he said he lived in the tower. It's a long way up. Do you think he can make it all the way? And what if he gets sick on the way there? You going to clean it up?"

The old guard turned to the sick man with an assessing gaze and judged. "What if he just got it all out of his stomach?"

"Well, what if he was to get sicker?" Lucas asked, pressing his cause. "I mean look at him. He was fine a moment ago and now, this. What would happen then if he was to get sicker? Him being all alone in his room. I know what would happen if it was me."

"What would you know?" the guard asked. "You a physician or something? I've never seen you before."

"Or something," Lucas replied with a slight smile, though quickly hid it. "No, it's just, I don't want him getting worse in the middle of the night. But, most of all, if I'm being honest, and you can trust me, I don't want him causing trouble for all the women in waiting. The lady I'm with will punish me all the way back to the capital if that happened. I know that much. If they get woken up in the night for anything other than their own wants. You're a guard here, you know what I'm talking about. Ever seen any of the guests cause trouble? Ever get caught in it?"

With a heavy sigh, the guard nodded. "Yeah, I do. I have seen it myself. Done to me even. You ask me, some of the guests that come here are worse than a common pickpocket. They don't—"

"I don't care, just get me somewhere where I can lie down before I die," The Castilian suddenly ordered, groaning.

"You got him from here, yeah?" Lucas asked, stepping back from the two.

"I got him," the guard replied. "I will take him to the infirmary."

"I'm never drinking again…" The Castilian said to himself, as he was led away. "Never drinking that Hungarian poison again…"

"He will be fine," Lucas said with a nod, watching the two men slowly fade away. Left to a momentary stillness, his eyes turned up towards the dark tower. Its shape melded with the very night, as its presence created the only space devoid of stars. "Not a bad start, all things considered. Now just to get in there."

Chapter 41
The Plan in Motion

The excitement of the hall dwindled down to a near stop, as those that remained either were asleep where they sat, or in the process of bidding their final farewells. Candles stood as remnants of the towers they had once been, their heights of pride but stubs and pools of wax. The Count's chair sat empty; his presence gone when the last of the women in waiting vanished before him. What music there was, only drifted in memory, as those with instruments found rest for their fingers and tongues by letting slumber take them. In all, the night had claimed its victory over those that had reveled in the festivities and its abundance.

Though, for what calm consumed the once busy and excited place, a motion was seeded. It grew with every whisper and every moment that passed, as those that were the source, tended to it with the caring of a farmer, until it stood ready to be plucked.

"So, he won't be a problem?" Helene asked softly. "You made sure he won't be in his quarters?"

"I took care of it," Lucas replied with a prideful grin. "I took him outside when he was sick and convinced a guard to take him to the infirmary. Pretty smart, yes? I think I deserve a little bit of a reward for my quick thinking."

With a faint nod, Paulus paid him silent recognition, before turning his attention to Helene.

"Do we continue then?" He asked.

Helene leaned forward and closed the gap between her and her would be accomplices. With a gaze that studied each of them, she watched, as though looking for something.

"It's time," she finally whispered, pushing herself off the bench and waiting for the others.

Her words reverberated with the two men, who for a moment were lost in the maze of their minds.

"Right," Paulus said, bobbing his head and rising, ready to follow.

There the two stood, waiting with their gaze turned to the source of the delay.

"Oh, you mean now?" Lucas asked, finally grasping the situation, as he pushed himself off the bench and clapped his feet loudly against the ground. "Yeah, right, ready. Let's go."

"Go and get your tools that you brought," Helene ordered softly to Paulus, before turning to Lucas. "And you, go get the cloaks. Be quick both of you. But, be discreet. Do not draw the attention of anyone. We can ill afford company in the tower. I will meet both of you by the entrance, after I get a few virgin candles and the pillow."

They left the hall in unison, but barely had they departed, when they broke apart and went off to their tasks. Moments passed, as Helene, the first to arrive, hung to shadows and awaited the others, her hand's grip holding tightly two candles. The faint sounds of the castle whispered, as most abandoned the night and its opportunities in favor of their slumber; though not all.

With steps guided with the purpose of a patrol, Demeter made his way through the halls. His eyes leaped at everything that appeared out of place, mimicking a hound on a hunt. Those that wished to avoid his sight clung to the shadows, as breaths were held and hearts drummed out of their chests in trepidation.

Past by the entrance where he had escorted many through its gate, and beyond the mud of the courtyard, he looked for anything that hinted at mischief or worse, but seeing nothing, he quickly vanished to search the rest of the structure.

For a while, only the whispers of the wind dared to speak, as Helene clung to her hiding place and did not risk to abandon it. There she waited, trying to calm her breathing with long breaths and closed eyes, until another sound called her attention.

The patter of feet grew in the hall, as Lucas was the first to make his way to the arranged location, his hands laden with the objects of his assigned quest. He lulled by the entrance in confusion, as he looked around, unable to see anyone.

"Lucas," Helene suddenly called, waving her arm out of hiding.

"Oh," Lucas said in suspense. "Scared me… I got them."

"Were you seen?" Helene asked, with a whisper.

"By who?" Lucas asked back, turning his eyes back the way he had come. "You saw something?"

"A shadow," Helene replied, looking down the halls at what was no longer there. "Now get out of sight."

The two stood still in obscurity, watching and waiting for any sound, be it salvation or condemnation. Finally, with a lone sound from the deep that forced both pulses to rise, their eyes shifted and lay fixed on a shadow as it climbed its way on the wall and advanced towards them. The clanks of metal were met with the echo of steps, though as the one who cast them rounded into view, a relief was felt by all.

"Hey Paulus," Lucas quickly said, hopping out of hiding.

"I got the tools," Paulus whispered catching sight of them and quickly approaching. His hands tightly gripped a rolled, wide and bulky cloth, as the sac over his shoulder swayed, causing the faint rattle of metal. "Trouble?"

With a sigh and an abandonment of her hiding, Helene stepped forward, grabbed a cloak from Lucas and threw it on. Its darkness swallowed her and hid everything from her hair to her toes, and as she pulled on her hood, even her face lay hidden.

"You're late," she stated. "And your sac is making noise, give it here. I will carry it."

Paulus dropped his shoulder and swung the sac right into his hand, which he passed to Helene without so much as a delay.

Grabbing it, Helene held it tightly in her arms, eager to muffle the sound that had been birthed from it.

"Careful," Paulus warned. "They're heavy."

"Let's hurry," she ordered, leading the way.

"I was here first," Lucas stated with a toss of the cloak, smiling to Paulus. "Try not to fall behind, old man."

Helene led the company as they made their way through the castle, careful of every corner and of its uncertainty. Pressing past closed doors, with the gentle patter of their feet, they tried not to awaken what souls slumbered. Though, with a hard grip that forced veins to rise, Helene pulled against a seemingly plain door and forced its hinges to whine. A darkness enveloped the scene behind it, but as the gap grew, light flooded in and a winding narrow staircase took shape before them all.

In a single file, they quickly climbed the narrow spiral stones, abandoning the ground and reaching up into the heavens. Light vanished from them, as what illumination existed and fluttered in the halls of the castle, was rendered distant. With faltering steps that relied on sound and the guidance of their hands, they advanced higher and higher, until finally one of them spoke.

"I can't see," Lucas said, stumbling and nearly falling. "Told you no one was here."

"I got it," Paulus replied. "Helene…"

"Here," she replied, holding out a candle.

Casting a spark from stone and flint, the illumination of light flashed like that of lighting. It gave but a sliver of sight before vanishing just as fast, until finally, a candle was lit. They continued through the darkness casting it aside with each step, as their feet pressed softly against the retreating border that hid in the solitary flame of a single candle.

"Is it really necessary?" Lucas asked with the faintest of voices. "The candle."

"Can you see in the dark?" Paulus asked, trailing but a half step behind Helene. "And you were the one complaining."

"Well, I mean, sort of," Lucas replied. "But I can see better than most. But, I'm not worried about hitting my toe. More worried about someone finding us here."

"If anyone asks what we're doing in the tower, I just have to say that I am lost, that is all," Helene explained forcing the two to fall silent.

"That does make sense," Lucas said to himself, following in silence once again. "Wait, what about if someone comes when we are busy with the door? Or sees the two of us?"

Helene continued to lead them forward, ignoring the question, for as long as she could. Stopping, she turned back and whispered. "Pray that does not happen."

Steps continued, moving to find their way to the stairs' accumulative end, as they went through another door and made their way down the hall. With each step forward, a large mass of darkness took shape and caught each of their eyes.

Yet, as they reached an open space, the candle's light climbed up, and their eyes stared at the final obstacle that was theirs to overcome; the vault door. Its black locks appeared to swallow the light, as each piece of metal stood defiant and ready for seemingly anything that would challenge them.

"Is this really the door?" Paulus asked in disbelief, as he was left slack jawed at the bent metal, bound wood and the locks that hung from it. "Is that really the door you want us to get into? That door?"

"Holy... Shit..." Lucas added, stepping up to it. "Any chance this is the wrong door?"

"This is it," Helene replied. "No mistake about it. I've seen inside it myself. This is the vault. Behind this is the Crown."

"Of course, this would be the door… I wouldn't be that lucky that it was another," Paulus mumbled to himself. Finally, with slow steps and a flustered sigh, he advanced, running his hand over the locks, as he studied their each and every grove. A gentle flick of his fingernail chimed, as he continuously hit it, all the while looking into the singular gap meant for the keys. With a gentle touch, he released it and moved his hand over the timber and metal that was the door. "No easy way past these locks… No way past the door…"

"Go and check the room." Helene ordered Lucas, pointing towards The Castilian's quarters. "Make sure no one is there."

With a heavy sigh, Lucas dragged his feet, shuffled over, and did what he was told. "It's clear."

A sigh of relief left Helene. "That's good."

"Before you do your thing, let me try something," Lucas said, quickly returning and stepping towards the vault. He placed his hands on the door, and with all the force he could muster, he pushed against it. His face grew red, while the obstacle and the locks did little, other than remain still. "Come on… Open, open, open."

"You know you have to pull…" Paulus said sighing, as the faint indication of a smile blossomed. "You probably just made it a little bit harder to open. But, before you try that again, maybe take the seven keys we have and get some of the locks off. I have to get my tools ready for what comes after that."

"I think I should have made more people sick," Lucas mumbled staring at the door, before beginning to do as he was told. "It is going to take a hundred years to get into this thing. Even if we take these ones off first."

"You got rid of the one who could do the most harm." Paulus explained, taking the sac Helene had carried and placing it carefully and quietly onto the floor, before pulling from it the keys, as well as the replacement locks. "The Castilian. No point in looking back at what we should have done differently, just do what you can now." He brought three keys to Lucas and pressed them into his hand, "start with these three, figure out where they go, and don't drop them. I will take the other four. Don't forget which key goes where, we need to put them back when we are done."

One after another, the long keys were pushed into the locks and slowly turned, some were met with resistance, as they dared not budge, while others let their teeth loosen. Though, with each turn and every attempt, progress was made, until clicks and snaps echoed down the hall and all seven were unlocked.

"That was so fast," Lucas said with a grin that did little to hide his excitement. "If only we had all of them, we would be done in no time."

"Keep your voice down," Paulus ordered, standing still with his gaze nailed to the remaining locks. "Even with seven of the locks removed... We are short on time." He turned his sight to his bound tools and quickly made his way to them. With his knees on the ground, he revealed them to the night and the candle. The harsh black pieces of metal did not glisten, shine, or sparkle, but simply held their dull demeanor in a still and unimpressive wait. Nearly a half-dozen of them lay spread out, including three files and two nails the length of the entirety of a man's hand. Beside them all was a small timber mallet, which was splintered and aged to the point that it seemed it would crumble at the first swing.

"Wait, wait, wait," Lucas ordered with bewilderment, pointing to the door, locks, and then back to the tools. "That is what's going to break through that vault? Those? Against that? Those?"

"Did you forget something?" Helene added with a hushed voice, as she too shared a bewildered look. "Maybe something else in the sac? Or back in the sled? We could risk it, if it meant getting in the vault."

Paulus said nothing, as he simply took one of the files, kneeled before a lock and began to move it back and forth over the defiant metal. The barrier sounded with each sway of his wrist that caused the lock's metal to scratch.

"That's the best way in?" Lucas asked, his jaw hanging slack.

"This is the best way in," Paulus replied.

"I thought he was going to pick the lock or something," Lucas said to Helene, as the two stared at him. "You know, like wiggle something and make it open."

"Well, maybe he…" Helene tried to reply, but drifted off, until she shook her head in disappointment. "Are you being serious right now? Are those all the tools you brought? Is that the way you intend to get us in?"

Paulus ceased his labor, as he turned around to the others with one hand clutching his tool and the other a secret, that could vanish in the faintest of winds. Opening his hand, he revealed the faint traces of a few metal flakes, before blowing the small nestled pile away.

"Is that…?" They asked in unison.

"If you have time to talk, then you have time to help." Paulus stated. "Now I would have tried to get in another way, but I would need more time to get in than just one night, especially without knowing these three locks beforehand. Each one is different and made by someone with more skill than I ever had. So, here we are. Lucas, get a tool and help me. Helene, keep watch and pray that no one comes. If someone sees you, they might not see us. It might just give us a chance to hide all the proof of what we are doing. And if you see or hear them first, give us a warning. Maybe we can blow out the candle… or find a place to jump…"

Chapter 42

The Nail

Drops fell to the ground, as water breached the sanctuary of the highest tower of the citadel. One after another they fell in a scattered fury that did not merge into puddles, but simply remained as lone droplets. Though, it was not the perspiration of clouds that dampened the floors before the vault, just as there were no rains that made their way through the defenses. Rather, it was all the sweat that fell off the brows of those that labored.

"This is taking too long," Lucas finally said with a flustered huff, as he ceased his labor and slapped his file against the ground. He quickly moved to wipe his face, finding comfort laying on his back, before rubbing his sore knees.

"Quiet," Paulus ordered, stopping to raise his fingers to his lips. "Quiet…"

"This is taking too long," Lucas echoed with a harsh whisper. "How long have we been here? Too long. And we're what? Not even past one of the locks. Not one. My hands hurt. And so do my knees… Like I took an arrow to them."

"Everything takes time," Paulus replied, clearing his forehead. "We just have to keep at it."

"Is this the only way?" Lucas asked, grabbing the lock he had toiled over and pulling at it with all his strength. "Is this how it is really done?"

"This is the easiest and quietest way," Paulus replied. "If I had done it like this... Well, I think the chances of me being caught would have been far lower. Might not even have this scar on my hand, but I did deserve it."

Lucas stared out into the distance, struggling to grasp the words spoken. "Wait... are you saying that you haven't even tried to do this before?"

"I am trying to say that we have better chances of not being caught because of what we are doing," Paulus explained. "Now, enough talking. Get back to it, time is pouring away."

With an incomprehensible mumble under his breath, Lucas turned his hands back to the file, lock and labor.

Time continued to pass, the celestial bodies growing in brightness and the night only seeming to darken. Drops of sweat once again rained onto the ground, while hands cramped, and flakes of metal fell softly like scattered snow.

"It's time," Paulus suddenly said, as he studied the shaved metal and the gap that he had made in it. "It's time."

"What?" Lucas asked, ceasing his labor and staring at him. "Giving up?"

Paulus moved away from the lock he worked on and made his way back to his tools, all the while ignoring Lucas. Form the laid-out tools, he exchanged the worn file for one of the nails and the mallet, before shuffling back to continue. Raising the long nail, he held it before the lock at a downward angle, before waiting. Finally, with a slow nod, he moved his hand over the ground grabbing the mallet, and with a slow extension and a stern expression, pulled his arm back and readied to strike. Moving the mallet forward and back, he practiced the aim eager to be precise.

"Why are you taking so long?" Lucas finally interrupted with a flustered whisper. "Just hit it!"

"Quiet," Paulus replied, letting his hands drop and turning to glare at him. "If I hit it wrong, it will not only make more noise than a church bell, but it may damage the door and worse yet, it may lock itself in place. Then we will have to really labor to break through this vault. You know what… come here."

"What?" Lucas asked.

"I need your help," Paulus explained, staring at the lock.

"Me?" Lucas asked. "For what?"

"I need you to hold the lock," Paulus explained. "And I need you to hold it still. Especially when I beat this nail in the lock. We cannot afford to damage the door. It will risk too much to do that. Come on, hands."

With skepticism and caution, Lucas wormed his way forward, eager to turn back at a moment's notice. He grabbed his cloak and wrapped it around his hands, before cupping the lock. "You sure this will work? You sure this won't hurt my hands? I am a master thief. I need my hands."

Paulus stared at him for a moment, before giving a solitary and definitive nod. Once again, he narrowed his eyes, aligned the nail and raised his mallet, ready to beat it in once again.

Lucas readied his hands and the cloth between the lock and his skin, as he swallowed deeply and tried to calm his nerves. Taking a deep breath, he held it in, watching as the mallet and the hand that gripped it found its path.

With a sudden quick breath that forced his companion's eyes closed, Paulus moved to strike.

"Stop!" Helene suddenly ordered with as soft and as harsh of a whisper as she could muster. "Stop!"

The two men ceased their labor and looked to her in startled confusion as she stayed by the stairs. Her eyes gazed down the spiral, though it was her ear that held her focus, as she tilted her head to hold her hand up to it and listen.

"What?" Lucas asked softly, though there was no immediate reply, as she continued to listen.

Suddenly, Helene's eyes grew wide, as she quickly turned towards the others and waved vigorously with her arms.

"What?" Lucas questioned.

"Company," she said silently with only the movement of her mouth before she pointed to the candle and ordered its light expunged.

Lunging, Paulus and Lucas both reached for the fluttering flame, stumbling over each other, as they both blew at the light. With a sudden disappearing act that rendered the night near absolute and engulfing, the glow of the red wick dimmed and the smoke faded into desolation.

Helene pulled back away from the staircase with the last embrace of light to guide her, as she made her way to her accomplices.

"What do we do?" Lucas asked with a whisper, standing by the others. "Should we grab the stuff and hide? The Castilian's room?"

"We can't do anything," Helene whispered so softly, that the breath of those by her side nearly drowned it. "Whoever it is will hear us."

Chapter 43
The Shadows on The Wall

Far in the deep, the clanks of heavy footsteps sounded, and forced to endure, Helene, Paulus, and Lucas were unable to do nothing more than stand still. With each beat of their hearts, a step seemed to sound with a great fervent approach and like a drum in the deep, its echo reached out, until they saw the dim light of a candle extend its search from the staircase, and with it, a shadow.

The candle's light grew into a fire that would swallow them whole, as the shadow cast on the wall drew closer to the thieves. Breaths grew shorter in anticipation, and the air thicker, as darkness once more battled for its dominance.

"It's him," Helene whispered to herself. "The Count's shadow, Demeter."

No reply was given, only their hearts, which struck with such a fury that it seemed they would burst at any moment. Hands became clammy, and eyes as wide as they could open, as the shadow before them grew closer.

Demeter stood but a few steps away, with only a final bend to reveal the would-be thieves and send them to a fate becoming of criminals. Thought for what cruelty fate can wield, it brought forth mercy. For just as the last step fell prey to his advance, he stilled.

"There you are," a soft voice echoed, as each soul present, was overwhelmed with fear.

"Duchess," Demeter replied baffled as he turned his sight down the steps and upon her.

"There you are," Barbara said again with a smile, as she approached. Each step she took clanked, as the heel of her boot met the ground with a firm and definitive purpose. "I think I told you, you can call me Barbara."

"W—what are you doing here at this hour?" Demeter managed to ask, as his eyes continued to wander her curves and exposed skin, with the added aid from his high step. "Lady Barbara… Are you lost?

Barbara took slow step after slow step closing the gap between them until their very shadows became one. The warmth of her exhale could be faintly felt, as well as her scent, which he devoured with each breath.

"Is there something I can do for you?" Demeter asked.

"I already told you, I was looking for you," Barbara replied.

"Right," Demeter said, turning his eyes up the last curve to where the vault lay just beyond his reach of sight. "All the way here?"

Barbara said nothing, as she simply raised her hand and put it on his chest. "If you want me to go, I can."

"What, wait, no," Demeter quickly replied, turning his eyes back to her and making her his focus. "I was just taking a walk. You caught me before I could finish."

"A walk at this time?" Barbara asked. "Sounds like you have something happening with your head. Maybe I could be of some service and relieve the strain."

"What?" Demeter asked with such a fluster that even his shadow seemed to shift its shade.

"How about we just start with you walking me back to my quarters," Barbara said with a slight smile. "We could try that again. Though, I suppose I could make my way over myself, or at least until I find someone else. Don't know, maybe the Count is still around. I suppose he could guide me the rest of the way if I knocked on his door."

"No, no, no," Demeter replied with urgency. "I will take you. I mean—I can take you again."

"Just one thing," Barbara said, stepping even closer towards him.

With a gentle touch, she ran her arms around the back of his neck locking her fingers together, and before he could even protest, she pulled him so close that there was no escape. The reach of their breath lay exchanged in an instant, as their lips pressed against one another.

"I expect to be escorted all the way to my room," Barbara stated. "Not like last time. I expect to be led all the way back to my bed."

Demeter stood with a shocked expression, blinking repeatedly, before finally moving his lips again with a smile that could not be restrained. "Right… Yes… Right…"

With a soft, yet dominating grip, she pulled him away from the vault and began to lead him back the way they had come. Their steps faded away, each one softer and more distant, until the creak of the tower's door whispered their final farewell. All the while, those who had remained hidden were at last given the overlooked pleasure of a sigh and a breath.

With relief that caused their limbs to nearly fall out from under them, the three could finally move, as they turned their heads and looked to one another in the darkness.

"Well, that was close," Lucas finally said with a laugh, slouching down onto the ground. "That's good news," he added with another mumble, the sweat still on his brow. "That was too close. I mean, I thought we were done for. Was thinking about where we were going to jump. Look at my hands, they're shaking."

No words followed his, as those by his side simply released a soft chuckle.

"Wait on the candle, I'm going to check," Helene ordered, as her feet stumbled their way through the dark hallway back to the steps. "He's gone, light it."

With slow hands, Paulus once again moved to light the candle. Sparks flew, as strike after strike illuminated the scene, though it seemed none would take hold.

"But, did that guy really just get a kiss from one of the women in waiting?" Lucas asked, waiting for the light. "Talk about luck. I wish I could be that lucky. Did you see the Duchess in the hall earlier? She is a crazy beauty. A one of a kind beauty. I would give anything to have her do that to me."

Paulus continued, the banter of his tools the only reply that was given to his companion. Though with a touch of luck, warmth in the form of a flame returned.

"Nice, you got it," Lucas said.

"Take it, and light the other candle," Paulus ordered. "I need more light."

Paulus turned to the locks once again, holding the one he had labored against, before turning to the one Lucas had. With a slow nod, he finally moved to his unswung tools and plucked from them the nail and the mallet.

"Do you think we should wait a little bit?" Lucas asked, standing in the way of the vault with the unlit candle in his hands.

"You want to wait?" Helene asked. "What do you want to wait for?"

"Maybe they are still around, or they might come back," Lucas explained.

"It's time," Paulus said, ignoring their words. "Helene, I need you to go and check that no one is around again."

Her eyes sat on him for a moment, before she stole a glance to the items in his hands. Finally, with a nod, she moved her feet and hurried down towards the steps.

"Lucas, I need your hands," Paulus said, staring at the lock. "Hold it like you were earlier."

Lucas stood idle for a few short heartbeats, staring at the mallet, nail and the lock before nodding. "Yeah, alright."

As if the sands of time had been reversed, they once again took their stance. The lock was again held in the self-professed master thief's hands, the nail and its counterpoint aimed, while the watch tended to the stairs. All fell still and silent, as they watched with wide eyes as the mallet charged forward.

Resonating like a storm it thundered, its force shaking the very air and testing the resolve of all present. Yet, there was no protest to it. With an echo of the strike, Paulus quickly pulled the mallet back and drove it forward again. The metal nail drove through the keyhole with a few sparks, while the hardened and molded remnants of the earth bent. Strike after strike, he followed through and forced the nail deeper again and again.

The shackle of the lock shook with each blow, as it struggled to hold its place, but the gap that had been driven by hours of the file's labor slowly made it wane. Strike after strike, he followed through and forced the nail deeper again and again, as Lucas struggles to keep still.

With each strike, the time between them grew in length as Paulus's arm grew weaker, though he continued to deliver the blows. The touch of perspiration emerged on his skin, as the candles' wax dripped away, and his hands began to seize with cramps. Suddenly, with a glancing blow that sent the mallet stumbling to the floor, a faint chime touched the air as the metal finally gave way.

Paulus's limbs fell still, staring at what lay before him, while Lucas seemed frozen by the weight in his grip.

"Did you get it?" Helene asked, slowly stepping closer to her accomplices.

Holding her hand out in a silent request to have her curiosity confirmed, she stood like a statue, still and immobile, only to come alive when Paulus turned to face her with a smile on his face and an item in his hand.

"The lock…" she whispered with a smile, taking it in her own grip with, the nail still protruding through it and the shackle snapped where the file had worked.

"One down," Paulus replied with heavy breaths, allowing a slight smile to grow on his lips. "One down…"

Chapter 44

The Stolen Crown

Lips pressed against one another, their hearts rising, as the passion of the night took hold of them, and one after another their attires were thrown to the ground. Like a celestial body that glimmered and shined, Barbara's revealed skin stole the eye and kept it fixed. Yet, with a press that drove her night's companion to the bed, the moment of silent admiration passed. She climbed her way on top, their limbs wrapping around one another, as two became one and the soft moans of pleasure could not be restrained. Though, while their lust was being indulged, far above, in the lone and unguarded tower, another craving continued to advance.

A file worked its way back and forth, as the flakes of its labor fell like snow to the ground. Sweat clung to the brows of those nearby, as the one who toiled away in a seemingly trivial tribulation was left with a river to run down his cheeks and fall like scattered tears. His hands cramped to the point of deformity, while the grip of his fingers faded, and slipped stops halted his progress.

"Damn it," Paulus said, his hands cupping his face in silence, while his breath calmed and fell docile.

"Two locks down," Lucas said, pacing back and forth behind him. "Just one to go. Just one."

"I don't know why, but this lock is perverse," Paulus mumbled, as beads of sweat pervaded his brow even after a firm wipe. "Made better than anything else. Better than anything I could have hoped to make. The trick with the nail did not work and now it is stuck. I can't drive it in further and we are running out of time."

"Well, I'm sure the sun will rise slower for us," Lucas joked and added a laugh to it that only he shared.

"Look," Paulus said, moving his fingers in frustration over his face. "This is hard enough without having to hear about how we were almost caught, or how this is taking too long. And this would be over by now if you had just held the lock like I told you. So, do me a favor and go and keep watch with Helene."

With slow steps, Lucas moved away and made his way to Helene, as he let forth a mumble. "I held it right…"

There the two stood, as they watched and waited for progress to once again advance. Nonetheless, the one they waited for did nothing other than sit. Finally, with their patience tested against their nerves, they tuned to one another and shared a brief silent exchange.

"Paulus," Helene said, advancing and taking a seat beside him. "What's wrong?"

Paulus did not reply, as he simply sat still with his eyes on the lock. "Nothing… Just this lock."

"Just the lock?" Helene asked. "Think you're going to break through?"

With a heavy sigh, Paulus looked to her and gave her a slow, but definitive nod. "We will get there."

"Good," she quickly replied, standing up and beginning to move back, though not before he had spoken again.

"You know you didn't have to sit with me," Paulus said.

"At least it was not in the mud this time," Helene replied with a smile.

With a grunt, and a crack of his knuckles and neck, Paulus moved to the vault door again. Shaking his hands before grabbing his file and making for the lock, his fingers gripped the metal, and with a loud sigh, once again his labor progressed.

The repetition of it all sounded faintly down the hall, yet those who could only wait, began to whisper to one another.

"How long until the sun rises?" Lucas asked.

Helene did not reply, as she simply kept looking forward. "It will happen soon. Last I checked, the stars were vanishing and the darkness with it."

Lucas bit his tongue and held it between his teeth, as he turned back to Paulus. "I know it's not something you want to hear—"

"Then don't say it," Helene interrupted.

"I think I have to," Lucas replied.

Helene shook her head in a state of unrest.

"It's a good plan," Lucas stated.

"Speak then," she finally ordered.

"Do you think we should just act like nothing has happened?" Lucas asked. "You know, pretend to be asleep until it's time to go and just go?"

"And what about the Crown?" Helene quickly asked back. "Just leave it? And what about the locks that we have all but destroyed? Won't take long for someone to put the pieces together. No. We succeed here, and we do so soon, or else. Now, if you want, you can pray. That will do more than just complaining and coming up with bad ideas."

Lucas turned forward and began to nod slowly with pouted lips. "Yeah, alright… Just one last thing."

With a heavy sigh, Helen turned to him. "What?"

"Remember when I said I wanted to pluck one of the keys?" Lucas asked, with a slight grin. "Would have been useful, no?"

With a slow turn of her head, Helene shifted her gaze onto him and quickly made his curved lips vanish, as a glare shimmered from her eyes.

"Yeah, I'm just going to be quiet," Lucas mumbled as he retreated from her.

Time continued to pour away, as sweat continued to fall to the ground and the sounds of labor dominated the otherwise calm of the night. Seconds turned into minutes, and minutes into another hour, but as Paulus paused to inspect his work, the progress was found to be demoralizing.

"You know what…" Paulus finally mumbled in frustration to himself, as he once again grabbed his mallet, which only seemed to have grown closer to crumbling. Without delay, he used it and quickly struck his file like a nail in an attempt to bend the shackle. The loud bang resonated, and all those present shifted in discomfort, though there was no relief. With another strike followed by another, the sound only grew louder, as the lock shook and bounced against the metal of the vault door.

"That loud," Lucas said, rushing over to Helene, who still watched the stairs. "Should we do something? Someone is going to wake up."

"Pray," Helene replied, glancing at Paulus and then back down the stairs. "Or help keep watch."

"But—" Lucas protested.

"The sun will soon be up," Helene interrupted. "We're running out of time."

"Right…" Lucas mumbled, biting his lip in unease and staring at Paulus who continued to strike the door. "Right…"

The strikes shook the air and wiggled their bones, as time again moved with its slow progress, each blow to the lock choking the sands. Slowly the night was pressed back and the darkness that had given life to the stars, was driven away.

With panted breaths, Paulus tried to recover his strength. He stared at the lock, which held its place in defiance, though it lay battered with scratches and dents. With a grumble, he reached for his mallet and moved to continue. Blows struggled to meet their mark, as the file wobbled and pivoted, until finally, with a strike that hardly met its mark, the tool fell from him and tumbled to the ground.

It chimed along the way, each bounce echoing, as it summoned the attention of his accomplices and forced them to wince. And yet, Paulus cared little for the tool's protest or its noise, doing little to move, as his eyes remained focused on what lay before him. With a slow extension of his tired arm, he reached up, and took hold of what consumed his sight, and with a sudden click that comes from only metal's touch or its departure, the teeth opened.

"It's done…" Paulus mumbled in disbelief, as a sigh of relief left his lips and his shoulders slumped. "It's done."

"What?" Helene asked, taking a closer, and abandoning her post on watch. "What did you say?"

"It's done," Paulus replied.

Helene and Lucas simply stared, as they watched in disbelief. With slow steps they approached, the sight of the metal hanging precariously where it should have been, swallowing the entirety of their focus.

"I never doubted you," Lucas quickly said with an extension of his finger and a nod to accompany it. "Stick to the plan I did. That's what I always said."

"Open it," Helene ordered with a whisper so soft, it hardly survived to deliver its message. "Open the vault."

With a gentle grip, Paulus grasped the broken lock and pulled it off its nestled place in the center of the door. He put the last lock on the ground and admired his work for a moment, as the three instruments of denial lay cast asunder. Finally, and with a faint smile, he did as he was told and reached for the vault. With all the force he could muster, he pulled against the unlocked door and made the hinges move.

No barriers remained to hold the bound metal and timber in place. No tricks to hold the vault door in place. And so, without so much as its weight to delay the inevitable, it was opened.

The light of the candles creeped its way into the vault, illuminating the gold that shimmered in the warm light. Yet, all was cast aside to the marvel of one item. There before them all, sat atop a pillow, was the precious piece of metal they had come for, the Crown itself.

It sung to them, calling out, as the precious stones and ornate enamels tempted them with a desire for attention, though not all could be distracted for so long.

"So, are we sure all we can take is the Crown?" Lucas asked, slowly drifting towards the rest of the wealth that lay within the vault. "Like, maybe just a little of some of that?"

"Take even a piece of anything and you won't get a piece of copper from the Queen," Helene warned.

"Yeah, alright," Lucas mumbled, continuing to admire the wealth. "I hear you, stick to the plan and what not…"

"I have to ask," Paulus said, stepping closer to the Crown. "This is what we came for, right? There isn't a second one hidden somewhere else, is there?"

"This is the Crown that only the King of Hungary can wear," Helene replied, stepping towards it. "No mistake about it. It is the Crown that they say chooses the rightful King. And I can honestly say, that I am ashamed that I must touch it, for I am not worthy of the honor."

The three stayed there, simply staring at the item, and for a moment losing sight of everything else.

"The Queen chose you," Paulus finally said, nudging her.

"I can grab it," Lucas added. "I could just—"

"Go get the pillow, Lucas," Helene ordered, stepping closer and resting her hands on the pedestal.

Quickly he went, bringing the pillow forward and holding it near the Crown, as they all eyed it, looking for something that only they could see.

"It looks like it will fit," Paulus said, holding his hand out. "Give it here." He took the red pillow in his hand and wiggled his finger in between the stitching that kept the soft feathers from their escape. Suddenly, with a hard pull, he broke the bindings letting the soft stuffing fall softly to the floor.

"Collect every feather," Helene ordered Lucas, quickly following through with her own words. "I want to hide the shape of the Crown and leave no evidence of our deeds here."

"Right," Lucas said, doing what was needed.

"Ready?" Helene asked.

With a gentle touch, Helene lifted the Crown and moved it into the partially unstuffed red pillow. Its weight tested her gentle grip, as the chains and decorations shifted and swung with each movement, though she managed to guide it into its desired place.

"Maybe we should have brought a bigger pillow," Lucas commented, staring at the lump brought about by the high golden cross that protruded from its center. Holding his hand out, he pressed the feathers he had collected from the floor inside. "Here, try stuffing more of this in."

"You can sow, right?" Helene asked, her eyes never leaving the Crown and pillow.

"Yeah," Paulus replied, stuffing the last of the feathers into the pillow and trying to use them to hide the bumps of the Crown to a moderate success.

"Good, then you will take care of it," Helene ordered. "And do be careful when you do."

"Yeah," Paulus replied with a nod.

Helene turned her eyes to the last of the candles, the stubs of the wax and wicks vanishing with the arrival of the early sun's light. Though, she did not remain on them for long, as the faint sounds of dawn caught her attention.

"Let's hurry up," Helene ordered, pressing the others out of the vault. "Last thing we need is to get caught now. Let's get out of here and put the locks back on. Hide anything that may give anyone a reason to check the vault. We go to my quarters, where we will prepare the last of it. I want you to then bring it to my sled and stay with it. No distractions, and no leaving it. I will bring you something to eat."

With hurried, yet quiet limbs, they rushed out taking their previous posts. With a hard push, Paulus closed the vault door and rendered the treasure hidden once again. Clicks followed clanks, as the locks were placed back on and the keys removed. Though, as the last one was positioned, and the door returned to a state of untouched manipulation, those that had taken part vanished, and with them, the most treasured item the vault had held; the one that could decide the future of the Kingdom.

Chapter 45

Farewell

With a slow ascension, the sun reached over the horizon, and with a gentle touch, one after another all the stars but the sun vanished from the sky. The ice and flakes of snow began to melt, as figures began to emerge into the courtyard through the false rain that fell from the roofs.

The warmth of the day was quick to greet all, as the last of preparations were tended to without delay. Though, while the turbulence of the measures taken were in their final stages, there were two who lingered by a sled in a still and tired state.

"Should we help?" Lucas asked, nodding toward the others with bags of exhaustion under his eyes.

Paulus looked to him with the same look that mirrored his lack of sleep, before turning back to the pillow. "We have to wait for her. That's what she said. No exceptions."

"You really think she's going to bring us food?" Lucas asked, his stomach grumbling, and a yawn following. "I don't know if I'm more hungry or tired... Been here for hours already."

Paulus' jaw tightened, as he tried to fight what would inevitably part his lips. With a sudden crack, a groan emerged, as he brought a hand up to his face and tried to hide his open mouth. "You made me yawn... Why don't you ask her yourself?"

Lucas turned to greet Helene with a hungry smile, though before he could, he fell still.

With slow steps through the courtyard, Helene made her appearance known to those who readied their last tasks, though by her side stood her host, Count Gorge. Her expression was stoic, the marks of a lack of sleep hidden from her face, in a composure befitting of her company and rank.

"It is such a shame to see you all go so soon," Count Gorge said, as his eyes leaped from one woman to the next, though not before studying each one of them with a lingering stare. Though, as he ran through to the last, a look of confusion sat on his brow. "Is Barbara not here? Maybe in the carriage?"

Helene looked to him, as she readied to reply, but was interrupted before she could.

"We were grateful for the hospitality," Duchess Barbara replied, summoning all eyes to her descent down the stairs. A bright red gown wrapped her body and seemed to aide in raising the temperature. "I know that I will not soon forget the fantastic time I spent here. The Queen will certainly hear of it, won't she, Helene?"

"Indeed, she will, Duchess," Helene quickly replied, bowing. "I am sure she will always look back on this trip with adoration."

With a wide smile, Gorge let out a soft chuckle. "I would be grateful for any kind words. And I would be eager to tell the Queen that she can send all her women through my citadel. I would be happy to always host them. I would share my own room to accommodate any young woman. Though, I would be lying if I said I did not want to have another night with all of you."

"I'm sure you would," Barbara replied with her coy smile. "But I think that if that were to happen, our modesty would be tested."

Gorge grew a grin that could not be contained, as he chuckled and nodded. "That is my curse, I fear. I have such a powerful effect on women. I think even my men, younger and all, are made jealous."

"I'm sure they are," Barbara replied, gently patting his chest.

"I have prayed that the weather stays cold until you have crossed the river," Gorge added with a soft nod, raising his arm to look at the sun, before moving it to touch the woman beside him. "I sent scouts this morning. It may be a little risky, but if you have any trouble and it becomes too much to try and cross, you can always come back. My home is yours. Regardless of my men's jealousy."

"We are grateful," Helene replied, subtly separating the two. "But, the Queen is awaiting our company very soon, as she is soon to give birth. We would do all we can to get back to her. Even if the ice is soft, we would try a crossing."

"Of course," Gorge said with a series of nods. "Of course. It will be exciting to see if it will be a boy or a girl. I know a few of the other Counts have placed hefty sums of wealth on it. Myself included. Here's to praying it will be girl."

"And healthy," Barbara replied. "Most important that the child is healthy. Though, I would like it if it was a girl. I could see myself as a great influence on her if that is the case."

"Only time can tell for certain," Helene said, hinting at their need for departure.

With a soft sigh, Barbara moved towards her carriage. "I suppose we are short on time…"

"Duchess Barbara," Count Gorge said, quickly following her, just as she delayed beyond the shelter and cover of her carriage. "It was a great pleasure to have you in my company. I am saddened that you are leaving."

"As am I," Barbara replied. "I made some good memories here. I will especially remember last night. What a fun night it was, wouldn't you say, Helene?"

Helene was taken aback, as she stumbled for a moment to hide the tension and surprise that lay in her eyes. "Of course," she stated, bringing a hand to her brow and hiding her eyes momentarily. "I was just thinking the same thing. What a night it was, and what an impressive feast."

"I can't even remember when I went to bed," Barbara added with a grin. "Though, I spent most of the night tossing and turning. It seems the morning still managed to rise before I knew it."

"It is the air," Gorge replied with a nod. "The wind carries the water up the mountain and into the walls. Even with all the fires and carpets, I find it almost impossible to create a warmth that gives a gentle slumber. It is why I have always said, company is the best defense in winter."

"Perhaps that's what it was," Barbara agreed. "Well, whatever the reasons, it was an enjoyable night. Tell me Count, where is your shadow this morning?"

"My shadow?" Gorge asked, a hint of confusion on his face. "Oh, Demeter? He likes to do his rounds. Goes and checks all the posts of the men and any place of importance."

"Importance?" Helene inquired.

With a finger extended, Gorge waved his little limbs about the courtyard. "The gate, the tower, the vault… Things like that."

"Vault?" Helene whispered to herself, raising her voice. "Well, we have been here long enough. All the preparations seem to be in order. We really should get going. Especially if it's going to get warmer, like you think Count."

"I have said it before," Gorge explained, turning to each of the women who had shared his table. "I have said it before, but I am sad to see all you lovely ladies go."

"As are we all," Barbara replied climbing into her carriage. "As are we all. Do send my regards to your man and to all those who saw to us."

"Of course," Gorge said.

Helene waved to the others and made them begin to move. Those who had not mounted their sleds, mounts or carriages quickly found their place, as the last of the loose ropes were thrown into place. With a final wave to the Count, she leaped into her sled, right besides the red pillow and its precious stuffing.

"Safe journey," Gorge said, waving goodbye to those that had stayed, and unbeknownst, to him the Crown as well. "Farewell. I hope to see you all again soon. Farewell Duchess Barbara. You're always welcome. Farewell."

And with words and waves given, all those who were guests, moved to depart. They passed through the open gateway and quickly began their descent down the citadel and towards their escape, while the gate behind them closed.

Though, there was one who was truly displeased with the departure and mumbled repetitively to himself.

"What about the food?" Lucas asked.

Chapter 46
The Hunt

With panted breaths, steps echoed like thunder, as the one who cast them rushed through the citadel towards the light. His sword swung from his side and his left hand lay clenched tightly, as he pushed through the hallway and the threshold. The cold air of the courtyard quickly filled his senses, while his eyes bounced from every soul present, except for those he searched for.

"Where are they?" Demeter demanded, charging down the steps, his appearance rattled.

"Ah, Demeter," Count Gorge said. "Where were you? Our guests have left, and you were not here to tend to it. You are supposed to be my shadow. I expect—"

"Open the gate!" Demeter ordered, ignoring the Count, rushing through the courtyard and mounting the nearest horse. "HURRY! NOW!"

Those he shouted to rushed forward, as a sense of turbulence descended on them all. Chains rattled, timber was pushed aside and the gate to the citadel lay open. Demeter's horse breathed heavily, as its hooves burrowed into the muddied ground and carried him forward, snorting, as it tried to momentarily resist.

"Demeter?' Gorge asked, standing in solitary confusion.

Some half a dozen other men quickly leaped up, as they rushed in a hurry to their mounts, though they could do nothing to close the gap that grew between them and Demeter. Like a madman he charged down the mountain, each stride forcing him precariously closer to disaster.

"I have to catch them before they get farther!" Demeter said to himself, squeezing his legs and forcing his horse forward with even greater speed. He abandoned caution and braved a gallop against the hill, mud and ice.

Though, as he descended with a haste that could not be matched, his presence did not go unnoticed. From far below, the procession moved at a slow and easy pace, as caution guided their every move. The sleds and carriages shook and rolled, with every lump in the road forcing them to slow even further, and in turn admire the view.

"What's that?" A voice suddenly asked from the rear.

Eyes were slow to turn, though did so nonetheless, as the traffic before them did not demand much attention.

They stared at the view of the citadel high on the hill, watching what appeared to be a peaceful and scenic sight. Though, as they continued to stare, each content with what they had accomplished, three hearts collectively dropped as they saw a ridder rush down, with a group of horses further behind, drawing ever closer to them with the sound of thunder under their hooves.

"Shit," Paulus mumbled, catching a glimpse of the lone horseman before turning to Helene. "They're coming."

Helene turned to share his view, but quickly turned before her, to the long, muddied and icy road that led right to the final gate between them and freedom.

"If we just get through there quickly…" she whispered.

"What's going on?" Lucas asked, looking to the others and releasing a yawn.

"Company," Paulus replied, as he continued to look back.

C.A. MOLTZAU

"Should we do something when he gets here?" Lucas asked, drawing the attention of his accomplices.

"We're still in the castle," Paulus quickly reminded him. "We are still in the walls. We're still in the reach of an army. Don't be stupid."

"Stay calm and don't do anything," Helene ordered, as sweat began to work its way onto her skin. "Let's just see what he wants. Let's just see."

Chapter 47
The Broken Water

The cold air blew softly as the warmth of the day advanced slowly. Ice shifted its form, as piece after piece of it slowly fell away. Yet, the cold seemed to hold an aspect of its strength in the wind and its cold sting caused bones to shiver, assaulting all those who tried to hide. Though, within the shelter of stone and warmth, a splash fell to the ground and drops soon followed.

No instrument in the form of a chalice or cup sat on the floor, yet a puddle formed on the ground and drops continued to fall.

Elizabeth turned to stare at the ground, the puddle growing larger just beneath her. "Oh…" she mumbled. "It's time…"

She stood there momentarily, watching ripples form on the surface, and with slow steps, began to move her feet, her breaths strained, as she tried to make her way to the door. Her hands held the access for a moment, as her face wrinkled, and a few breaths were taken before she finally swung it open. In an instant, her eyes met those of a young guard, as he quickly took notice of her.

"My Queen?" he asked, noticing her distress.

"Find my physician," Elizabeth ordered, slowly abandoning the door and moving through the room towards her bed. Her pace was slow, her breaths rising and falling, the contractions her momentary blight. Her hands grabbed at the walls, a low gamble to leave her, as the voice of the young guard cast an echo into her ears.

"Right away, my Queen."

Grunts accompanied each contraction, as time poured away and Elizabeth was left to herself and that of her pressing company. Yet with quick steps that echoed throughout the halls, company was soon to join her.

Two souls made their way to the threshold of the Queen's room, the physician and the guard, practically side by side, with only a momentary pause to delay their progress.

"My Queen," Janos said as he came into the room and closed the door on the guard. "How may I be of service?" he asked with his usual calm and composed demeanor. Though, as he stared at her his voice fluttered with uncertainty. "My Queen?"

"It's time," she replied with a soft laugh that shifted into a grunt of discomfort and pain. Her hands pressed against the plastered stone walls, as her nails scratched the timber post. "It's time, I'm sure of it."

"It's not in me to argue with a woman," Janos explained, sharing in the remnants of the light laugh. "Especially one who has done this labor successfully twice before. Well, you know the process, it will take some time before you are able to push and until then, there is not much we can do other than letting your body do its work."

"That's why I like you," Elizabeth said. "You say things as they are."

"Where is your woman?" Janos asked, making his way back to the door, though stopping before opening it. "Where is Helene? Have you sent her to begin preparations?"

Elizabeth continued to breath with heavy breaths, as the discomfort of her labor was all but apparent. Nonetheless, she grew a smile. "She is away on an errand. But, she will be here soon. I am sure of it. She will be here soon, as we have planned."

"This is not your first time," Janos said, swinging the door open and throwing his head out of the threshold. "Guard!"

"I want the bells," Elizabeth said reaching out to him from across the room. "Make sure that they know."

Janos gave a slow nod, as he aided the Queen into bed. "I will pass it on,"

With the clamor of feet their attention turned to the young guard who made his presence known again with a stumbled stop.

Janos stared at the youth for a moment with a look of doubt, before finally nodding.

"I need you to bring me water," he ordered. "And have it be warm. I then need cloths and I need them to be clean. I would advise you to call one of the Queen's helpers to aide in the tasks. And if I were you, I would hurry. The Queen and the birth of your next King may hang on your actions."

With a multitude of nods and a pale expression, the young guard turned to leave. "Right away."

"And one more thing," Janos said, making his company fall still with another order. "See to it that the bells are ready to be rung. This is news the Kingdom must know about. Whatever its outcome. It is the Queen's wish."

With a final nod and as great a speed as he could muster, the young guard rushed down the hall, his voice calling out, as one after another the souls of the palace came alive with excitement at the news. All the while, within the royal quarters, only the sounds of labor filled the air, as the long and painful matter of succession was at hand.

Chapter 48

The Consequence of The Night

The heavy panting breaths of the large horse sounded in the air, as its hooves pummeled the ground with a quick approach. The mud climbed on its high legs, as its rider suffered a similar fate. Yet, his speed was undaunted, and like a hunter, his sights fixed and his purpose absolute.

In anticipation of his arrival, Helene had descended from her sled and left the treasure she accompanied in its untouched disguise. She took a few careful steps forward, ready to greet her would be pursuers, fully aware of where she stood, and what could happen. Her eyes lay nailed to the curve of the muddied road, as she waited for a sight that she was all too certain would come. Though, with each moment that passed, with each second that was lost, a sense of uncertainty climbed up her spine.

The sudden whine of a beast had all eyes drawn up to the slope in anticipation, and it did not take long for the mount and its rider to storm around the bend and charge forward with urgency. Each gallop shook the horse's muscles, as with each stride it closed the gap until it was right upon everyone. With a hard pull, the mount came to halt with a whinny, as its front legs swung in the air.

Demeter quickly threw his eyes from one person to the next and heavy breaths momentarily stole his means to speak. All looked to him in silence, wonder, and curiosity, as he wiped his face on his sleeve and smudged a streak of mud across his face.

"What's wrong?" Helene asked calmly, as Demeter and the beast he rode upon drew closer to her with heavy breaths. "We're barely out of the shadow of the citadel. What has you coming down so fast after us? Why would that be?"

Demeter said nothing back to her ignoring the questions, while the sound of his horse's hooves met the mud in an eerie silence. Rather, he remained focused, as he looked over each sled, carriage, and those who remained within.

"Where is Barbara?" He demanded. "Where is the Duchess?"

"The Duchess?" Helene asked taken aback. She turned and looked over her shoulder, back to her accomplices and those they escorted. "She is in her carriage. Is that really the only reason you have come down here?" she pressed for an answer, as her eyes clung to his slumbering sword, suspicious of his intentions.

"I, ugh, I want to see her," Demeter explained.

"This is hardly the right order of things," Helene replied, her gaze drawn to her sled and the pillow that lay in sight.

Demeter looked to her with sorrow in his eyes that reached into the very essence of his soul. "Please, I just need to see her. Just once more."

Helene moved to open her mouth, the words chosen just shy of falling from her tongue, but before she could reply, the soft yet commanding voice of another stole the scene.

"What is it you want, my shadow?" Barbara asked, revealing herself with a smile. "Here I was ready for my long journey. Did you know, I managed to fall asleep already. Must be because of the lack of sleep."

"My lady," Demeter said, leaping off his mount, and quickly going down upon his knee while he lowered his eyes momentarily. "Forgive me. I did not mean to bother you after our farewell… But—"

"Come now," Barbara interrupted with a gentle reeling finger that whispered what was to be said. "Do you intend to have this conversation kneeling in the mud? Get up and come into my carriage."

With quick limbs, Demeter rose from the ground and moved to the carriage, leaping into its shelter and privacy, as he left Helene to hold the reins of his horse.

"So, what has you charging down the mountain?" Barbara asked coyly. "The Ottomans invading?"

"No, it's just…" Demeter began to explain, though was silent, as a wide smile grew over his face and he could do little to hide it. "I know that I am underserving of it, but if I may have a moment more of your time, there is something I must say."

"I already let you in," Barbara replied. "Speak, before those in our company decide they want to hear it too."

Demeter shifted his weight, readying to speak, as the light creak of the carriage announced his impending words. "I am sorry for the disturbance my delay has caused. I am sorry for not having been in the courtyard."

"I missed you when we were saying goodbye," Barbara replied. "Here I thought you were going to appear before the departure. Almost inexcusable."

"I was held up," Demeter explained, with a saddened expression. "My own fault. I fell asleep after you left. Such a deep sleep, I didn't hear a sound until it was too late."

"I guess I wore you out," Barbara replied with her coy smile.

"But, I had to gaze upon you once again. I just had to. And I had to give you this." Demeter quickly explained, as he held out his clenched hand. Uncurling his fingers, he revealed to the light the object in his grip; a ring of silver and a precious blue stone. "You left that in my quarters. After the night we…"

Barbara stared at Demeter with a faint smile before she turned her eyes to the possession in his hand. Taking hold of it, she stared at its every shimmer and shine.

"You forgot it…" Demeter concluded.

"This was mine," Barbara explained, putting it on her finger and admiring its perfect fit. "But, not anymore." She removed it and returned it to his hand.

He stared at her with a blank expression, as her words added to his confusion. "But… I don't understand. This is your—"

"It was a gift," Barbara explained. "One of my favorite rings. Something for you to remember our time by. After last night, whenever I look at my hand and see the ring is missing, I will remember the time we had. I hope when you look at it, you experience the same."

Demeter stared at her with a gaze of wonder, as he was left slack jawed. "I will treasure it, forever."

"Then this must be our final farewell," Barbara announced, running her hand softly alongside his face. "The Queen is waiting."

"Right…" Demeter responded with a whisper that weighed on his heart. "Farewell, Barbara."

"Farewell, my shadow, Demeter," Barbara said, as a momentary lull hung between them.

With a soft nod and a heavy plop into the mud, Demeter leaped from the carriage and made his slow walk back over to his mount.

"Is that everything?" Helene asked, stealing a glance back at the high fortification and catching sight of the other men on their horses as they rode down towards them. "We really must be going if we are to beat the setting sun and what trouble can come with the night. You wouldn't want all these women called by the Queen to have to deal with that, would you?"

"I am sorry for the delay I have caused you," Demeter apologized, as he took the reins of his horse and stared at the horses that continued to descend from the citadel. "I will take care of them; you don't need to worry. You are all free to go."

Helene, Paulus and Lucas stared at his back with heavy eyes, as he moved to climb back up the mud-covered hill. With his arm extended, and a wave that forced the other riders to a stop, he signaled them to turn about.

"I couldn't help but overhear," Helene explained, stepping towards the Duchess's carriage, though she kept her eyes on Demeter and his men. "You gave him one of your rings?"

"What's a small trinket in exchange for something greater," Barbara replied. "I have more rings than I have fingers already. Besides, it made him happy. Can you really ask for more in life? Well... I suppose I can. So then, shall we advance, or do you wish to gossip?"

"Forward," Helene ordered, moving back to her sled, the pillow, and the Crown that lay within.

Once more the procession advanced towards the final barrier that kept them prisoners, and with a final swing of the castle's hinges, its gate, high walls, and army all fell prey to the deception. They had allowed the thieves and their most precious treasure to pass right by.

Chapter 49
The Labor and The Knife

Feet paced in uncertainty, while a few to ran up and down the hall, as a shout of agony echoed through the halls.

"AAAHHHHHHH!"

Sweat poured from the one being assaulted, as those who tended to her echoed the same message yet again.

"It's going well," Janos said with a soft nod, waving off a woman and silently sending her onto the next task, as he stayed by a table scattered with his possessions. "Taking its time, more than the last times. But it's going well."

With a heavy grunt, Elizabeth clenched her fists, digging her nails into her own skin and nearly bringing forth blood. Sweat fell from her like the tears of a widow, saturating the warmth of her bed. Her hair stuck to her back, while the rest of it lay scattered and chaotic. "This is worse than the two times before... Far worse."

"It does sound like a boy," Janos replied with a calm and slow nod. "Not the first time I've seen it happen. Boys tend to cause more trouble."

Elizabeth lay with heavy breaths, as a momentary respite in her body's siege left her tranquil. "How long has it been? I feel like I have no strength left in me."

C.A. MOLTZAU

"Just so long as you don't fall asleep, or pass out," Janos replied calmly. "I won't have to do anything. If you do, and I can't wake you up... Well, I'm sure I don't have to warn you again."

"If that happens, just make sure you save the child," Elizabeth ordered, gritting her teeth and preparing for what was to come. Her hands grabbed at the fabric of the bed, though her nails did not burrow, and the wrinkles were far softer. "Whatever happens, just make sure you save my son. He is destined for great things. Greater things than me..."

"Just keep listening to your body," Janos replied, moving to fill a cup and bringing it to her. "Keep breathing and pushing. And keep drinking. You run dry and you're going to be in a real problem." Though, as he turned back to her, his pace faltered at the sight before him.

Her head was tilted back, and a soft groan was forced from her lips. There she remained, her eyelids faltering, until they were pressed closed and her body fell still.

"My Queen?" Janos asked, approaching her with suspicion. A few calm, but quick steps sounded, as he made his way to her side and placed his hand on her clammy skin. "Ah, that's not good... Breaths shallow... Pulse soft... My Queen?"

To the lack of a reply, he abandoned her side and made his way to the table he had labored over moments before. His eyes turned their focus from the Queen to his tools, as he uncovered the objects and allowed their sharpened metal to shine in the light. Six edged tools sat side by side, their hungry blades whispering of a desire for a stain and labor. With a slow hand, he gripped the handle of a long knife, and with steps that dawdled, he returned to the Queen.

"Queen Elizabeth?" Janos asked loudly, the blade tip pointed towards her, while his free hand shook her. "My Queen, I would rather not do this... Please wake up. My Queen!"

Chapter 50

The Crack

With a calm and reassured pace, the Queen's women and their escorts were making progress to return to the capital. They moved through the shadows cast by the trees, as the warmth of the sun fluttered about. Though, while hooves battered, wheels turned, and time dwindled away, a distant sight caught the wanderers' eye. One after another the sentinel of trees diminished, until nothing obstructed those who advanced, except a barren space of snow, ice and water.

The wide river held the attention of all, as they watched the bleak and still scene before them. There, on the frozen water's edge, each was left to wonder on the strength of the ice, as a few began to descend and inspect for themselves.

"You sure it's safe?" Lucas asked, rubbing his eyes awake and nearly stumbling to the ground while descending from his sled. "Maybe you think she will give the order to go around?"

Paulus stared out into the wide icy scene, as the faint sound of the river below it forced it to creak like an old ship. "I don't know, but I'm sure that it will be alright. We crossed it once."

"Yeah but," Lucas said, turning his sights to the others present. "We didn't have so much weight last time. And look…"

he exhaled a quick few breaths, as each one only highlighted his point. "See? No smoke. It's too warm."

"That's not smoke, it's fog," Paulus replied with a faint laugh. "You're not a chimney."

"What about the weight?" Lucas pressed. "We got a whole lot more this time. A whole lot more. We're heavy."

"I don't pretend to know much about women…" Paulus began, as a slow smile grew over his face. "But, you better hope none of the women hear you complaining about the added weight."

Lucas stared at him with a blank look, as he slowly grasped the words. With a sudden curve of his lips and a loud exhale of air, he laughed loudly, a few tears forming in his eyes. "That's a good one!"

There the two stayed, their shared joke blossoming before dwindling to a soft chuckle. Though, before the embers of their comedy could be expunged, a third soul joined their side.

"How do you think it looks?" Helene asked, stepping past them and pressing her foot against the ice.

"Like I told Lucas, I think it's safe," Paulus replied. "But we won't know until we get out there. I would advise to scatter the weight a little, if you don't want to send out a scout to check."

"Last time we tried to cross there was a bit of water," Lucas chimed in. "I remember it. And it has been warmer. Tell her about the smoke."

"It's fog… And we could go around," Paulus added. "Would put us back a bit, but it would be safer. I would advise you to consider it."

"It would be slower," Helene quickly replied. "And I have been considering it. Why do you think we've fallen still? But, it would be so much slower, that we might not make it back to the capital in time for what is to come. It would be so much slower… Time is of the precedence; time is always the precedence."

"And what if the ice gives way?" Paulus asked. "How much would be lost if someone fell through?"

"I understand what you are saying," Helene replied with a firm voice. "I do, but to abandon before trying is not something my Queen would do. It is not something I can do. We will take precautions and advance slowly."

"Alright," Lucas agreed, when Paulus nodded.

With a loud voice that echoed over all present, Helene let her intentions known. "We go forward," she ordered with a wave. "Leave space between each sled and carriage."

With slow steps, man and beast advanced, an air of caution around them, as they abandoned the firm ground under them and replaced it with what they hoped would hold. Faint puddles drew the eyes, as the unsettled oasis rippled with the force of each step. Yet it was the sounds of ice and spewing water that summoned all attention and pulled forth a gasp with each whisper.

Despite the momentary anxiety that filled the air, a hint of relief began to spread its way through them and smiles commenced to grow anew, as the white surface of snow and ice seemed to hold.

"Nothing to worry about," Paulus said in reassurance to himself and that of his companion, as they continued their crossing. "Nothing to worry about..."

"Yeah, maybe your—" Lucas began to reply, but was silenced by a sound that sent a shiver through each being's soul.

A loud creak echoed across the space, as its whine came forth like a foul omen. Cracks soon followed one after another, demanding each person's eyes, as they all fell still. Breaths were held, while jaws went tight, and an absolute silence descended upon the group that would not release.

The moment held, as suspense descended into doubt and then impatience, all eyes turning to the one who led them forward. With a silent wave, Helene ushered them forward again.

With slow steps, eyes shifted to stare at the surface under them, as their delayed progress grinded against the ice.

"I think we're about halfway," Lucas whispered. "No return..."

Each step sounded in their ears like a beat of their heart, while the frozen road below them shook with the wobble of a ship.

Once more they fell still, their eyes watching in uncertainty for any indication that they prayed would not come. Though, like preachers rambling into the silence, their thoughts and prayers were not answered. Water bubbled up beside them, as small geysers found their way through the ice.

"Back!" Helene ordered, watching the water rush through faster and faster. "BACK!"

Though it was too late. With a sudden snap, the ice below them began to move with a whine filling each person with dread. A crack as loud as a tree's collapse screamed, startling the horses who whinnied and whined, conflicted by the orders of those who held them and their instinct to flee. The fissure rushed its way under the sleds and carriages, passing all those who found themselves on the ice. Yet the worst was yet to come, when splinters erupted and cracks branched off, filling the air with shouts and cries, as the icy waters opened up all around them and to some, just below them.

A sudden collapse swallowed a handful of the sleds and carriages indiscriminately, as even the wheels of the Duchess' carriage fell prey to the whims of the ice. Rank lay a distant thought, as survival took precedence, leaving none to rush to Barbara's aide, each person worrying about their own fate before that of another. Water climbed up limbs, and all those in the grasp of the dark hole were nearly swallowed into a cold and watery fate. Not even Helene, her sled, or the item she escorted were spared the turbulence. With a hard thump, the pillow and the Crown that lay sewn within, crashed onto the fragile ice with such a force, that the three who knew of its value were momentarily rendered frozen despite the chaos surrounding them.

"Forward!" Paulus shouted at the top of his lungs, turning his sights to those who stared at an icy grave. "Spread out and go! Go!"

A fury of feet and hooves pressed their way forward, as all rushed to escape, though Paulus did not move in their direction. Leaping off his horse, his feet cracked the ice beneath him as he quickly rushed towards Helene.

"I got your back," Lucas shouted, hurrying to his side, though neither reached their destination.

"Save the Duchess!" Helene ordered, leaping out of her sled and following after the pillow and the Crown within.

"But—" Lucas began to protest, his eyes on the precariously balanced pillow.

"GO!" Helene ordered.

Lucas and Paulus rushed over the ice, each shift of weight screaming of the peril and planting the thoughts of an early death.

"Get the horses," Paulus ordered, as he made his way to the rear of the carriage and the heavy chests.

"On it," Lucas replied, rushing to the horses. The ice cracked under his weight, as the swinging limbs of the beasts kept him back. "Jesus mother of—" he mumbled, as he kept glancing down at the cracks that formed under his feet and the hooves that flailed precariously close to his face. With a sudden leap, he grabbed at the reins that bound them and pulled the startled horses forward with all his might. "Come on you beasts! Come on before you drown me!"

Paulus meanwhile charged into the rising icy waters grabbing at one of the chests, and with all his strength, throwing it off. It cracked the ice with a thump, as it partially sank, though the carriage did not move. With a second toss, he grabbed at another one of the chests and did the same, though still the carriage did not escape the grip of the ice and water. Finally, with a third toss, the carriage leaped from its fate.

Drawing the carriage and the Duchess forward to safety, their eyes quickly turned back to Helene, who lay alone and precariously close to being swallowed herself. With all their haste, they rushed to her.

Laying on the ice, Helene's arm extended as she tried to reach for the disguised Crown. The ice under her began to fracture and spew forth more of the cold water through each of its cracks. Yet, the masked Crown lay defiantly just out of reach and on the edge of falling into the depths of the river, as with each passing moment, it stood closer to being forever lost. With a final lunge, Helene challenged fate in both desperation and hope, as she reached across the ice covered by water.

Her hands held it for a moment, as the cold water shocked her very soul. Though, for what celebration she could have, it was short lived, as the ice under the Crown gave way and the strength of her grip was tested.

A cold as sharp as a dagger stabbed at her unguarded hand, as she submerged it into the water, desperate to keep her hold of the pillow. Plunging her other hand in to aid in her struggle, she grappled with each passing moment, as her grip lessened. One finger after another, they began to uncurl, the numbing pain too much to maintain with the weight of the heavy Crown. Though just as it seemed she would falter, a pair of hands grabbed her ankles, and in single heave, pulled her back to safety.

"It's a miracle you still have it," Paulus said with a light laugh, as he aided her up. "Well done. Let's get you something to dry you up."

"Is it alright?" Lucas asked, staring at the pillow. "You know, the Crow—stuffing?"

"I think it got bent," Helene whispered, patting the wet heavy pillow and struggling to hold back her shiver. "The top of the Crown. The cross... it's been bent."

Paulus and Lucas turned to one another with a look of horror on their faces.

"Can you bend it back?" Lucas asked.

"I don't want to break it," Helene quickly replied. "Besides, it's not really the moment."

With a heavy sigh, Paulus finally chimed in. "It was not lost, and everyone seems to be alright. That's all that counts."

"And you could always say we found it that way," Lucas added with a series of nods. "I mean, the Queen doesn't have to know we were the ones that added a bit of charm to it. Does she?"

"Quiet," Helene suddenly ordered, as she caught sight of an all too familiar figure.

"Well, that was exciting," Barbara said with a coy smile, as she approached. "I think some of my things got wet, but I am happy to see my main chest of clothes are undamaged. A shame about my carriage. I don't know how long it will take to fix it. It seems it might have been faster to go around, but such things are only in hindsight."

"I suppose you could ride with me," Helene said, leading her away. "There is room in my sled. We could take those who are still able to move with us. The rest may stay to fix their carriages and sleds after resting and recovering."

"Well now, that sounds like a fine plan," Barbara replied. "But, I think it would be best for you to get warm."

In each other's company, they quickly made their way to warmth and to prepare for the rest of the journey. Though for the two that were left behind, they simply looked to one another.

"We didn't get a thank you," Lucas said. "And I think she thinks we risked our lives for her gowns. And we saved Helene too."

"Yeah..." Paulus replied. "Come on, before we catch our death. We still have a long way back to the Queen."

Chapter 51
The Capital

The sound of hooves battering the ground echoed, as the procession of horses, sleds and carriages advanced forward. Their pace was fast with no delays, as they passed the trees that hugged the road. In the distance, plumes of smoke could be seen against the blue sky, the faint sight a clear sign of civilization. Though suddenly, horses faltered, and those that were carried by them turned to each other with doubt and suspicion, as a faint, but undeniable sound echoed.

"What's all that racket?" Lucas asked, as they continued to move past the trees and closer to the very shadow of the city walls, while the sound grew louder. "Those bells? I think those are bells."

"Fire?" Paulus asked. "No, can't be. We're downwind, no smoke, or heat, or mob. Something else?"

Each passing moment made them grow louder, the high bells ringing with a fury that called out to the world, and reverberated and thundered well out into the countryside and forests.

"The Queen…" Helene whispered, as it dawned on her.

"It must be," Barbara replied from beside her, a shared blanket between them.

"The Queen and her unborn child," Helene shouted. "Something has happened! Make haste! Make haste!"

With all the speed they could muster they advanced abandoning caution and subtlety for progress. Roaring past the last of the trees, the sight of the city quickly swallowed their view, yet they did not slow. They rushed with even greater speed, each trying to keep up with Helene who led the way storming into the very courtyard of the royal palace.

With a leap out of their transport, Helene, Paulus and Lucas rushed into the halls as fast as their feet could carry them. They paid little attention to anything, ignoring the ongoing ringing bells, and abandoning those they escorted. The only proof of their journey was the heavy pillow in Helene's hands, as they pressed past those who labored and guarded the way.

"How much further...?" Lucas asked through panted breaths, as he slowly fell behind.

There was no answer that accompanied him, as the others simply continued forward, the bells still audible even within the strength of the walls.

"Move," Helene ordered, reaching the Queen's room and pushing against those that loitered in the hall. With a hard shove, the door swung open for her to gaze upon all within as a gasp slipped past her lips. "My Queen..."

"You're too late," Janos quickly replied, wiping the blood from his hands with a once white rag. "You missed the birth."

"What?" Helene asked.

"It took a while," Janos replied. "The birth took its course, as it should. Be it a little slow and an almost close call. But, all is well now."

"He means to say I'm fine," Elizabeth replied with a light laugh from the comfort of her bed. Her hair lay in a mess, the remnants of her labor still holding her, though an air of calm and relaxation had settled. Nestled in her arms was a small bundle which her eyes remained fixed on. "Come and say hello."

"Hello?" Helene asked with a soft whisper.

"Come and say hello to my son," Elizabeth replied. "Come and say hello to my little boy."

With slow steps that sounded, Helene drew closer, the pillow still under one of her arms. Extending her free hand, her fingers graced the skin of the unnamed infant.

"Your husband..." Helene whispered. "His father would have been proud. It's what he always wanted."

"It's what we always wanted," Elizabeth replied.

"It is as I predicted," Janos said chiming into the conversation. He placed the last of his tools away, untouched by blood, and made his way to his employer. "A boy. I take my leave, my Queen. Should you need anything I will be close, though I doubt you will need anything."

With a soft smile and a softer nod, Elizabeth looked to him. "I thank you for your assistance and clarity. Things could have been far different."

"My Queen, I did little to nothing, it was all you," Janos replied with a bow before making for the door.

With a whine from the door the physician made his way to depart. Though, before the door could be closed, Paulus and Lucas looked in with curious eyes. They watched just beyond the threshold, trying to catch a glance, though not much came of it, as the door was closed on them and their snooping left unanswered.

Elizabeth smiled, as she released a soft laugh. "I see the men you hired still with you."

"They did well," Helene replied, a smile growing on her as she glanced at the closed door while the precious red pillow rested over her lap. "They did very well."

"You could almost say that I have been awaiting your return," Elizabeth said, as she let out another laugh, yet she followed its fade with another question. "Did you get it? Did you succeed?"

Helene nodded, with a smile, and took hold of Elizabeth's hands.

"Yes," Helene stated proudly. "We did. We did. We succeeded in everything we went to accomplish. I would not have believed it possible if I was not with them, but they got it out of the vault." She glanced to the pillow with a smile and a laugh, moving to present it to the Queen. Yet before she could, the sound of another reminded them of where they sat.

With a loud whine that called for a mother, the newborn made his young voice heard, as he dashed the celebrations before they could begin.

"That's a familiar sound," Helene said with a laugh. "Haven't heard it in a few years. It's a nice sound."

"You say that now," Elizabeth replied with a laugh of her own, gently calming her newborn. "I think I remember all too well the last time we heard that sound. Still, would not change a thing."

Extending her arms, Helene presented the pillow weighed by the treasure within, and with a nod of affirmation, the quest was rendered complete. In silence they remained there, though like all missions the execution of its completion lay heavy with the promise of reward.

"Helene," Elizabeth said, running her hand over the lumps of the pillow, the Crown undeniable. "You have written yourself into history... I need you to do something for me."

"Anything," Helene replied, as she held the baby boy's little hand.

"I need you to write a letter for me," Elizabeth explained. "I need you to write a letter to the council and have them assemble. I think it is time we showed them what we have been working on."

"Of course," Helene replied, readying to move.

"But first, I need you to do something else," Elizabeth explained. "Bring your two accomplices in, I wish to give my thanks, and what is due."

With a smile and a wave, Helene moved to the door, cast it open and called her collaborators forward.

"On behalf of the Kingdom I thank you both," Elizabeth said, as their eyes fell on her. "We thank you both. You have done a great service for the Kingdom. You have given it a chance. As we discussed, I have already assembled your payments. I did that as I went into labor. You never know in life. Either way, you will find what was promised to you both outside. Thank you."

"It has been an honor, my Queen," Paulus replied, lowering his head and bowing.

"Yeah," Lucas added, doing the same.

"I wish you both the best, Helene will see you out, farewell accomplices of the stolen Crown," Elizabeth added with a smile.

Chapter 52

A Reward in Waiting

The vivid warmth of the slowly falling sun shone brightly, as the remnants of winter dripped away, and the cold of dusk slowly stretched its reach. The bells still echoed loudly, calling all those who waited within sight of the city for the news to be relayed. Yet, while all things moved forward, within the royal structure there were two who moved to depart.

"It got a little colder," Paulus said, a slight chill touching his skin.

"Those bells ever stop?" Lucas asked himself, stepping out into the courtyard. "Going to make me hear them in my sleep. If I can ever fall asleep. Oh, who am I kidding, after all we did, I am going to sleep for days. Days!"

"I want to thank you for your service again," Helene said with a smile, as she led them out towards the stables and ignored their rambling. "The both of you. It would not have been possible without the both of you. You have given it all a chance. As we discussed with the Queen, your rewards are waiting for you."

"We're happy to help," Lucas replied. "And if you ever need anything else, like another stolen Crown, or a poisoned drink, maybe something completely different, like seducing one of the women in waiting... Well, you know who to look for."

Helene let out a laugh and the hint of a snort. "I will remember that. And I will put in a good word for you should the opportunity arrive. But, I hope you don't forget and are both aware that you must keep silent about what has transpired in relation to the Crown."

"We know," Paulus replied. "Don't we?" He asked, turning towards Lucas.

"Yeah, yeah, yeah," Lucas said. "Not a word. Not a word. Not a word while in the Kingdom. Not even to meet some women. We will be as quiet as a mouse in a house. A very quiet one."

"Good," Helene replied. "I am glad to hear it."

"So, what will you do now?" Paulus asked. "Will the Queen need more assistance?"

"Well, now that she has another child, and a newborn at that, I am sure I will find no shortage of tasks I will need to tend to," Helene replied with a smile. "Though, it would be a lie to say that I am not excited."

"You should write about what we did," Lucas suddenly said. "Write about an old man and a young master pickpocket. I would, but—"

"He can't read," Paulus interrupted.

"I can, I just choose not to," Lucas replied.

"Maybe one day I shall," Helene said with another laugh. "Maybe one day, but not yet… Well, it has been a pleasure. I did not think that I would be saying that after meeting you both that first night, but I am happy to say that now."

"That was a good night," Lucas replied.

"She means the night we were in chains," Paulus explained.

"Oh, that night…" Lucas said, as it dawned on him. "Still a good night."

In silence they entered the stable and their sights quickly fell upon two readied wagons with a chest in the back of each of them. With a look to each other, Paulus and Lucas were still at the shock of the scale of the chests, though Helene did not pause and continued to lead them to their reward.

With a swing of the lid, she cast one open and then the other, as the reward of their labor glimmered and gleamed under the light.

"That all for me?" Lucas finally asked, a wide smile growing over his face.

"This one is, yes," Helene replied with a light laugh escaping her.

The two men stared at the treasure of precious metal before them; their weight in silver just before their eyes.

"I must be dreaming," Lucas finally said, reaching forward with a laugh.

"Thank you," Paulus added, closing his chest and looking back to Helene.

"It is what you have earned," Helene replied, giving them each a soft nod. "I need to get back to the Queen. It has been an adventure."

"We wish you and the Queen the best," Paulus said. "And in all seriousness, you know where you can find me if ever you need anything.

With a final nod, Helene turned and departed back the way she had come, quickly vanishing into the royal residence.

"Looks like our part in this story is at an end," Paulus said with a laugh.

"Yeah," Lucas replied with a laugh and a smile of his own, though it quickly faded and a look of confusion replaced it. "Wait, what story?"

Paulus stared at the man for an instant, yet it did not prosper for long, as with a sudden curve of his lips and a laugh, he broke it.

"What?" Lucas pressed.

"Forget it," Paulus replied between laughs. "So, have you decided what you are going to do?"

"With my fortune?" Lucas asked.

"With your life," Paulus replied.

"They are one and the same," Lucas said. "Life is short. It is something that should be enjoyed. It is something that should be celebrated and spent well. So, I was thinking of going to the next Kingdom in the West where I am going to start something fun. Free from all consequences."

"It sounds like you're just going to waste the wealth you worked for," Paulus replied with a laugh.

"Well, that's what it's there for," Lucas explained, slapping his simple wagon. "You can't take it with you. I mean, you can take it with you, as you move, but not when you are still and gone. And besides, when it gets to the year fifteen hundred, there won't be anything left anyway. Going to eat and drink well along the way. What about you?"

Paulus turned his gaze into the distance, lost in his own thoughts. For a moment he delayed, as he slowly grew a smile. "I think I will be going home, back to the family I have left. I have a lot to make up for. I did a few things that hurt people. I stole from people, robbed them of their dreams with my actions. I want to make things right. I'll use the wealth to make amends and return what I took. But, after that, I think I will be getting into something a little simpler. Farming."

"Farming?" Lucas asked with a laugh. "You? A farmer? Well, if you were a beggar for coins, it's not that much of a change to be a beggar for a good harvest."

Paulus let out a soft chuckle, "Yeah… But what about you? What else will you do?"

"Honestly, I think I will try to find a meal that will make me remember my past," Lucas explained. "I think I would like to remember something. And who knows, maybe I will."

"Live well, my friend," Paulus said, putting out his hand.

"You too," Lucas replied, moving his limb to meet him.

With a shake of their hands, they exchanged a gesture, though not a final one.

"Oh, get over here," Lucas added, throwing his arms wide and giving Paulus a hug. "We're family. You're like the grumpy grandfather I never had."

"Funny," Paulus replied with a pat on the back.

"Until our paths cross again," Lucas said, as they pulled apart. "You never know in life."

"You never know…" Paulus echoed.

Chapter 53

The True King

The sight of a hundred banners hung in the air, as the limbs of a hundred armed and armored men held them. Their armor glistened, each piece of defense polished to perfection, while the hilts of their slumbering swords held the stains of their labor. Their expressions were still, their eyes gazing at a sight beyond any horizon. Though, it was those who marched past them moving under the banners and invited to witness, that made the decisions that would shape their world.

"What do you think this is really about?" Fodor asked with a light laugh, as he walked beneath the banners and past those who held them. "Do you think she is going to just parade her newborn, or do you think she is really going to ask that we rescind the vote? Or something entirely different?"

"Probably just more ceremonies that are a waste of our time," Istvan replied, glancing to his corrupted entourage that followed. "A royal procession… It seems she has gotten a royal procession ready. Probably for the birth… Maybe a second posthumous. But, we have to be here. I think just about everyone is. Except for John Hunyadi that is. He must be with our next King by now. We will see what this is about. Either way, it seems she is really wasting our time. All she can really do since the vote."

"There are quite a lot of guards…" Fodor commented. "Quite a few of them."

"I had to waste a small fortune to bribe her guards." Istvan said, catching sight of Victor whispering to his men. "Did you know that? They have been feeding me information this whole time."

"You did?" Fodor asked with a shocked laugh.

"Of course," Istvan replied with a grumble, as he gave the man a nod and had it returned. "Who do you think they are loyal to? The one whose hand feeds them. Been at my whim all this time. I can only hope that she is fool enough to try something. It would give us an excuse to tighten our grip on her."

Forward they all went into the hall, its doors left fully open, and its walls decorated from one side to the other with an assortment of soft smells and ornate décor. Every expense that could be granted was, as the scene demanded it. More guards stood with banners in their hands, while the women in waiting stood at the forefront, their rich colors, fine clothes, and hints of sweet scents distracting all those who entered.

In a moment that became long, the Queen's guests simply stood and waited, turning to one another in impatience. Their whispers sounded, while their eyes fell on the young and beautiful women, all unaware of the closing of the great door they had casually passed.

With the sound of loud music that shook the hall and startled all who had begun to chatter, a faceless announcement demanded undivided attention.

"Her Majesty will now enter!"

All eyes watched as Elizabeth emerged from the door closest to the thrones. Her rich gown flowed like a river, its touch of blue holding each guest's gaze, as her slow steps echoed loudly. Sitting slowly, she took her place comfortably on her throne, a perfect vantage point over all those in her presence. She gazed over each and every noble before her, a smile growing over her lips, before finally speaking.

"I am glad that so many of you are gathered here. And I would like a moment to say something that is on my mind. Death leaves a hole in one's heart. It leaves something that seems capable of swallowing us whole and I have no shame in admitting that I too nearly fell prey to this when the King, my husband, passed away. But, there is something that can fill the void in a heart. And even the customs, or even the laws, are all worthless in the face of something like love. I am delighted to say that I found love in the labor of my friends, as I also found it in the child I gave birth to. My son. As such, I can now not only say that I am Queen of Hungary but, that I am the mother of her King." With a wave, she called forth Helene who had remained on the precipice of sight with her hands full.

Whispers once again blossomed from those who had been summoned as they turned to one another, before catching the sight of the child in Helene's hands that demanded undivided attention. His blue eyes stared over each of them, as golden hair occupied his head and his pale skin whispered of winter's first snow.

"This is my son," Elizabeth explained, taking hold of her child and sending Helene off to the next task, as the voices of her guests dwindled. She played with the boy for a moment and planted a kiss on his forehead before looking back to her guests. "And as even Helene would testify to, he has the strength of someone far older. Capable of holding the weight of the very Kingdom, if not the Crown."

Once more whispers filled the air, as their chatter and restlessness grew more pronounced.

"What is she doing?" Fodor asked with a hint of uncertainty.

"I couldn't have been lucky enough that her and the child would have passed in the birth?" Istvan grumbled to himself, as he pushed away from the others and drew closer to the Queen and her child. There he stood, half a dozen steps away, as the hall slowly returned to a calmer state.

"Istvan…" Elizabeth said with a smile. "It seems you have something to say."

"I am not sure what it is you meant with your little speech, Queen," Istvan said, taking another loud step forward and pulling all the attention to himself. "I would like to begin by saying, I am happy to give you our collective congratulations with the birth of your child—your son… apparently. We are delighted by the news of his birth, as well as your invitation here. Your new husband, the elected King, the one we determined would be the most appropriate figure to rule, will be pleased by the news that you have had a child safely."

"I am sorry," Elizabeth said, holding her child on her lap while he stared out to Istvan and then into the audience. "I thought I made myself clear. It seems I did not. I will not be taking a new husband. I will not marry again, and I will not strip my son, the King, of the right to wear his Crown."

A momentary pause filled the air, as all those who had been invited were rendered mute. Slack jaws practically settled on the ground, as those that owned them could muster no sound.

In silence, Fodor threw his eyes over his shoulder to those who stood as statues. His eyes watched their slumbering swords, the hands that would man them hanging precariously close to the hilts. He quickly moved to speak to Istvan, though before he could, Istvan moved further beyond reach.

"Comical," Istvan said, taking another step closer to the Queen and her son. "It is a late hour for you to be telling such jokes, Queen. I applaud your efforts. Your very tenacity makes me want to laugh and scream. Though, you forget yourself. Do you really think that you are in control here? Do I really need to explain to you that there is only one Crown that can make one the rightful ruler of the Kingdom? No ordinary circlet can do that, regardless of what you want. And that Crown, is locked far away from any of you."

"Do you mean this Crown?" Elizabeth asked, giving another signal to Helene.

Hearts fell still and eyes wide as Helene returned carrying the Crown they had procured, a slight bend to its high cross the only mark of its acquisition. Its ostentatious display left no doubt in any a mind of its validity. No longer did whispers blossom, but rather, the unrestrained sounds of wise men's voices.

"This is the Crown of Hungary," Elizabeth explained, standing tall with her son in her arms. "And this Crown has already been used by the archbishop of Gran in the coronation for the one in my arms. So, in every sense of the word, this is your King."

An air of silence consumed the hall so voraciously that not even the beating of a heart, or the wailing of a soul dared break it. None but one.

"You have made my day," Istvan suddenly said with a sinister laugh, accompanied by an even more malicious smile. "You have given me the excuse I need. I thank you for that."

"I would advise you to submit," Elizabeth replied calmly. "I would advise you to recognize my son, the true King. If you do not, your fate will be sealed."

Istvan's low grumbled laugh could be heard by all in the hall. "My fate? It is yours that is sealed. You have really made things easier for me. Now, I don't have to go myself to get the Crown for our next King, Wladislaus of Poland. Now, I will gain even greater rewards because of you. But first, I will remind you that you are in my company. All those before you, they serve me. These guards, the men of the hall who you believe serve you, have been recruited to serve the Kingdom, they will not aide you. They answer only to me." He turned to the guards and with a commanding voice, made his will known. "Men at arms, I call upon you to detain the Queen, her son the false King, and anyone else who is with her!"

None moved, as the silence that had descended on them moments before held its grip.

"I order you!" Istvan commanded again. "You serve me! Arrest her!"

Still none moved, as his words vanished, like shadows in the night and dust in the wind.

"My loyal men," Elizabeth said, turning her attention to her captain of the guards. "Tell me with your actions, what is it you protect? Tell me what is it you serve? Is it the defense of walls and stones? Is it the Crown? Is it the royal blood that flows through my veins and that of my child? Or is it a future for Hungary and all her people? A future free from the dominion of corrupt men. Men such as these. There is only one answer that I will accept! So, I ask you, will you protect me? Will you be ordained to the service of the Kingdom? If not, I ask that you put your swords through my heart, for I would rather be left to the ground then serve the will of soulless men."

All eyes fell to Victor who stood by the wall and slowly made his way towards the Queen, the King, and Istvan.

"Who are we?" He finally asked his men loudly.

"The necessary!" They replied in unison, as they beat the base of the banners they wielded against the ground and forced an echo like thunder.

"And what is our role, being necessary?" Victor demanded, his presence but a few steps shy of his mark.

"It is our role to protect you, my Queen, the true King, and their children!" the guards answered in unison, as they thundered once again.

"We serve the Queen," Victor said, staring Istvan down. "And we serve the King!"

"Then, by my authority as Queen, and that of my son, the rightful coronated true King, I order you to arrest these traitors!" Elizabeth ordered.

In an instant, banners fell, as all those within the room drew their weapons into the light, their tips focused on the nobles before the Queen and the little King. A few rushed to the door, yet it stood locked, and the Queen's men quickly fell upon those who tried to escape. Istvan himself was met with Victor's blade, which was pressed to his neck with just enough strength to draw a few drops of blood.

"This will not stand!" Istvan barked. "This will not stand! Whatever this movement is will be crushed! Savor your moment, for none of this will endure! You will be wiped from history, and that boy will serve as nothing more than a pawn!"

"Perhaps," Elizabeth replied calmly. "Perhaps you are right. But, even if that happens, your King, my son here, will one day know what those who loved him did for him. That is enough for me."

With a blank stare, Istvan and the conspirators could only gape in silence as the Queen marched back to her throne to stand by Helene and the Crown.

"Behold your True King!" Elizabeth ordered to both her loyal followers and her enemies who lay subdued. "Behold my son, behold Ladislaus."

"Hail the True King! Hail the True King! Hail the True King! Hail the True King!"

Their shouts like thunder sounded far beyond the hall; cries of victory shaking even the skies. Though, their words alone could not break the storm that gathered beyond their reach. For far away beyond the borders of the Kingdom, the whispers of war began to blossom for another King who wished the stolen Crown for himself.

THE STOLEN CROWN

ABOUT THE AUTHOR

Chris A. Moltzau is a historian, a writer, a traveler, and a storyteller who graduated with honors in Medieval History with a minor in Classics from the University of Arizona, USA. He then went on to receive a diploma in Viking Studies from the University of Edinburgh, Scotland.

During his studies, he participated in several on-site research projects. This includes Greece, where he studied the history and impact of the Mycenaean's to the Ottomans, in addition to seven other countries in Europe where he investigated the Dark Age and the Middle Age. Chris was also part of an archaeological expedition in Gotland, Sweden, which uncovered a farmstead that had been used during the Viking Age and throughout the Middle Age.

A prolific writer, he is passionate about making history fun and telling the 'untold' or 'forgotten' tales.